THE FESTIVAL OF THE DEAD
THE COMPLETE CHINATOWN CASES
OF JIMMY WENTWORTH, VOLUME 1

THE FESTIVAL OF THE DEAD

THE COMPLETE CHINATOWN CASES OF JIMMY WENTWORTH, VOLUME 1

SIDNEY HERSCHEL SMALL

ILLUSTRATED BY
JOSEPH A. FARREN

COVER BY
LEJAREN HILLER

POPULAR PUBLICATIONS · 2022

TABLE OF CONTENTS

THE FESTIVAL OF THE DEAD

To Solve the Murder of a Brother Cop, Jim
Wentworth Fights His Way into the Fanatic
Rites in the Black Building of the Dead

1

FOR BETTER THAN forty years, in sunshine, rain, and fog, with never a single black mark entered against his record, George Bannion had walked his Chinatown beat.

From the Hall of Justice he would start, marching along Kearny Street to California. Then, more slowly as the years turned his hair to gray, he would climb the steep hill. Halfway up, where Chinatown begins, he would stop, look out over San Francisco Bay to see what the weather would be. Then, from a tiny stall, he bought a package of gum, which he chewed to take the taste of cheap perfume away when he must pass the houses of joy.

After that he began his slow zigzagging back and forth. Dupont Street… Waverley Place… Fish Alley… Bannion knew every merchant.

During tong wars, when the streets were deserted, and hatchetmen imported from the shadow of the Great Wall sharpened their weapons and their courage in damp, hidden cellars, Bannion walked his beat as placidly as when the New Year lilies were in bloom. The red paper placards announcing tong vengeance meant no more to him than the more customary advertisements for *ginseng* or dried shrimp. He could not read either. His job, and he did it well, was to keep peace. The tongs laid murderous plot and terrible counterplot, but never during Bannion's hours.

Why? Clear from Grace Cathedral to the dirtiest, rattiest hole where raw squid were sold by the clammy inch of tentacle, Bannion was liked and trusted. If he helped himself to as little as a bag of *li-chi* nuts, down into the grimy paw of the vendor went George's dime.

The heads of the Six Companies felt the same way about George Bannion as did the sweepers of the pork-and-duck shops. He did not have an enemy among the thousands of Chinese…

And yet, just the same, after forty years of uninterrupted service, and four gold stripes on the sleeves of his blue uniform, George Bannion was found in a dark doorway on Waverley Place with a knife in his chest.

There had been no struggle.

Bannion's uniform was not dusty, save where his back had been propped against the door of the empty house. The uniform was not disarranged. The gun, every chamber full and the barrel clean, was in the holster. Bannion's cap was even on his head.

The knife, a common, nine-inch blade, such as fish-cleaners use, had been driven clear through the wall of his chest and into his heart. Bannion must have died instantly.

The Six Companies, honestly disturbed and sorry, sent a huge floral star to the funeral, and a purse to Bannion's widow. His fellow officers marched beside the hearse. The newspapers, suddenly discovering the veteran's record and fame, printed his picture. The detective bureau, lashed by the selfsame city editors, grew more harassed every hour.

The Chinatown detail did their best, and learned exactly nothing.

Bannion's body had been found by a couple of Chinese

youngsters. Shopkeepers on the opposite side of the street said that Bannion had passed with his customary hand wave. None had seen him attacked.

And yet a full week after the veteran's murder, the best the Chinatown detail had been able to do was to bring in a frightened waiter-coolie, who, in carrying his tray of hot, covered dishes from Hang Far Low to a dealer in pickled eggs, had said that he had seen a very big man following Bannion along Waverley Place.

None of the shopkeepers could verify this; the coolie did not know if the man was black, yellow, or white.

By the eighth day Captain Dunand was past anger.

"Take a look at this, boys," he said cheerlessly to three of his Chinatown detail. He held up the newspaper for them to read.

POLICE WITHOUT CLEW
IN BANNION MURDER
Shakeup on Force Hinted by
Mayor Welsh in Case of Failure

"I'm not blaming you boys," he said finally. "If there were any other news, the papers'd forget this. Not that I don't want to get whoever killed Bannion. If one of you fellows, who've been making arrests every so often, had been murdered, I could understand it. But Bannion's dead… and he didn't commit suicide!"

"It took a big man to drive that knife in," said one of the detectives. "Right up to the hilt."

"You can't finger-print every Chink in San Francisco," said Dunand. "That's another thing which bothers me,

Blake. The murderer was so sure he wouldn't be discovered that he didn't trouble to wipe off the hilt. You know how careful a hatchetman is."

Nodding, Blake said, "I've talked with every stoolie and with the Six Companies. They don't know a thing—"

"We're only going over what we already know," broke in Dunand wearily. "Well, you boys might just as well get going—"

"Not much sense in it to-day," suggested another of Dunand's picked men. "It's some sort of holiday in Chinatown. Everything shut up, except a few shops for suckers—"

"What holiday?" asked Dunand crossly.

Blake shrugged.

"Darned if I know," he said. "A sacred day of some kind."

Dunand's temper boiled up.

"You fellows expect to catch a Chink murderer, and you don't even know what their holidays are!"

"They have 'em every week or so," apologized Blake. "The Pekingese and the Cantonese celebrate different ones. And sometimes when a big family's putting on a show for the birth of a son, you'd think it was the 4th of July—"

Dunand said, "Forget it," realizing the difficulty of understanding Oriental customs, and, because he had already told his men everything he could think for them to do, turned toward a window.

At a desk there a young officer sat, busy at a typewriter.

Dunand stared at him a full minute, said, "Don't go," to his men, and then called, "Oh, Wentworth—come here a moment, please."

The young officer stood up.

*Wentworth's fist
smashed out fiercely*

He half glanced at the reports he had been writing on the Bannion case, but as his superior had said nothing about them, he came empty handed.

"To-day's the 14th of April, Wentworth," said Dunand. "What would that be in China?"

"*Tsing-ming* period, sir. To-day's called *Siu-fan-ti.*"

"Is it? What's that mean?"

"A day for the worship of ancestors. Literally, it means 'the sweeping of the tombs.'"

Dunand nodded, and then said abruptly, "Your father resigned from the force at the time of the Boxer Rebellion, didn't he?"

"Yes, sir."

"And then stayed in China—married there?"

"He married a nurse in Shanghai, captain."

"Umm… you're registered as a member of the police department clerical staff, Wentworth. If I had you transferred, do you think you could find out who killed Bannion?"

The young officer flushed.

"I'd like to have a try at it," he said.

Dunand, liking the answer of the younger man, nevertheless growled, "You've seen all the reports, Wentworth. Just because the boys here don't speak Chinese the way you do, don't get the idea into your head that they don't know their business."

Wentworth said quietly, "You were angry, sir, because I had a little influence used to get me into your office. I didn't want to patrol a beat. I wanted to be where—well, where I might be able to do some good. And dad wanted me to get on the force. I don't think I've a chance at finding who killed Bannion, but I might be able to pick up something—"

"Where?" demanded Dunand.

His own honesty made him go on:

"I don't know where to turn," he said. "We're baffled. But perhaps... a new viewpoint... will you let people know, in Chinatown, that you understand Chinese? You might hear something. And yet the Six Companies tip us off to anything. If they are in the dark... oh, go have a shot at it, Wentworth!"

"Yes, sir... I'll wear the uniform, if you don't mind."

"What?"

"Couldn't I be assigned Bannion's beat?"

Dunand looked at him coldly, and then suddenly began to laugh.

"That's one on the force," he chuckled. "Nobody'd ever

think a harness bull was a detective—or had any sense. I'll arrange it for you Wentworth—right now."

The lean young officer grinned.

"Don't get a knife in your heart," said Dunand. "Keep an eye out for big Chinks. Watch both ways, d'you hear?"

"A little man could do it just as well," Wentworth went on quietly, for all his elation at getting the assignment he had hoped for. "If he knew exactly how. I think Bannion was killed—"

The four men leaned forward eagerly.

"—by the lightning stroke," Wentworth concluded. "Why—by whom, of course I don't know."

"What's this lightning stroke?"

"The quickest way to knife a man. You get the knife—a sharp one with a very thin blade—in as far as the ribs, and then give it a little hitch, and then slide it along farther, with quick, sort of slicing jerks, until it penetrates the heart. One jam—the way a big man'd do it—always tears the flesh. It takes practice, this stroke. An assassin's way of killing. When I was a kid, a man lost his head in Hang-kow for knifing people on the street. Just as Bannion was murdered—"

"Why'd this assassin kill 'em?" Dunand demanded swiftly.

"He was only a robber," said Wentworth. "He was clever; he must have practiced a good deal. He could kill 'em and rob 'em without being seen at it. He was—"

Wentworth became silent.

"Got a hunch?" Dunand asked.

The younger man nodded.

"Hop to it," said his captain. "Now, listen. Whoever's on

Bannion's old beat will be told to meet you at the Cathedral. He goes off, you go on. I'll fix it. But why didn't you give me this dope before, Wentworth?"

The newly-assigned detective looked at his superior frankly.

"Part of it I just thought of," he said. "If I'd said anything to you, you'd have thought I was a fresh young squirt, sir."

Dunand liked him better than ever. "Good luck to you," he grunted, and, his hand out, "don't get the department in another mess by getting killed, Jim."

2

EVER SINCE JIMMY WENTWORTH had been assigned to the force, he had hoped for a break like this. As he walked soberly enough through the down town shopping district, jammed with automobiles, he wondered if the women hurrying to keep tea engagements or to make purchases in the department stores knew that only a block away strange Oriental intrigues were planned and consummated, often bloodily... like poor old Bannion's death.

Wentworth knew the Chinese too well to believe that the veteran officer's death was accidental.

But why had Bannion been murdered?

The powerful Six Companies, with their feelers in every part of Chinatown, did not know—or didn't want to tell. The Chinatown detail had drawn nothing but blanks.

Wentworth, from the report on Bannion's death, which traced exactly the dead man's beat, repeated to himself the route the veteran had followed for so many calm years. Dupont Street... Waverley Place... over to Jackson... down Fish Alley... across Dupont again... down to Kearny...

The patrolman was waiting in front of the Cathedral.

"Quiet as th' inside of th' church here," he said to Wentworth. "All except a little singin' goin' on—"

"In Waverley Place?" Wentworth asked.

The relieved officer grinned.

"Got Bannion on th' brain, lad?" he asked. "No—down on th' Alley. Yowlin' as if th' fiends was on earth."

"Thanks," said Wentworth.

"For what?"

Wentworth almost said, "For the tip." What stopped him he did not know. No one was near them except a vender of *li-chi* nuts and coconut sugar candy. Instead, Jim said, "Hanged if I know… well, here goes!"

The vendor waited until Wentworth had turned, and then said: "You want mebbe-so nlut? Prenty good."

"No, thanks," Wentworth refused.

The Chinese grinned toothlessly, and then crackled into shrill Cantonese; an emaciated porter-coolie grinned at what was said.

"What's all that mean?" Wentworth asked.

"I say tlo-day good luck."

Again Wentworth said, "Thanks." He smothered his own grin. What the vendor had said was, "Look at this babe, with milk still in his ears! He stands as erect as if he were all of the Seven Sages of the Bamboo Grove about to travel the hundred moon-lit miles. Mah! He thinks he is a dragon, but he is but a swollen silkworm instead of being the Devourer of the Sun. The ways of the white men are assuredly strange when they send this infant among us."

So that was what they thought of him? Then perhaps he had a chance at finding something out!

Thoughtfully Wentworth walked slowly along the street, sniffing smells few white men knew. He might almost have been back in China.

At a corner he paused, apparently busy at selecting an orange from the food merchant's stall, but actually scanning the placards on the wall behind it. Nothing of importance. A baby in the family of Ng K'iu Po. An announcement that the daughter of F'ung Chi Loung was ready for marriage, and that the proper offers would be entertained by Chi Loung; there followed an account of the girl's habits, beauty, and filial piety. The prices of jute. A statement that a merchant desired a young assistant, versed in the business of wringing ducks' necks and chopping up their livers. Only the usual thing.

Tourists stared in the windows; once a man asked Wentworth if anything ever happened in Chinatown, or if all the stories were bunk.

Wentworth said, "Everything's peaceful here," which answer, he felt, would have satisfied regulations. (Down in a basement a council of the Hip Suey Sings were deciding when to start their career of vengeance; up on a top floor two men were bargaining with two others—hatchetmen— about the price for the abduction of F'ung Chi Loung's daughter, who, if shipped into the interior of the State, would bring an excellent price.) "No excitement here any more," Wentworth said cheerfully, and wondering himself what devil's broth was being brewed at the exact moment, strode along the street.

From an upper story of a restaurant thin, minor music from a *san-hein,* that round-bellied guitar, drifted down, the cadence broken by the irregular tap-tap of a skin drum. Whine… ting, ting, ting… tap-tap…

Pausing, Wentworth decided that it was only, again, the usual performance to attract white tourists.

Here he was walking along, just as Bannion had walked. Would the next few minutes verify his suspicion?

Past the fish stalls, the pork shops, the drug stores with curious articles in the windows—embryo chickens, in alcohol, powdered snakes' heads, dried yak's blood, *ginseng*—Wentworth strolled.

The shops were silent; only one man dozed or stared at nothing in those which were truly Chinese; to-day was *Siu-fan-ti,* sacred to one's ancestors. No Chinese made purchases, but one never knew when a white fool would enter, and add coins which some day would enable the merchant to be returned—either alive or dead—to the Celestial Land across the water. And accepting money from a white man was no insult to one's ancestors…

Music of a different caliber filtered through the street sounds. Some one was chanting nasally to the accompaniment of flutes, and Wentworth, not stopping now, listened closely as he approached a sordid, black building in the heart of the district. Some one was singing—a man—in falsetto, singing the song of the builders building the sacred dwellings of the dead:

"Khi' tchi ying-ying!
To' tchi houng–houng!
Ai! Ai! Ai!
Tcho tchi tong–tong!
Sio Hu ping–ping!
Ai!"

Wentworth had heard the song many times in China.

He was a good four blocks now from Waverley Place, where Bannion had been found murdered—killed with the lightning-stroke.

What was going on inside the black building Wentworth knew also; incense would be rising. From the sacred chests would be taken the precious ornaments and robes sent from China, to be used when the nine hours of singing and devotion had been completed. In a corner of the room would be the carers for the dead—men apart in their lives from the others, who, for a consideration, would be reviled and cursed during the ceremony.

The lives of these men couldn't be very happy, Wentworth knew, or the fellow in Hangkow would never have deserted it for that of an assassin and robber. From men of this caste hatchetmen were recruited.

The black building seemed ominous, although Wentworth could see no one near it. What had happened when Bannion walked past over a week ago? Anything? Or was Wentworth all wrong in his guess?

Across the street was a bowl shop, where common porcelains were sold at six for a quarter to Chinese, and for twenty-five cents apiece to tourists. Wentworth hesitated at the window, walked past, looked back, and then slowly opened the door.

The aged Chinese sitting behind the counter looked up, and, impassively, bowed to authority.

"How much?" Wentworth asked, pointing to a bowl.

The old Oriental stared at the window.

"You like, you take," he said pleasantly.

Wentworth shook his head. "How much?" he repeated.

"Fi' cent." In a sing-song mutter the Chinese mumbled, "So we have another honest officer of the law? I am beginning to reverse my opinion of these men-in-blue." Then, in English, as if he doubted Wentworth's refusal, "You like, you take. *Maskee*."

Wentworth went to the window, and picked up the bowl he had seen.

It was a common blue porcelain, with several poorly-painted figures on the side. One, that of a stork, had been so hurriedly done that the leg seemed broken in the middle.

"It looks like a stroke of lightning," Wentworth said coolly.

Was he right? Did the old merchant's impassive eyes flutter toward the black building across the street?

Wentworth leaned on the counter, seemingly examining the bowl.

The merchant's voice lifted; Wentworth understood every word he cried.

"My son, here is a very young and innocent policeman. Come and tell him that the longer he remains here, the poorer his health will become."

So the merchant knew something!

From the rear of the shop came a man of Wentworth's own age, dressed in a suit as well tailored as any white man's.

"How do you do," the young Chinese said. "My father tells me you like the bowl. May we send it to your home? We'll be glad to. But—if you don't mind my saying it—this is the time the sergeant makes his rounds...."

Wentworth put the bowl down. He said truculently, "Want to get rid of me?"

The young Chinese said quietly, "You never can tell what happens in Chinatown, officer." No mention of Bannion, of course. "And my father and my house were always friendly with... the police."

3

THIS TIME WENTWORTH looked at the other squarely. The father was staring at a fly on the wall, and yet Wentworth knew that he was badly troubled.

Inaction, hesitation, was something Wentworth was never troubled with. For some reason he liked the young Chinese who spoke English so well, and appreciated the decency of the old man in warning him, or at least in getting him away from what was certainly a dangerous neighborhood.

Yet the detective knew enough about the Chinese to make his question indirect. In English, calmly, he said, "Are you afraid my coming here will bring trouble to your house?"

"How much do you know?" the Chinese countered.

"How much can I tell you?" demanded the white man.

Wentworth had decided to trust father and son.

"On Christmas, Wang Yu, my father, went with our family to the house of Bannion to see the grandchildren's tree," the son, Wang Chen-p'o, retorted. "Do you think we are happy because he is dead?"

"And why is he dead?"

"Because..."

"Out with it!"

"And be taken for questioning to the Hall of Justice?

Nothing doing. For when I came back, my honorable father would probably have a knife in his back—"

"Made with the lightning-stroke," snapped Wentworth.

Wang Chen-p'o made a noise in his throat.

"Why'd you come in here?" he pleaded. "Now, you've been in the store so long that… you can guess what will happen to us!"

Wentworth believed the Chinese was entitled to know. "I came in to find out if Bannion had gone into the place across the street—if you'd seen him."

"He did."

"You saw him come out?"

"Yes."

"Alone?"

"Yes."

"Nobody followed him?"

"Not that I saw."

Nodding, Wentworth said, "That's enough. Now—I'm going. You've got to save face, Wang Chen-p'o. When I go, yell at me in Chinese. Tell me I'm a thief and a robber and all the rest… it may work."

No sooner had Wentworth stepped outside than Wang Chen-p'o sent Chinese curses after him; the young Oriental had picked up a really valuable bowl, and the idea being conveyed was that the policeman had insisted upon being presented with it—with an ancient *Tching-hoa-yao,* prize of the establishment, pictured with grapes and poppies and worth a fortune.

Wang Chen p'o's snarls could be heard for a full half block, and certainly by any watcher or listener in the ominous black building's windows.

Now Wentworth had three things open to him.

He could telephone Dunand, and have the black building surrounded. He could go in himself. Or he could continue along his beat and see what happened.

It was the third thing which Wentworth decided to do, partly to protect the Wangs.

He didn't look toward the place where *Siu-fan-ti* was being celebrated; he walked placidly down the street, not turning until he reached the corner where Bannion had always turned.

Before he had gone a hundred feet he knew that some one was following him with ceaseless catstep.

The hairs on Wentworth's neck rose like hackles; he could almost feel the swift plunge of a blade in his back, but, whistling softly, he marched along Bannion's beat, with the slip-slip of padding feet somewhere behind him. More than once Wentworth half decided to go for his gun, swing around, and drop his follower—if only he knew who the man would be! He might as easily shoot some perfectly innocent Chinese.

When he turned the corner into Waverley Place he managed to get a glimpse behind him, and saw no one at all.

More, before he had gone far he knew that he was no longer being followed.

Why?

It came to the detective like a flash.

His pursuer—his murderer, perhaps—knew that the new patrolman was following Bannion's regular, accustomed beat, and would now go three blocks—slowly— along Waverley Place.

Bannion had been knifed in front; In the chest!

If this assassin had determined that Wentworth had heard anything in the bowl shop, and that it was necessary for the patrolman to die before he was able to hand his information to headquarters, *he*, Jimmy Wentworth, would be stabbed in the precise same manner.

Wentworth suddenly grinned.

Not fifty feet from the scene of Bannion's murder was a police call box! That was why Bannion had been killed on Waverley Place—when the old man had gone to the box to ring in, whether or not he had any information about the ominous black building where the rites for the dead were performed!

Wentworth knew now exactly what he would do.

As he walked—slower than ever, to give the pursuer plenty of time to circle the block, he saw to it that his gun would slide swiftly from the holster, although he wanted to get his man alive and not dead.

From an open door Wentworth could hear a grandfather reading from the Book of Li Po to his brightly dressed grandchildren:

> "Surely the Earth-sorrow
> For the Passing of Spring
> From her Quiet Places
> Is indeed overwhelming"…

Was *he* going to be overwhelmed? Not if he could help it.

Unconsciously Wentworth's steps quickened. He wanted to see what was going to happen, and his eagerness for action could not be held down.

Across one more street—there, in the middle of the next block, was 1145 Waverley Place, where Bannion had been found dead. There, a little farther down the street, was the blue call box, toward which methodical Bannion had been plodding, perhaps only to ring in, perhaps to tell about some strange thing he saw or wisely guessed at.

And, coming up the street, toward the call box, ambled a little Chinese, black, like all his countrymen, from coat collar to shoes; no more innocent-looking Oriental could have been found from one end of Chinatown to the other. His hands were folded together in his sleeves. In the right hand, Wentworth felt sure, was a counterpart of the slender-bladed knife which had drained Bannion's life.

Wentworth continued whistling as he walked. His nervousness left him.

The Chinese was cleverly suiting his pace to the white detective's; they would meet just a few feet away from the call box.

Wentworth began to play a part. He gave the appearance of an excited man as he neared the blue box on the lamp standard. Whether the Chinese was observing him Wentworth didn't know, for the fellow kept his head down, ambling along as if headed for his room after a day of work.

Now they were just about twenty feet apart. Wentworth walked patrolman fashion near the buildings, and then suddenly swerved out toward the call box. The Chinese swayed toward it also. His head was still down.

Just as he must have met honest, unsuspecting old Bannion.

When they were three feet from each other, the Chinese looked up for the first time. He gave a little ejaculation of surprise—*hai*—enough to set any one off guard, and then an apologetic smile swept over his face.

Just as he must have smiled at Bannion before he killed him so cleverly that it was not seen even across the street!

Wentworth's mouth smiled also.

Then, just as the Chinese's hands were leaving his long black sleeves—in another half-step, unless one man stopped or backed away, they would have been breast to breast—Wentworth's eager fist smashed out, a fierce, hard-driven blow.

It took the Chinese squarely under the jaw, lifted him off the pavement cleanly. Before the black clad body dropped to the ground, there was a tinkle of a long-bladed knife as it fell a dozen feet away.

The would-be assassin was out—cold. Opening the call box, Wentworth spoke rapidly. "Wentworth. Tell Captain Dunand to get down to the black building opposite Wang's shop on Dupont. I'll be there!"

Had any one who'd seen what had just happened already reported it to that same black building? Or could Wentworth get there before what had taken place was known to the performers of *Siu-fan-ti?*

Wentworth dragged the Chinese to the pole holding the call box, cuffed the yellow man's right hand, snapped the other cuff closed, and then hooked his extra handcuff through the steel circle, fastening it waist high on the standard, where the metal of the pole was narrowest.

Stooping to pick up the Chinese's long-bladed knife, Wentworth continued walking along Waverley Place as rapidly as he dared. At Dupont he veered from Bannion's old route, and started swiftly toward the ominous black building.

4

AT THE DOOR of the black building Wentworth turned and looked back along the street. How long it would take Dunand to get the wagon there the detective could not guess; five minutes, perhaps ten. If he waited that long before entering, the news would filter, probably underground, to the men inside—and nothing more would be learned.

Wentworth was sure that he had caught the actual murderer, but not the men behind the assassin.

He wanted them.

As his hand went to the door—unlocked, for what good are locks against the evil spirits who flit about the dead?—he already heard the nasal whines of the carers for the dead:

"Khi' tchi ying-ying!
Tou tchi hong-hong!
Ai… ai… ai…"

The foreign sound took Wentworth back across the Pacific… If he had been there, he would never have dared intrude on such a ceremony, but here it was different. Back of him, also, was the thin blue line of policemen, standing between Orient and Occident, keeping the peace.

Gently, Wentworth pushed open the door.

He was in an unlighted box of a hall; a Chinese, able to see him against the outer light, said sharply:

"No can do! Go 'way!"

Since Wentworth knew that some hidden observer had seen him come in, probably from a window, he wasted no time.

"I've got paper for you," he said.

"What plaper?"

The half minute had accustomed Wentworth's eyes to the gloom; inside the horrible chanting continued, so as yet no alarm had been spread.

With his right hand the detective reached inside his coat, and then struck out viciously with his left at the dim, approaching figure of a Chinese. The man gasped as Wentworth's fist drove against his middle—the sound covered by the noise in the inner room—and then Wentworth had him by one arm.

It took the detective only a fraction of time to bear his man to the floor, and then, since he no longer had his cuffs, he half-throttled the Chinese with one lean hand, while with the other he jerked off the Oriental's silken jacket. Wentworth hurriedly gagged the watchman, and then bound him rapidly. He did not dare leave an enemy behind to knife him from the rear, nor to give the word.

What would happen if his figuring were wrong—if the performers of the sacred *Siu-fan-ti* were innocent—Wentworth knew. He would be broken for intruding, for attacking this very man.

But he wasn't wrong. He was positive he had come to the right place.

Out of the inner chamber came the chant:

"Tcho tchi tong-tong!
Sio liu ping-ping!

Ai!"

And then, just as Wentworth straightened up, the singing stopped abruptly, and a voice screamed:

"*Sha* L'ung Yen is dead! L'ung Yen has been killed! Vengeance! *Sha!* Kill!"

Jimmy Wentworth, gun out, pushed open the inner door.

His first glance was enough to horrify even a man who knew of the strange places and doings of the hidden Orient.

Through the open door Jim Wentworth saw a confused mass of bodies—men who had died since the last *Siu-fan-ti*, and who had been disinterred to be shipped across the Pacific to the sacred soil of China. About this terrible heap of dead stood the evil-faced attendants. But even this was not enough to turn Jim Wentworth's blood cold, to set his lips to a hard white line.

Swinging from the rafters, a long, black gown over his immaculate American clothing, was Wang Chen-p'o.

The young Chinaman's father, Wang Yu, was forced to sit below and watch his son's death agony.

A series of teakwood chairs had been placed one atop the other, so that young Wang's toes barely touched the uppermost chair. Only its support kept him from strangling instantly. As he swayed, and fought to keep balance—and life—the chairs teetered and rocked. The observers howled with joy and excitement at the performance.

Old Wang's face was impassive.

He stared steadily at the suffused face of his son. Old Wang Yu prayed that no word, no plea for mercy, would escape his boy's lips.

Wentworth's fingers tightened about the butt of his gun.

A big altar had been clumsily made of wooden boards

and draped with blood-red cloth. Behind it were arranged a long row of hideously painted gods and demons—the water-snake god—the dread-dragon-king of the lowest hell—the living-fire-goddess.

Sticks of incense flared and stunk.

Bowls of sacrificial rice were all over the room; on the floor, the altar, on top of some of the bodies.

Wentworth had been desperately trying to single out the leader of the body of fiends. With Wang in the air, simply because the young Chinese had spoken to the white detective, Wentworth had no time to spare in which to attempt to decipher the mystery. Later, perhaps. Not now.

He roared in English:

"Nobody move!"

Straight through the chant the white man's words hammered.

For an instant, while heads twisted about fearfully, the room was silent. Young Wang's hard breath sounded like wind in the reeds of Lake Hui Ch'ung....

Then some one shrieked, "*Sha!* Kill! Kill!"

Wentworth's gun darted from side to side, in a vain endeavor to find the man who had shouted.

"Back against the wall," he cried.

Wentworth's eyes were never on one place for more than a split-second, but they were on a level with the horde of Chinese.

He was about to order that Wang Chen-p'o be taken carefully down from his gallows, at the same time knowing instinctively that any overmuch interest shown in the Chinese would result in his being killed, undoubtedly before nightfall; his lips were actually open, when a

Chinese, creeping along the bare boards of the floor, leaped up, seized him insanely by the throat and hair, and tried to tear him to the ground.

Wentworth felt the hot sear of a knife in his shoulder, the fury of quickly drawn breath in his very ear, and then his finger tightened automatically.

Biting smoke swirled up to his nostrils.

The Chinese, a giant in stature, made one clutch, ripping his fingers down the detective's cheek, and then staggered back. He fell on his knees, talking strangely to himself, with his voice sliding up and down as if it already refused control.

He shook once, and then crashed down, face forward, stone dead.

Up went Wentworth's gun as he backed toward the wall.

A wizened Chinese—Wentworth's quick eyes caught the wrinkled monkey face—shrieked:

"*Sha!* Kill! Kill the white devil! And these two renegades! Then we can say we were attacked in *Siu-fan-ti,* and we will be all let go! *Sha!* Kill!"

Wentworth's gun roared a second time, aimed at the fiendish carer-for-the-dead who was screaming, but the onrush of Chinese, armed with knives and sacrificial swords and hatchets blessed by the chopping-life-tree-god, tore forward, over the bodies of the dead…

Dunand's voice was the most welcome sound Jim Wentworth had ever heard as he waited for death:

"Back, the lot of you," Dunand shouted. "Line 'em, boys… look out for knives… cut down that Chink who's in th' air…."

The riot squad wasted not an instant.

Some of the Chinese swarmed up a stairway at the rear of the room and ran for the roof, where the Chinatown detail grabbed them one by one.

One officer was stabbed in the thigh before he got his man to the floor.

Yet among the captives Wentworth did not see the wizened Chinese with the evil eyes.

The leader of the carers-for-the-dead had escaped.

"Now, young Jim, tell me what it's about," Dunand said grimly, when the last of the Chinese had been placed in the wagons. "If you've no good reason for this—it'll break you. And me, for backin' you up."

"Can I have a half hour before explaining?" Wentworth asked.

"Be in then… no… finish your beat, Jim. That'll look better, eh? And then drop in and make out your report."

Wentworth saluted.

As he walked past old Wang Yu, at the door, who watched two of the officers caring for his exhausted son, he said.

"You can tell me, honorable Wang. A debt is due me. A life was saved. I must know what happened."

Wang Yu said tonelessly, "Can do," in English, although Wentworth had spoken in Chinese. Then, in his own tongue, "A debt is due. I will pay. Behind the great red church of the white men is an alley. Go there. A member of my family will await you. When it is dark."

Wentworth, nodding, went outside, and started his steady pacing up Bannion's beat.

By the time he again reached the call box, and rang in, "All's quiet," as Dunand had requested, to headquarters, the murderous Chinese was gone. Perhaps they would not be able to pin Bannion's death on the assassin, but "attempted murder" would certainly stick. And that meant a ten-year stretch at the Point, San Quentin—making jute sacks.

5

IT WAS WELL after eight o'clock before Jimmy Wentworth stepped into Captain Dunand's office.

The captain of detectives had already plenty of time to think things over. He had given out the story to the morning paper boys—the capture of the assassin, who was Bannion's murderer, and the riot at the black building; but to their questions as to what it all meant he had merely looked wise, since he knew nothing.

And so he said to Wentworth now:

"You're either a hero, Jim, or a fool. Which is it?"

Wentworth grinned.

"We won't be broken, sir," he said. "I've got the whole story—"

"Shoot," said Dunand. "But if we've messed things up—broken into a temple, or something like that, without cause, heaven help you. And the department."

"Had any kicks from the heads of the Six Companies?"

Dunand frowned.

"No…I haven't. No kicks from any one! Get going, Jim! The newspaper hounds have been baying on my trail—"

"Couple of 'em outside," Wentworth admitted.

"What'd you tell 'em?"

"To see you. That I was only the cop on the beat."

"Good boy! Now—start at the beginning, Jim."

Wentworth sat down wearily in the chair toward which his chief waved, and lit the cigarette Dunand pushed in its packet toward him.

"I'm tired," he said suddenly, and then plunged into his story.

"Catching the little Chino—the one I locked to the post—you don't care about. He followed me, and then when he knew where he would meet me, ran around the block, or took a hidden passage, and tried to treat me the way he did Bannion—"

"Why was Bannion killed, boy?"

Wentworth said, "After the fracas, captain, I went to meet old Wang—"

"It's Bannion I want to know about!"

"Everything dove-tails. I've got to give you the details, sir. That's the way with Chinese happenings. You see, old Wang owed me a debt for saving his son. He's paid it to-night. After I walked my beat, I went past the Cathedral, clear out of Chinatown, and then doubled back the little alley. At the end of it is a shed—"

"Department's reported it as a fire hazard—"

"Yes, sir. You go in the shed, and pull away some of the dirt and stuff on the floor, and you find a trapdoor. A member of Wang's family met me; we went through the tunnel—it's got branches, probably leading to all of the Wang family houses—and ended at old Wang's.

"Three of the Six Company heads were there.

"Everybody did a lot of bowing. We drank the ceremonial tea. Wang knows I speak Chinese, but the good old boy never opened his head about it. He let me hear all the comments and asides without batting an eye. Then came the customary compliments. 'The honor of the family of Wang had been saved.' That sort of stuff. I could hardly wait to have 'em get started. Then one of the Six Company men said that the department had saved the peace of the district—"

"I wish th' mayor could hear that! He told th' commissioners that if we didn't get action by to-morrow, he'd make a few changes!"

"We've got all the action any one could want," Wentworth said. "Then, after darn' near a half hour of guff, we got down to business. The man who murdered poor Bannion—"

Dunand's hands gripped about his chair arms.

"—did it to prove his complete bravery. He—"

"Nonsense!"

"Wait, chief! He proved it by killing a white policeman who has been believed invincible and all-seeing. Bannion stopped at Wang's before he was killed. I don't know whether he looked at the black building too long or not. Anyhow, the carers-for-the-dead must have been suspicious of him, and let the assassin go to work."

"Why?"

"In China," Wentworth said slowly, "there's a class of such men. Pariahs. Over here, they were tired of seeing the hatchetmen—pariahs also—getting all the glory and the gold. So they went to the tongs—I got this tonight, of course—and made them an offer. To become hatchetmen. The tongs laughed at them. Spit at them. Called them a lot of cowardly dogs. And then they decided—the whole company of amateur undertakers—to prove what a courageous bunch they were.

"They talked it all over in the black building. And when Bannion stopped and looked at the outside of it, they must have been afraid that he was sure something was up."

Dunand nodded briefly.

"My guess," he said, "was opium. Maybe in the coffins."

"You knew about the black building?"

"Knew what was usually done there. But the coffins were made right here in the city, so I passed that up, naturally. It's the damnedest thing I ever heard, Jim. The way Bannion was killed started you on the right track, didn't it?"

"Yes, sir. That was the tip. And when I was followed, after I'd passed the building-of-the-dead, I was pretty sure I was right. Old Wang, the decent old cuss, warned me about it, too."

Dunand looked steadily out of the window.

"You don't get any credit at all on this job, Jim," he said quietly. "None. I think we'll try the Chink for murder, and also for attempted murder. We'll nail him on the second charge. You'll testify—and for heaven's sake try to seem dumb, boy—that he attacked you with a knife. That way, we're sure he won't get off. If we tried him for straight murder, a jury might let him off—to kill more cops! And don't mention the Wangs to anybody, eh? Keep 'em, and the Six Companies, out of it. As to the riot… hmm… we can't convict those Chinks. We'll deport 'em. Fast. The Six Companies won't want 'em here any more than we do, and we'll ship 'em out of the country in a hurry. And you, Jim— you continue being a flat-foot, and go back to your beat, boy. That's where you belong—but don't ever forget that you're working for this department from now on!"

Wentworth lit a second cigarette; his hand trembled a

bit as he did so. Dunand's telling him that he "belonged"—that he was one of the inner circle of the Chinatown detail—was everything he had hoped for.

"Nobody but the Wangs know I speak Chinese," he said. "And I wouldn't mind having a look at a certain wrinkle-faced Chino… I'll feel safer when we start him, steerage, for Hong-kong. Anything else, sir?"

"Hmm," Dunand said under his breath. "When a Chinaman likes you, he likes you. Be friendly with young Wang, Jim. He may be able to do you, and the department, some good. Now—yes, there is something else, young fellow. It's this: if you think you've fooled me, you're all wrong."

"About what, sir?"

"Lay off the 'sir' when we're alone, Jim. I was christened William for the convenience of my friends, but whoever heard of a policeman called Willie? Bill's better. About what? *I* know you've been knifed in the shoulder, even if it hasn't bled all over your uniform. I'm that good a dick, anyhow! And I know, now, that you've got nerve." His hand gripped Wentworth's "Good boy. Go down to the Harbor, and have the cut dressed. Then… want to eat with me?"

Wentworth's face flushed with pleasure.

"And if it hurts when they wash your wound," Dunand said grimly, "think of me, working up an appetite for dinner by trying to answer a thousand questions from the newspaper boys—trying to tell 'em the truth, and yet protect the Wangs, and you, and it'll be a wonder if I'm able to eat at all! Meet you at Jack's in an hour, Jim."

Wentworth discovered that all his weariness had left him. His shoulder did hurt a bit, but he was whistling as he walked down the corridor toward the elevator. This morning he had been a uniformed clerk. Now he was Jim Wentworth, of the Chinatown detail. And back in China-town, to keep him busy when he walked his beat, would be the necessity of watching a certain wizened Chinese—of seeing the evil-faced man—first.

CRIMSON CIRCLES

In the Secret Cellar of a Chinese Dope Joint Kong Gai, Arch-Killer, Sentences Jimmy Wentworth to Death

1

THE HAZE OF twilight was settling down over Chinatown as Jimmy Wentworth was pacing the final round
of his beat. Cymbals clashed and flutes wailed dolefully
where white men and women ate chow mein and chop
suey. Where the Chinese themselves sought entertainment, *san-hein* plucked by the pointed nails of singsong
girls sent out thin squeaks. To the detective's right, as he
walked up the hilly street, the mechanical pianos of Waverley Place blared.

Through this maze of sound a gun cracked. Swinging
about, Wentworth heard the shrill summons of Malloy's
whistle—one hasty, urgent blast. Jimmy jerked out his own
gun as he ran. Riots in this district could be serious. Malloy
was not the officer to ask aid unless he needed it.

Almost a full block down the street Wentworth could
see Malloy's bulk, moving toward him. Between them
were several shadowy forms, which seemed to be bent over
something on the sidewalk. In the fraction of an instant
that Wentworth's eyes took in the scene, he heard his name
called, the shout ending in a horrible scream. He knew
that Malloy was down, even before he saw the patrolman
plunge forward.

Racing down Waverley Place, Wentworth fired into
the air. Despite his cry of "Stop!" the stooping men were

dissolving into the fading light. Wentworth fired a second time, over their heads. He hurdled the prostrate form the men had been bending over and knelt beside Malloy. A pool of blood was spreading beside the patrolman, and his face was gray as ash.

"Chinks, Jimmy, Chinks," Malloy whispered. "Some one… got me… in the back. When I was coming to see… what was up."

Slipping his arm under the dying officer, Wentworth called to a woman who stared from a doorway.

"Tell Central to send a police ambulance!" he shouted, and then said softly to Malloy, "Get you fixed up right away, Pat. Just a scratch, old man. Lie still—"

"Got me," Malloy whispered. He coughed, and fresh blood welled to his lips. "I never seen who did it, Jimmy. Man came out of house. No. 41. Chinks jumped him. They were"—Malloy coughed again—"doin' something… to his… knee, Jim. Or leg. I dunno. Then I got it… in the back."

Wentworth said softly, "Don't move, Pat. Just lie quietly."

The other man on the sidewalk was dead. The men who had killed him were already far-away. If they were Chinese, and the motive had been robbery—something concealed under the dead man's knee, possibly—the Chinatown detail would ferret it out later. The first thing was to make old Malloy easy.

The old officer's eyes were closed. Suddenly his hand tightened on Wentworth's.

"They're comin'," he said clearly. "I can hear 'em."

Wentworth bent closer. Malloy would never hear anything more, for he was dead. It was almost a minute

*Jimmy's left took the
hatchetman on the jaw*

before even Jimmy's sharp ears caught the clang! clang! of the department ambulance as it roared up toward Waverley Place.

Identification of the dead man was easy. The woman in No. 41 admitted that he had worked for her.

"He never had a dime," she told Wentworth. "So robbery couldn't be the motive—unless the fellow had done some robbing himself and was robbed in turn."

Quietly, efficiently, Wentworth set out to dig up the dead man's past. What he learned helped him little. The fellow had lived in San Francisco all his life. He was in the middle twenties. He played the pool rooms. He had once won a couple of hundred dollars on the ponies. He had never been arrested nor suspected. Just a bum who, for cigarette money, was known to sell lottery tickets and make a little money in other unsavory ways.

No one had seen him killed—or admitted seeing it. No one had seen Malloy stabbed. On the face of it, the man had been murdered, reason unknown, by Chinese, and Malloy had been killed when he started running toward the scene of the crime. But Wentworth was not entirely satisfied. Ordinarily the Chinese would have disappeared when Malloy discovered what they had done.

After going off duty, Wentworth reported to Captain Dunand.

"We want to get whoever got old Pat," the head of the detective bureau said. "My guess is that the dead man won on the lottery and some Chinese knew it. They did him in. Malloy was just unlucky enough to arrive at the wrong time. The Chinks had a watcher, and he got Malloy."

"Pat blew his whistle," Wentworth said grimly. "That means he must've known he was being followed. As for the guy being robbed of lottery money, the Chinese would never do that, chief. It would give the thief a hundred years' misfortune." Almost to himself he added, "Yet, maybe I'm wrong. Malloy said the Chinks were doing something to the dead man's leg. Or his knee."

Captain Dunand looked squarely at his detective. "Hmm," he said. "The autopsy surgeon said that he noticed that one leg was clean and the other one pretty dirty. What d'you make of that, Jim?"

"You mean one leg looked as if it'd been washed?"

"Right."

"I never heard anything like that," Wentworth said. "But Malloy did say they were doing something to the man's leg."

"You'd better find out what they did," suggested Dunand.

"You and I know what sort of man this chap was. But watch the papers jump us. They'll fake the story so it'll appear as if he were a prominent citizen and that old Pat wasn't on the job or the murder would have been prevented. Gives 'em a fine chance to give us hell, Jim."

"Hell may break out in Chinatown," Wentworth replied. "There's something funny about all this. If it'd been robbery plus murder, I don't think Malloy would have been touched. And this clean leg affair... I thought I knew a lot about the Chinese, but that's one on me."

"See what you can find out—to-morrow," Dunand ordered. "I'm putting the detail on the case immediately. Don't go back yourself to-night. It would make the Chinese wonder if you aren't more than a patrolman... And keep your eyes open, Jim. Two murders at one time is a little too many. We've got to find who did 'em."

"And why," said Wentworth.

2

IT WAS THE Chinatown detective's custom to have his lunch on the third floor of a Chinese restaurant, where no "slop-for-white-devils" was served. Here the more important merchants met each noon to eat and gossip. Wentworth was accepted as merely a police officer, and therefore a necessary evil. That the owner allowed him to lunch on the third floor meant only that the wily proprietor wanted to keep him away from the rooms below, where white men and women were able to buy *ng ki po* or vile electric brandy served in teacups.

Wentworth knew all about this, but his job was preventing tong warfare and other forms of Asiatic murder, and, when murder had been committed, finding the killer. By keeping his ears open as he ate he was often able to pick up something helpful. Having been born in China, Wentworth understood Chinese and its dialects, could speak it, and could almost think in Oriental fashion.

The day was again warm and close. In the big room, overlooking the Barbary Coast, were many Chinese, engaged in exploring the centers of doughy dumplings with their chopsticks, endeavoring to extract bits of stewed duck or pickled fish.

Perched on a high stool, Jimmy had been eating only because it was time to eat, and for the good reason that he wanted the Chinese to think he did everything on schedule. He wanted to be expected places at an exact time. Some day that might come in handy.

Across the round table on which Wentworth's *foo yung* congealed was Tsing K'ung himself, the owner.

"Verry hot," he announced, as Jimmy sipped tea. *"Foo yung* good? I eat *foo yung* many time with Bannion."

Bannion, a veteran patrolman, had been murdered. Wentworth's first case was the solving of the crime, although none in Chinatown knew of his part in it.

"Bannion he like prenty hot tea. I go fo' hot watah fo' you."

"Send a waiter, Mr. Kung. That's the way white men do."

Had the proprietor shrieked an order, the nearest waiter would have rushed to obey, which was what Wentworth wanted. Wentworth had seen something. But Tsing K'ung desired to show the policeman every honor, a debt which he would some day collect, when there was a fight in the restaurant. The nearest waiter, now scurrying about with both hands filled with hot bowls of food, was the one who had aroused Jimmy's curiosity.

What had happened was this. Halfway up the side wall, where the restaurant was higher than the adjoining building, was a small window, covered with netting to keep out flies. Some one had told the waiter to open the window. Chinese fashion, the servant had not troubled to get a ladder. He had placed two stools on one of the tall eating chairs, mounted, and then pushed open the window.

In getting down from his shaky perch one leg of his wide, flapping black trousers had caught on the edge of the second stool, so that the sleezy fabric was pushed—for the fraction of an instant—up to the knee. And around the waiter's scrawny leg Wentworth had seen several brilliant red circles, a half inch wide.

As Jimmy quietly finished his lunch, he tried to recall which Chinese tribes employed anything resembling a caste mark. He could not. In western China, some of the racially intermingled tribes tattooed their faces. The Lolos did this, and the Kachins, but with blue marks, across the nose, or on the cheek-bones. Wentworth had never seen anything like these painted crimson circles, nor heard of any lore or custom justifying them.

With a bowl of tea in hand, Jimmy waited for a time when the waiter with the strange leg markings would be near enough for him to call, "Oh, boy!" in English. The fellow, however, went into the kitchen.

Ever since the day Wentworth had started on the obscure trail of some fiendish Chinese gang, whose head was a wizened ape-like Chinese called Kong Gai, he missed no detail which might give him a clew to the identity of these Asiatics. Here might be something tangible. More, he was increasingly puzzled by the "clean leg" of the dead man last night. Could there be any connection between a waiter and an underworld bum—a Chinese servant and a white man?

In the kitchen, behind flimsy swinging doors, there was a crash of dishes, followed by an apologetic, *"Hai!"* Tsing K'ung, standing near a table, cackled something explanatory about the incident, and then the waiter himself shot through the doors, empty handed.

Behind him, a vegetable knife brandished high, leaped the cook himself, screaming angrily, *"Sao ta tzü! Stinking

Tartar! Clumsy fool! My finest food on the floor! *Tong nui!* Ox-face! I will cut out your liver—"

Wentworth knew perfectly well that this terrific anger was assumed and that the cook had no intention of using the knife. However, in his part as a white man who understood nothing about the ways of the East, he jumped forward, pleased that he might have an opportunity to speak with the waiter.

Running between the two Chinese, he took the knife from the cook.

"That fool of a servant thinks the ten fiends are all after him at once," a merchant laughed, and another Chinese giggled that the white policeman had an equal amount of intelligence. The waiter had not stopped when his attacker was disarmed. He had continued running. The patter of his feet could be heard as he raced down the stairs to the busy street below.

"Now, oh cook, see what you have done," Tsing K'ung grumbled. "Are you the god of vengeance? He is gone and how will I be able to pay him for the week's labor?"

"His labors have been little. We will not miss him. His hands have a palsy. I should have killed him for spoiling the bowls of shredded chicken. You will thank me for getting rid of him!"

Wentworth, in English, broke up the argument. "What was his name, Mr. Kung? I ought to make a report of this."

"His name? When I called, he came. A servant is not known by name until he has proven his value. Name? I not know. Report? Must do?"

"Well," Wentworth said, "maybe not. But if I've got to know, tell me where he lives, and I can find out."

Tsing K'ung shouted at the cook. All of the merchants joined merrily in the discussion. But none of them knew the waiter's name, nor where he lived. When Jimmy was convinced of this, he warned the cook to leave knives alone in the future; he accepted Tsing K'ung's imitation apology for the disturbance; he grinned at the merchants as if he did not realize they were secretly amused at his excitement, and then started down the stairs leading to the street.

Crimson circles! What meaning could these marks on the waiter's leg possibly have? Some meaning. In Chinatown nothing ever happened by accident.

3

AND YET SOMETHING had happened by accident. A glance told Wentworth what it was, even before the jabbering group of Chinese melted away at his approach. There, opposite the doorway to the restaurant, was a big truck, with the white-faced driver staring at the circle of Asiatics. On the ground Wentworth saw the same waiter who had fled so swiftly from the restaurant. Fled, to be struck down by the truck as he dashed to cross the street.

Even while the detective dropped to his knees beside the crushed body, the truck driver pleaded with him. "I was takin' a load of hides to that Chinee leather maker. I was goin' slow, officer. You know how slow a guy's got to go to get through this street. This Chink jumps off th' sidewalk. I never seen him until I hit him—"

"He's dead," Wentworth said.

The driver groaned.

"Go call police headquarters," Wentworth directed. "Tell 'em what happened—make it short. Say a man's been run over and killed. They'll know what to do. Tell 'em where it happened. Get going. Make it snappy."

Some one had already sent word to an apothecary's shop down the street. Powdered lizard's feet mixed with *ginseng* and diluted snake venom was being rubbed over the dead man's chest, where his heart no longer beat. The apothecary mumbled the Six Sacred Words, but even so the breath of life did not return. The waiter must have died instantly.

Wentworth kept a close watch that no one touched the dead man's sleezy black trousers. He listened intently to the conversation about him, but heard nothing to indicate that any of the Chinese had seen the crimson markings. Nor was there any trace as to the identity of the dead waiter. He was only a coolie, living in some unknown rabbit hole.

But nevertheless a coolie with crimson circles painted around his leg! Wentworth intended to have a good look at the strange marks, but not here, not where he would attract attention. Methodically, he saw the dead man placed in the wagon; methodically, he explained to the truck driver what to do.

"Ain't you goin' to handcuff me?" the man asked.

"You've got a fine opinion of cops, haven't you?" Jimmy grunted. "An accident's an accident. Even going to the station's only a formality. Get going. I'll phone in about it when I can."

When Wentworth returned to the restaurant, the sorrowful Tsing K'ung, knowing what had happened, said that the dead man was technically still his servant, and that he himself would arrange all funeral expenses. From the kitchen the cook screamed what most white men would have considered obscenities. Actually, feeling guilty, the cook was reciting the Hundred Apologies for Causing Death, which would take him the rest of the day to complete.

Wentworth left with the wailing of the cook in his ears. He walked soberly along his beat until he came to the shop of old Wang Yu. Wang Chen-p'o, the son, a Chinese of Wentworth's own age, sat out of range in a corner of the porcelain shop, while two thin faced Orientals—hatchetman guards—made believe they were stacking a shipment of jars. The Wangs, fearful of their lives because of the unseen, unknown Kong Gai, were taking no chances. Wentworth knew that the flower vendor across the street was another hatchetman acting as a spy, who would warn his mates in the shop if any one doubtful approached.

All this was none of Wentworth's concern. He, also, would protect the Wangs, who were friendly to the police. Since there seemed no excitement about, Wentworth entered the shop. Every one in Chinatown already knew that the Wangs aided the American police.

"I hear a waiter was run over," grinned young Chen-p'o. "Was he another bad boy, James? That what you come to find out?"

"Know who he was?"

"Never heard of him. Why?"

Wentworth said, "Do your men know any English?"

"Damn and hell. That's all. Safe to talk, Jim."

"Good. Now why do Chinese have red circles painted around their legs?"

"Hanged if I know. But I've had the misfortune of an American education. I'll ask my father." Chen-p'o crackled into Cantonese before Wentworth could stop him. The detective was glad that neither of the guards seemed interested. When old Wang shook his head, and whispered a few words, his son said, "He has never heard of such a custom, Jim. And what he doesn't know isn't worth knowing. He's even wise to me. Is there anything else I can do?"

"Plenty. But you know who I want to find already. Tell me, how does it feel to get a knife in the back?"

"Stick around Chinatown long enough and you'll find out. So far you are lucky. When you entered, even these dumb guards, who only know how to kill an enemy, said something uncomplimentary concerning your brains."

"Suits me," grinned Jimmy. "Keep that stuff about red circles to yourself."

Following his customary route, Wentworth left the part of Chinatown crowded with bazaars and shops, and began to climb the steeper hills, north of Waverley Place, where fish merchants, on the roofs dried whitebait and long-tailed shrimp. Halfway up the hill a rumbling truck caught up with him. A hundred feet ahead, at a smelly gray wooden building, the truck stopped, and the half-caste driver and his assistant got down, slowly, carrying inside a bundle of nets. Both men seemed very tired.

Wentworth turned down an alley, walked to the end, doubled on his tracks, and finally continued his climb up the hill. He turned at the next corner. Below him, he could see the open space in the rear of the gray building. Here bare bamboo poles were thrust into the ground, on which the nets were hung to dry after the morning's fishing. As the detective glanced down, concerned more with passing the time until he could get to the station and have a good look at the crimson circles, a man carried an armful of nets into the yard. The same fellow who had sat beside the driver of the truck. However, he seemed tired no longer, for he sang nasally, and his movements were quick and alert.

Wentworth watched him stretch his black nets between the twenty-foot high bamboo poles, until the result was like prodigious cobwebs. The coolie worked with sinuous grace. With his very rapidity, he caught one of his bare feet in the meshes which lay before and around him. Wentworth saw him struggle to disentangle himself. Again, the Chinese seemed curiously fiery in his movements.

While the coolie grunted and snarled, his short fisherman's jacket fell away, and the white detective could see the muscular, hairless chest. Then, unlike any Chinese Jimmy had ever seen, the coolie lost all patience. He drew a short knife from his belt, twisting about to yank it out, and began to hack away the binding strands. With the upper part of his body released, he attempted to squat down and get at his legs and feet.

Without warning, he fell, entangling himself worse than ever. The air was filled with curses. Thoroughly enraged, the coolie slashed away at the net so unreasoningly that he ripped through the cloth of his flapping blue coolie-cloth trousers. And Wentworth saw, about the thigh, at least a dozen brilliant crimson circles! Crossing these, at right angles, was the bright mark made by the knife itself, already a streak of bright blood.

Wentworth wasted no second. He vaulted the fence against which he had been leaning, and raced through the empty space toward the bamboo poles.

The coolie, knife in hand, blinked at the approaching officer. And, proof again that nothing is unobserved in Chinatown, Asiatics began to slip from their dens and follow the running officer. Others slipped from the gray building itself. Noises broke out, shrill calls from a dozen directions.

As Jimmy dashed in, the coolie's knife flashed up. The

detective's left hand darted in under the stabbing arm. At the same instant he cracked the fish-coolie heavily, a short, jolting blow, in the man's middle. The descending knife missed Jimmy's head, ripping futilely through his uniform below the shoulder. Before Wentworth was able to get a finishing smash at the coolie's jaw, the pack was on him. The detective was hurled down through sheer weight of numbers.

In his nostrils was the stench of unwashed bodies. In another moment a knife would rip him wide. But, instead, hands lifted him carefully. Chinese clustered about, brushing dust from his uniform. Another Asiatic brought him his cap.

Wentworth went wild with anger himself. Only his training kept him from going into action. He knew, without glancing around, that the coolie with the red circles on his thigh was gone.

Most of the Chinese vanished as speedily as the net-mender. One of those who remained, a placid old Oriental with a shred of beard on his chin, said gravely, "Why you want hurt China boy?"

"I didn't want to hurt him," Wentworth said, as if he were puzzled by what had happened, for all his rage. "Why *you* come throw me down? You all want go jail?"

The Chinese shook his head. "We 'fraid mebbe-so you hurt China boy," he said. "Too bad."

Jimmy let the lie pass. "I think China boy hurt already," he said solemnly. "I watch him. I see him catch he-self on net. I see blood on leg. I go look-see. Then China boy he take knife at me. He very angry. He—"

"No. He 'fraid. He scared. Too bad." Brightly, "All over now?"

"China boy hurt," insisted Jimmy. "He go hospital. You take me where he stop. I take him hospital. Have leg fixed."

"He 'fraid Melican hosp'tal. Mo' betta China doctor fix leg."

"Where he live?"

The spokesman went through a pantomime, ending by saying sorrowfully that no one knew.

"Next time," Wentworth said, although he realized how all were laughing secretly at his words, "Next time you jump on policeman, all go jail. You hear?"

The abject apologies of the Chinese would have satisfied a less understanding man than Wentworth. He knew what they were worth. Any one else would have thought that the shrill cadences which followed him—uttered in Chinese—were only a continuation of the apology. Yet Jimmy's ears burned as every portion of his anatomy was discussed, unfavorably, and while his ancestors, himself, and any descendants foolish enough to acknowledge him as their father, were all considered in detail.

Now, what was there to this crimson circle affair? About the fish-coolie's thigh had been something like a dozen. Half as many had been painted on the waiter's leg. Why? How many—if any at all—had been removed from the white man after he had been killed on Waverley Place?

Wentworth wondered what would happen if, at random, he were to send the squad into Chinatown and pick up fifty Chinese. Would any of them have the crimson marks on their legs? Even so, would any of them talk? Wentworth wished the waiter hadn't been hit by the truck.

Four thirty came at last and Wentworth went down to the Hall of Justice. Without wasting time, he went directly to Dunand's office.

"I've run across a funny one, chief," he said. "Red rings—circles of crimson—painted around the legs of some Chinos. A new one on me. Even old Wang never heard of it. Come to the morgue. The waiter who was killed by the truck's got 'em on his leg. Another fellow got away to-day."

"Let's have a look at them," agreed Dunand. "Might solve a few things."

The Chinese waiter lay on a slab, naked as the day he had been born. But there was no trace of red paint or stain on either leg!

4

FOR ONCE, EVEN after renewed entreaties, the elder Wang was unable to give Jim Wentworth a single bit of information. Wang Yu had never seen crimson circles. He was able to add to the detective's store of knowledge about tattooing, but the marks had not been tattooed. They must have been painted about the leg, otherwise they would not have disappeared from the waiter's limb after he had been struck down by the truck.

Here was some sort of society, some new "tong," perhaps, with members all over Chinatown. The waiter had only been on the ground a few seconds, but some Chinese had removed the circles. Again, the fish-coolie was protected by a throng of Asiatics, who, like Wentworth, must have seen the bloody-hued markings.

Wentworth tried to puzzle it all out, but the next morning he was where he had started. Actually, the death of Malloy and of the tout couldn't directly be connected with the crimson circles. Yet the curious marks were never out of Wentworth's mind. As he walked along his beat, Chinatown was crowded, and as visibly peaceful as ever. Not one word did Wentworth catch, about impending trouble or the strange circles.

Since a dead waiter could tell no tales, the department had turned the body over to Tsing K'ung. When Wentworth left Dupont Street he heard the noise of the funeral on the street above. Only professional, paid mourners would follow the coffin to the temple, but nevertheless Jimmy decided to have a peep at the performance.

There was a priest ringing a little bell, first in line. A boy followed, carrying a banner inscribed with a fictitious and wonderful history of the dead man. Then came coolies bearing long, twisting paper monsters, before which any devils lurking in the street would crumble and turn to ashes. Next was the palaquin-coffin, carried on the shoulders of sturdy Orientals. Last came the mourners, chanting away fervently to earn their money.

Tsing K'ung had been as good as his word. His servant was being given a number one funeral, with no details forgotten.

As Wentworth watched the cortege approach, Chinese passed him, or stopped to watch. One of these Jimmy knew for a merchant in a small bazaar—a thin, quiet Oriental, nearing his seventies. Unlike the others, the merchant had come down the steep side street—from the direction of the house where Wentworth had attempted to catch the fish-coolie. The old man's face muscles twitched. His bony hands wriggled back and forth inside his wide sleeves.

The cortege, Jimmy knew, would meander to the temple, where vermilion-robed priests would plead with the rows of gods to send the soul of the dead man to heaven, instead of turning into a devil and tormenting people on earth. There would be plenty of wailing, plenty of incense burned.

Just as the procession reached Wentworth, where an alley crossed the side street, an alert funeral attendant decided that possibly demons might be hiding in the narrow way who might not have seen the dragons, so he gave a mighty stroke on the bell he carried, and almost at the same instant a second attendant touched a match to a string of firecrackers, so that the street shook and trembled with sound.

At Wentworth's side the old merchant gasped, so gently that it could not have been heard a foot away. Then he clutched at Wentworth with feverish force. His nails bit deep into the detective's arm, clear through cloth.

Jimmy whirled, one hand going for his gun automatically. Seeing what was happening, he caught the sickened old Chinese and tried to hold him. It was almost impossible. The merchant writhed and twisted, his face unrecognizable. He seemed to have the strength of a man in his prime.

Then, as swiftly as the seizure had taken place, the Chinese relaxed with a sigh. Wentworth eased him to the sidewalk, while two Asiatics hurried up.

"Our father sick," one of them said. "We take him home."

Jimmy was about to release his burden to the pair, when he remembered that no sacred tablet was in the merchant's shop window. The man was unmarried, and had no sons. However, "father" might mean any old relative.

"I get doctor," Wentworth suggested slowly.

The second Asiatic growled. "Get the old man away. Otherwise things may be seen." Said it in Chinese, and then added in English, "My father many-time too much sick. We take him away home."

Wentworth glanced about swiftly. His eye lit on a white man and his wife. The man was carrying several paper-wrapped bundles. Tourists. Now they were observing the procession with keen interest. Wentworth called to them, and ordered the man to go to a pay station a block south, telephone the police, and say that a sick Chinese needed to go to the hospital.

"And tell 'em to hurry," Jimmy added.

The man nodded, and with his wife holding his arm, turned to go. Just as Wentworth saw the white couple reach the corner, the merchant began to twitch again. At the same moment Wentworth heard the white woman scream, and saw several burly Chinese jostling her.

Gun out, Wentworth was on his feet. He caught up the writhing Chinaman, dragged him erect, flung his slight weight over his shoulder, and, firing once into the air, stumbled down the street.

"Stay with me," he shouted to the terrified pair. "Everything's all right. Walk in front of me."

The Chinese had expected that he would leave the sick merchant to stop the trouble at the corner. If he had, he knew that the merchant would be gone when he returned. And Jimmy believed now that the old Chinese would have the crimson circles around one of his legs. It was no easy matter, carrying a contorting man, watching two white people, and at the same time endeavoring to see who were in the pack about him, who kept away only because of his gun. All sorts of Chinese. Coolies, clerks, vendors.

How many were simply curious? How many knew what was up? In the throng Wentworth thought he caught a glimpse of a small, wizened Chinese with evil eyes—Kong Gai?

"Keep going," Wentworth snapped to the pair he guarded. "Now, stop. Get my keys off my belt. Open that police box. That's fine. Now, tell whoever answers that

Wentworth is calling. Good. Tell 'em I want an ambulance. Right. Now say I want help. Fine work, old man. Hang up the receiver and close the box."

Many of the Chinese edged away, leaving a ring of about a dozen yellow faces. The detective raised his voice. "What's the matter with you?" he asked. "Sick man must go hospital. Why you stay here?"

The ring moved closer. Two lean Chinese began to lick their lips.

"Get back," Wentworth snapped, gun ready. He knew that furtive movement of hand inside jacket. "Get ba—" he began, and instantly fired.

The Chinese shrieked, and grabbed at his wrist. His knife clattered to the pavement. One of his fellows snatched it up.

"Keep back of me," Wentworth told his companions. "If they rush, run."

A Chinese whined, "We must advance all together, brothers, or one by one we will be shot. When I give the word—"

If he gave it, the shrill blast of a police siren smothered the sound. Up the steep, cobbled street the wagon roared, with Captain Dunand himself urging the driver to greater speed. But before the officer at the wheel could jam on his brakes, or his mates leap from the rear of the machine, not a Chinese was in sight.

A moment later the ambulance from the Harbor Hospital hooted its way to the callbox. Captain Dunand asked quickly, "What's wrong, Wentworth?" And, before Jim could answer, both white man and white woman tried to tell him.

The hospital interne, kneeling beside the old Chinese,

said, "He's got a pulse like the beat of a hammer. He's quiet now, but he'll go off again in a sec'. Yep. There he goes again. Convulsions. Poison, I'd say. Better get him to the hospital in a hurry."

"Send some one with the ambulance, chief," Jimmy urged grimly. "And don't let any one see him when he's in bed, doctor."

The interne looked curiously at this young patrolman who was giving orders. When Captain Dunand made no objection or comment, the doctor said, "O.K. Want us to let you know when he dies, cap?"

"Keep him alive," pleaded Wentworth.

The doctor shrugged. "Couple more spasms and he'll be a dead Chink."

In a low voice, Wentworth said to Dunand, "Nobody's wise that I know something funny is up. When the old man's lifted into the ambulance, I want a peek at his legs. Have some of the boys stand behind me. I'll lift the bottom end of the stretcher. I don't want any one seeing me do it."

Dunand glanced about. "Nobody's looking," he said.

"All Chinatown's watching. I want 'em to think I'm dumb, or you might as well take me off the beat before I get a knife in the gizzard."

Several of the riot squad crowded about. When the front end of the stretcher was on the roller at the end of the ambulance, Wentworth balanced the other against his body, and swiftly pulled up the Chinese's trousers. Both legs were circled with crimson marks, from below the knee almost to the thigh.

5

"I THINK YOU'RE more of a Chinese than I," young Wang Chen-p'o said to Wentworth, after the waiter brought dessert and coffee. "You were born and educated in China; I went to college here. I think like a white man. To me those crimson circles are a joke. And yet, although you haven't connected 'em with crime, you can't eat a mouthful. Snap out of it, Jim."

"They've got me guessing."

His friend nodded sympathetically, and then said, "You rather have me guessing, too. How come you're a detective, old man?"

"Because I'm Chinese-minded, maybe. Filial piety. My dad was on the force. He went to China during the Rebellion, and stayed there. Wanted me to join the force. And here I am."

"A good steak was wasted on you to-night. Oh, well, go ahead and gab about your red circles. That's what you've been waiting to do." Taking a deep puff, Chen-p'o added, "If I were you, I wouldn't go sticking my nose into other people's business. You've been lucky so far. You're still alive. But even my honorable father is frightened enough to go into hiding just because he's threatened, as he did a few weeks ago. Watch your step, Jim."

"You think Kong Gai's back of these strange marks?"

"Not knowing if there really is a Kong Gai, I can't say. I'm not curious, either. But you are."

"It's my job," Jimmy said. "And I get a kick out of it. Now, about this red circle business. Firstly, I saw 'em on the leg of a waiter in K'ung's restaurant. Just a few circles on his leg. The waiter ran away, was hit and killed by a truck, and the crimson circles vanished.

"Secondly, a fish-coolie, who looked tired to death when he went to mend nets, comes out to work all pepped up. He gets caught in the meshes, goes berserk, and when I go to see what he's doing, a mob knocks me down. The fish-coolie had nearly a dozen rings painted on his leg. I think he knew I saw 'em. Anyhow, he gets away before I can grab him.

"Thirdly, when Malloy was trying to stop a murder on Waverley Place, the dead man had one dirty leg, and one clean one, and Chinese had been bending over him! Were the circles there, also?

"Next, while I'm watching the waiter's funeral, an old man standing beside me falls in a fit—"

"A perfectly respectable Chinese gentleman—"

Wentworth nodded. "That's what he is. When the firecrackers go bang, he almost dies on the spot. And we have to send for the riot squad to be able to take him to the hospital. Why? So he can be spirited away, or the rings wiped off. And *he* had fifteen or more circles on *each* leg! He's safe in the hospital, but he's so near dead we can't question him. Now, what I want to know is—"

"The connection between a tout, a waiter, a fish-coolie, and a respectable merchant?"

"Right. And why one was painted with a few rings, the next with a dozen, and the third with half a hundred or so."

"Maybe they're merit badges, Jim, and the fellows are all Scouts."

"Don't be funny, Wang. Here's another thing. The waiter runs as if the fiends are after him. The fish-coolie wants my life. And the old merchant tries to drop dead. Figure that out."

"Not me," Chen-p'o grinned. "I don't get paid for it. What you're really after, I take it, is to find who killed Malloy, and—" lowering his voice "—if Kong Gai the Dread is back of this business, whatever it is."

"I'm going to phone the hospital again," Wentworth said. "When I come back, you have a solution, or you can pay the dinner check."

"Fine break for me," grinned Wang.

The hospital reported no change. They had managed to prevent a recurrence of the merchant's convulsions, but the physician in charge said it would be murder to allow him to be questioned. "That's the way strychnine poisoning cases react," the doctor explained. "Any sudden noise starts them going again."

"It's strychnine poisoning, doctor?"

"It is." Soberly, "It might have been any one of several things, but now we are positive."

"How long has this poisoning been going on?" Jimmy asked.

"From the age and condition of the patient—" the doctor paused, and then calmly eliminated Wentworth's theory "—I should say it was the first time he was ever—er—poisoned."

"Could the strychnine been given him without his knowledge? While he was standing on the street?"

"No. And I understand you were beside him then. Extremely improbable. Just a minute, detective. His nurse is here." There was a considerable wait, and then the doctor said quietly, "I'm sorry, but the man is dead."

Wentworth smothered a curse.

"He had a slim chance," the doctor's voice continued, "but somebody threw a rock through his window, and the sound of the breaking glass sent him into another convulsion. Your detectives went outside immediately, but found nothing."

Wentworth said grimly, "You're positive it is strychnine poisoning?"

"I am."

"Can you tell me all about strychnine? How it is given, as a poison—"

"Come to my house later, and I'll tell you gladly." He gave Jim his address.

Wang Chen-p'o stared at his friend when Wentworth returned to their booth. "Have you seen the ghost of your ancestors?" he asked.

"Our old man's dead."

"Tough break, Jim."

"Break's right. Now we're where we were before. Pay up for our dinner."

"Not me. I've got a solution."

Wentworth asked, "You know the connection between waiter, tout, fish-coolie and merchant? Shoot."

"You've forgotten the Chinese saying, Jim. 'Between

men of varied degrees, there are two threads; firstly, the gods ordered the birth of lord and slave, and—'"

"Secondly," interrupted Wentworth, " 'the lives of all men are bound by the juice of the poppy.' You're all wet, Wang. Pay the check. It was strychnine poisoning."

"I answered the riddle. Why not split the check?"

Agreeing, Wentworth said, "You can't hook opium with this crimson circle business, Wang."

"Sometimes I think opium's back of everything in Chinatown. What do we do now?"

"Go see this M.D. Want to come? Get all the dope on strychnine."

"Why?"

"Because I haven't a single hunch on the case. I'm stumped. I'm fishing for some clew—"

They left the café together. The doctor was going straight home, and by walking the pair would arrive after him. Wang did his best to keep up a conversation, but Wentworth was deep in the mystery of the crimson circles. He realized that in visiting the physician he was going far afield, and yet what else was there to do?

Dr. Braydon was smoking a quiet cigar in his library when the pair arrived.

"Sorry to have lost your patient," he said to Wentworth, after Wang had been introduced. "Your Chink was poisoned, well enough. Strychnine. He may have been given it as a stimulant. Heaven only knows what these Chinese devil-doctors give. He was in no condition to stand stimulation. Any reason why any one'd want him killed?"

"None," Wang said. "He has no family. His money, what

little exists, goes to the treasury of the Six Companies for charity."

The keen-eyed physician asked, "And how about those curious painted rings around his legs?"

Wentworth, totally at sea, decided to trust the doctor. Swiftly he explained the entire circumstance. "Could there have been strychnine in the paint, doctor? Was it absorbed into the skin, so that a few circles were harmless, but a lot would cause death?"

Dr. Braydon shook his head.

"Another blank," Jimmy said. "That's all I seem able to draw in this game."

Looking at the end of his cigar, the doctor said, "Your friend, Mr. Wang. Can he offer no solution?"

"I would have won a dinner if I could," said Chen-p'o. "The best I had to offer was that 'the lives of all men are bound together by the juice of the poppy.' Opium, or its derivatives."

Dr. Braydon puffed on his cigar thoughtfully. "It isn't generally known, but the antidote for opium or morphine poisoning is strychnine."

Wentworth's eyes began to glow. Wang Chen-p'o smiled slightly. There it was!

"At a guess," the doctor continued, "the old merchant was an addict. Somebody gave him an antidote, becoming fearful he'd had too much of the drug. There was a noise— the firecrackers—and the old man went into convulsions. The crimson circles—"

"Show," Jimmy said swiftly, "that he'd taken opium for a long time. It's clear now. The waiter, on the other hand, had only a few rings around his leg. He was new to the business.

He hadn't had any dope all day. When the cook came at him with the knife, he ran, because he was low mentally—"

"Correct," agreed the physician.

"Then, the fish-coolie; he'd just been given opium or morphine. He was intoxicated by it—"

"Correct again."

"And the white man," the detective summarized shrewdly, "had only been initiated into the fraternity. He'd got a shot or two, and then tried to blackmail the Chinese for more!"

Dr. Braydon smiled slightly. "Whoever marks his victims does it, I should say, for two reasons. One, to recognize them as 'safe' to give the drug, the other, as the old Chinaman, to administer the antidote before an addict dies from excessive use. Had the merchant gone directly home, and not stopped to view the procession, he might have lived. Whoever is back of the scheme understands something of drugs. My guess is—do you want it?"

Wentworth said eagerly, "You bet I do." And even the bland Chen-p'o leaned forward.

"Whoever is responsible, has seen a victim die. It is not a pleasant sight. First, in an opium death, there is profound sleep. Slow pulse and respiration. Contracted pupils. Muscular relaxation. The sleep becomes coma. The eyes dilate. The skin is cold, and covered with perspiration. The face becomes livid and inhuman. I've seen one or two, and I don't ever want to see another!"

"Death is Kong Gai's meat," Jimmy muttered. "He wouldn't care how much his victims suffered."

"Who's Kong Gai?" the doctor asked.

"The man responsible for the death of Malloy, doctor.

Who is he? We don't know." Wentworth stood up. "I can't thank you enough. At last I've got something to work on."

"I'm interested, detective. What are you going to do?"

"Spoil my chief's evening, and then go to a shack where they dry nets."

"Can I go along?"

"Are you married, sir?" asked Wang Chen-p'o.

"Yes. Why?"

"Then stay here and be honored by your children," the Chinese smiled. When the pair were in the street, he said, "You owe me the price of my dinner, James. 'The lives of all men are drawn together—'"

"Here's your bet," Wentworth agreed. "Promise me this, Wang. Keep off the streets to-morrow. You're too curious. You'd probably get in the way of a bullet trying to see what we were doing."

"I prefer my hide unpunctured," grinned the Chinese. "Anyhow, count on me to bring a nice roast pig to set on your grave, Jimmy."

6

"I'M NOT GOING to have you risk your life unnecessarily," Captain Dunand said, late that night. "I can see you've planned so you won't be suspected, but nobody can ever tell what a D.U. will do."

"That's why I want it staged for four in the afternoon, chief. It's the safest time. Anybody in the gray house will either have taken their shot, or hit the pipe already. The night crowd of dope users won't have arrived."

Dunand's hand tightened about the arm of his chair. Then he said, "Have it your way, boy. I'll phone McCormack. He lives a few short blocks away."

While they were waiting, Dunand said briefly, "If they gang up on you, Jim, all you'll get is a fine funeral." After that, he sat in silence.

When McCormack arrived, Wentworth knew that his chief had chosen well. A member of the detective bureau, McCormack was a wiry little man, thin of face. For years he had been in the wholesale warehouse district, where he had done valuable service for the department.

"What's up, chief?" he asked, after Dunand had introduced the men.

"Wentworth 'll explain."

Briefly, Jimmy told about the crimson circles.

"Everything points to a house in Chinatown," he said

finally. "If we raid the place, every Chino will remember that I was in the yard where nets were dried, and that ends any good I do in the future. Here's what we do, if you're willing. It may mean a knife in the back—"

"Just as soon be knifed as shot," McCormack chuckled. "Let's hear it! What's the dope?"

"Dope!" Wentworth snapped. "The house is full of opium. Maybe morphine. I want a look-see. Here's how we do it. We'll pick out a shop down the street. You turn off Dupont. The third store on the right's a shoe shop. The owner's rich. You go in, ask for a pair of slippers like a man'd buy his girl. Then hold the old boy up.

"The minute you leave the shop he'll go to the door and yell loud enough to wake the dead. I'm always at the corner of Dupont at three forty-five. Be there on the dot to-morrow. I'll fool around until Foh Wak screeches, and then—"

"I run, you run after me. I duck into the gray house."

Wentworth nodded. "Give me a chance to get close. Otherwise they'll bar the door when you're inside, and argue with me until every one inside can be shaken awake, and all the evidence destroyed."

"Sounds good," said McCormack cheerfully. "I'll dress the part. I even leave cooties in a suit that's been in every flop-house south of Market." As if asking for further instructions, he said, "Suppose they jump you?"

"They think I'm a fool. If they got rid of me, they'd get some one with sense."

"This'll be the first time a cop ever chased me," admitted McCormack. "If you got to shoot, Wentworth, be darn' sure you miss me!"

After McCormack left, Dunand asked, "Jim, are you

putting your life in jeopardy to catch Malloy's murderer? To raid an opium joint?"

"I want Kong Gai! This wholesale drug racket sounds like him. I'm afraid of the devil, chief. I want to get him before he has Chinatown gripped in his claws—and me along with it."

"The Six Companies won't let him become too important."

"The Companies are honest; Kong Gai's malignant. And he hates white men."

"Why, Jim?"

Wentworth laughed ruefully. "If I don't know who he is, how can I answer questions about him? Well, here goes for some sleep!"

The next day Wentworth followed his regular routine. He was no longer looking for crimson circles. He only wanted peace during the day, so nothing would interfere with the afternoon plans. At lunch, at Tsing K'ung's restaurant, he complimented the owner on the waiter's grand funeral, and K'ung merely smiled. Over at the merchants' teakwood table, one Chinese remarked that a death at a funeral was unlucky; his companions glanced fleetingly at Wentworth, who continued eating as if he understood nothing.

"Sometimes," the man said, "the gods protect a fool."

It was no wonder that the Chinese did not expect him to know their language. Every day intelligent Americans spoke to them in pidgin English. Poor old George Bannion, killed to enable one of Kong Gai's hatchetmen to prove his bravery, had walked the beat for forty years and had been barely able to say "Happy New Year."

At twenty minutes to four, Jimmy turned into Dupont Street. He had no need to glance at his watch. The clock of the old cathedral told him the time. Five minutes later he was fifty feet from the appointed corner. The great clock, beneath which men were told

Son, Observe the Time
And Flee from Evil

pealed the quarter hour.

The echo boomed through Chinatown. Before it died away like a golden moan, a shrill Chinese voice shrieked, the wail breaking on the highest note, and then starting again, with revived vigor.

Wentworth stared about, as if unable to determine the direction of the outcry. Some Chinese at the corner pointed up the side street. The detective swung into his stride and reached the corner in an instant. At the sight of a wiry white man, in dark suit and light cap, running from him, Wentworth broke into pursuit, shouting, "Stop! Stop, or I'll shoot!"

When he was a hundred feet behind the "thief," McCormack stumbled realistically, to give him a chance to gain ground. McCormack raced across the street, toward the painted windows of Waverley Place, with Wentworth gaining at every leap. The Chinese watched with amusement at this game between the foreign devils. Bets were made, mostly on the "thief."

In the doorway of the gray house two Asiatics stood, attracted by the noise. These two guards also watched with amusement as McCormack ran up the opposite side of the street. The thief was breathing with obvious difficulty and playing his part convincingly.

Wentworth yelled, "Halt!" and fired into the air. Seemingly terrified, McCormack darted across the street. Before the two Chinese could guess his intention, he dived past them, with Wentworth not ten feet behind him. The Chinese tried to dash in after him. They were both trying to slam the door at the same instant. Wentworth smashed past them, sending the pair sprawling.

Tearing after the thief and calling for him to halt, Wentworth heard one of the guards shout a warning. He did not get what was cried. McCormack was giving him perfect assistance. Straight to the first door he ran. When he found it locked he raced down the corridor to the next, and hurling it open, continued down the hall.

Passing the open door, Wentworth saw a sprawled figure on a heap of quilts. An opium user. His guess about the gray house was right.

The place was stirring. Somewhere in its depths a sweet, curiously masculine voice sang out: *"Me yod! Me yod!"*

So that was the plan! Before Jimmy had reached the end of the hall, he heard the crackle of flames eating on the flimsy paper-and-wood partitions.

Me yod! Fire!

7

THE SOFT VOICES of women were plainly audible, as singsong girls were scurrying along hidden passages of the gray building. Wentworth shivered as he thought of sodden users of opium unconscious in their filthy cubbyholes. Already smoke was feeling its way into the hall.

McCormack called, "Don't shoot! I give up!"

Reaching the thief's side, Wentworth whispered, "The Chinese outside never turn in alarms. What a mess!" Loudly, he said, "Don't run again, or I'll drill you!" Clear above the crackling of the flames, he shouted, "Help get people out'f here, and you will get a light sentence, thief!"

"You bet," agreed his fellow detective.

Together, on their work of mercy, all else forgotten, the two men ran from door to door, trying to wake the sleepers. In one room—empty—Wentworth found a few crimson stains on a grayish quilt. Crimson like the circles. Pushing, pulling, urging, the white men managed to get some of the addicts to their feet. Then, to Jim's amazement, he heard the roar of fire apparatus outside.

"Stick with me," he said in McCormack's ear. "The fire gang 'll get the rest of 'em out. There'll be a basement—always is. Let's have a look at it. Won't be any one there now, but we might see something. That fire stunt was tough on us."

The first locked door gave to Wentworth's shoulder. The room behind it was empty. So was the second. But the third showed a stairway, leading down. More doors, always locked. Together the detectives smashed their way ahead.

Not even Wentworth was prepared for such magnificence as they found in the basement room. It was cool, fragrant. Screens, painted with silvery bamboo, with great butterflies of fiery color, hid the foundation walls. Gorgeous silks covered low teakwood chairs and couches. Thick Chinese rugs, marked with the dragon, the wheel of Law, with Yin and Yang, the male and female elements of being, made the floor soft and luxurious.

A lamp burned like a star on its chain, but the room was empty. Nor was there any sign of *yen-shi* to be seen. However, in a corner Wentworth saw a tall vase, of transparent glass. In the vase glowed a crimson liquid. Beside it was a brush. The tip was crimson from the stain contained in the vase. Here the crimson circles were painted!

Smoke swirled down the stairway while Wentworth searched the room, looking for a bit of evidence to connect Kong Gai with opium and death. Something to indicate that there was a Chinese named Kong Gai. Something to show who he was. There was not a single clew.

Then both white men heard feet on the steps.

"If it's a little Chino, shoot him if he turns and sees us," Wentworth breathed. "We'll get him alive if we can. But get him!"

Back of the great screen went the detectives. Four Chinese hurried into the supposedly empty room. Two of them were the guards from the outer door.

"Kong Gai is gone!" one of the Chinese cried.

"The house burns, according to order," growled another. "And some fool has told the white devils' fire machines. The place is overrun. We had better light fires here also. Then nothing will be found. And then depart speedily."

"Only not as we came," snickered a tall Asiatic. "Above is too much fire. And who knows,where that idiot of a policeman has gone?"

"If he burns," the fourth growled, "I need no longer remain hidden after killing the other policeman, who discovered you removing the circle from the leg of the man-who-takes-money-from-women, who told Kong Gai that unless he was given free *yen-shi* he would tell what he knew about the great Kong Gai."

"My party," whispered Wentworth. "Don't shoot, Mac. Not even the murderer. We want 'em alive."

Before McCormack could object, Wentworth hurled aside the screen and was in the midst of the Chinese. One of the guards went down as Jimmy cracked him over the head with his gun. The murdering hatchetman went for his knife, but not fast enough. Wentworth's left took him on the jaw.

The third Asiatic started for the stairway. He stumbled over one of his fellows and lost balance. Instantly he began to claw and rip at Wentworth's legs, to drag the officer down. The last of the hatchetmen on his feet had his long blade out now. Wentworth shot hastily, and missed. He barely avoided the upward death-stroke of the heavy knife.

As he ducked, the Chinese on the floor seized his hand, and tore at it with his jagged fangs. Wentworth was sick with pain as he wrenched away. At the same time he smashed down on the evil face with his gun.

McCormack saw the hatchetman's knife rise again, carefully, precisely. His gun roared. The murderer screamed once. His mouth filled with blood and he fell.

The detectives knew that there would be no surrender. Methodically, cold as ice since it was necessary, each fired once. The fourth Chinese they smothered together, handcuffed him, and then drew breath.

Then, in the little silence, Wentworth heard what made his heart stop.

"So James Wentworth is not the fool we thought?" he heard, in the same sweet voice which had called for the house to be fired. "He pursues a thief who is not a thief at all. I have been wondering about you, Mr. Wentworth. Detective Wentworth, I should say?

"Now, I promise you something. Not a knife in the back, detective. We will do better than that. I promise a real torture when the time comes and we meet."

There was a short, satisfied laugh, and, except the crackle of flames above, only the groans of the handcuffed Chinese. Both Wentworth and McCormack had stared this way and that, without seeing Kong Gai, or learning where the Chinese had been concealed. He had not been anywhere in the room. The detective's hasty search had been thorough.

"Trick panels," Wentworth muttered. "Or a peep-hole somewhere. No sense looking for it."

The Chinese hatchetmen between them, the detectives fought their way through the smoke. The other Asiatics had already been carried out by firemen. Wentworth, taking no chances lest Kong Gai attempt to rescue his man, was alert and ready. But where the smoke was thickest, and the flame hottest, a Chinese figure, dim and shadowy, slipped behind them, for all their care, and a knife was driven deep into the hatchetman's heart. It was accomplished so expertly that when they were in the air Wentworth's skin tingled. It would have been as easy to have knifed him. But Kong Gai, in true Asiatic fashion, preferred to wait and torture, as he had promised.

Outside, Captain Dunand walked over to his men. A trifle guiltily, he said, "I came to have a look, and got a little nervous. Turned in the alarm myself. Glad you are both safe. Any luck?"

"Rotten. Kong Gai got away. I was right about the crimson circles. Dope marks. Malloy's murderer is dead. Mac here got him. We were bringing one hatchetman with us, but somebody knifed him so he couldn't talk."

"Nice work, boys. Don't stay talkin' with me. Might put the Chinks wise."

Wentworth watched the firemen fight to keep the flames from spreading. A side wall trembled, and the roof fell with a spatter of sparks. Kong Gai, of course, was safe in some other burrow. Who was Kong Gai? What did the evil Asiatic want?

"I don't know about the others," Jimmy said, "but Kong Gai is wise to me."

Dunand snapped, "Then all the advantage is his. He knows you. You don't know him. The best thing for you, Jim, is to be put—"

"Not back in the suburbs, chief," Wentworth said grimly. "Kong Gai's boasted. Made a promise. Perhaps he can't keep it. I know his voice. That's something. Let me try to get him, chief!"

"If you insist on getting killed—"

"I don't want to miss any fun," grinned Jimmy Wentworth. "And"—he added quietly—"I'm not going to let Kong Gai say that a white man was afraid of him!"

KING COBRA

*Locked in the Depths of Kong Gai's
Lair, Jimmy Wentworth Is Doomed to
the Strange Death of the Snake*

1

"ARE YOU SATISFIED it's suicide?" demanded Captain Dunand. He stared down at the dead man on the floor as if asking him to solve the riddle. "Are you, Jimmy? If you aren't, now's the time to say something, before the newspaper boys are tipped off to what's happened."

"Not any more satisfied than you are," Wentworth said.

The two detectives were in a ninth floor-apartment high on Nob Hill, San Francisco's exclusive residence district. From the windows, had either man raised his eyes, could be seen the bay, and, nearer, the tiled roofs of Chinatown.

"I don't like empty safes," Dunand muttered.

"Clean as a whistle," agreed the Chinatown detective. The safe, hidden in a recess made to hold a radiator, had been concealed with a bright Oriental painting made on silk. It was closed, but not locked, when they had discovered it. Closed and without a scrap of paper inside.

"And yet this man Carrington might have been broke," the captain of detectives said. "Perhaps he'd spent every dime he ever owned. Maybe he had papers in the safe and wanted 'em destroyed before he shot himself—"

"He must have shot himself," Wentworth said, thinking aloud.

"Of course he did, Jim! The gun's clenched in his fist. That's unusual, but I've seen it once or twice before. And his head's powder burned. He must've shot himself. Every window in the apartment was locked. The entry door in the rear was locked. O'Malley had to smash the door down to get in, and it was not only locked, but the chain bolt was in position. As if—"

"As if he were afraid of something?"

"Maybe, Jim. I wish I knew."

The dead man lay face downward on the floor. The cold hand gripping the heavy automatic in its stiff fingers had aimed well. Undoubtedly the muzzle had been pressed against Carrington's forehead when the trigger had been pulled. And the result was not a pretty sight.

"Want to talk to the elevator boy?" Dunand asked. "O'Malley's waiting in the hall with him. The manager of the place is running the elevator until we're done with

the kid. He's a Chink kid. You might get something out of him."

In a pea-green uniform, buttoned to the neck, the nervous elevator boy looked very yellow.

"I bring number ninety-seven topside," the boy said unhappily. "I hear gun shoot. Number ninety-seven, Mr. Johnson, go telephone police. Tha's all I know."

Wentworth, born in China, could have questioned him in any one of a dozen dialects, but since the Chinese knew him only as patrolman, and not as Dunand's right-hand man in the district, he continued speaking in English.

"You were on this floor when you heard the gun?"

"I open elevator door," the boy nodded. "Gun he go bang."

"And then Mr. Johnson called the police?"

"He say, 'Something funny,' and telephone."

"The death is lingering and painful. I will thrust the needle into your veins—"

"You didn't try to open the door, or ring the bell, of this apartment?"

The China-boy appeared unnecessarily uneasy as he said, "No. I not want see," his eyes faltered, dropped, to the dead man. "I not want see Mr. Carrington dead."

"How'd you know he was dead?" Wentworth snapped.

"I heard gun."

"Didn't you think he might have been cleaning a gun and it discharged?"

"I not think what happen," the boy shuddered. "I very afraid."

Wentworth's question darted out. "Why were you afraid?"

"The shot," the boy said.

Jimmy was back where he started, and knew it. There was every reason why the Chinese boy should have been fearful at hearing the discharge of the weapon in a sedate apartment house. Wentworth understood well that fear, in a time of crisis, meant neither guilt nor concealed information.

"I'd like to talk with this Mr. Johnson," he said to Dunand.

"Know the firm of Johnson, Blalock and Freeland? Johnson's the retired president... O'Malley! Will you go to Mr. Johnson's apartment and ask him to step over here? And don't grab him by the arm, either, O'Malley!"

Mr. Johnson was a tall, spare man in his late seventies.

"Messy way to die," he commented. "Want me to tell what little I know? Gladly. Charley"—glancing at the elevator boy—"was running me up. Just as he opened the door, we heard a shot. Whether or not I actually heard poor

Carrington fall I am not certain. I may have erred in not attempting to open the door—not that it would have done any good—but it seemed that the police should be notified instantly. And after I telephoned, I found Mrs. Johnson—she is in ill health, gentlemen—rather upset, and did not want to leave her. And that is all I know… except…"

The detectives said, with one breath, "Except what?"

"Mrs. Johnson said that she heard some one scream. Our apartment is next to Carrington's, you know."

"The top of his head was blown off," Dunand grunted. "He couldn't have yelled. Your wife was nervous. She imagined it."

"The funny thing is that she said she heard the scream about two or three minutes before she heard the shot, captain."

"From Carrington's apartment? Or a noise in the street?"

"She insists that it was Carrington's voice, and that he cried out in agony. As a matter of fact, Mrs. Johnson was trying to get my son, at the office, to tell him, when I returned from my after breakfast walk. I spoke with her, gentlemen, and she is absolutely positive the scream came from this apartment."

"Only a few minutes before the shot?"

"Less than five minutes. Probably only two or three."

Wentworth whirled on the elevator boy. "Who've you taken up to Carrington's apartment this morning?" he snapped.

"Eight o'clock, I take downstairs Mrs. Cohn's maid and dog," the boy began in a singsong voice. "Next, Mr. Hotchkiss he go office. Mr. Wilson he go office. Miss Chase, she go get hair fixed pretty. She gave me fo' bits to find taxi.

Mr. Murphy, he go work too. Mrs. Murphy, she go with him. Only two I bring back up on elevator. Mrs. Cohn's maid and dog, she come back. Mr. Johnson, he come back from smoke cigar and walk. Nobody else. Nobody for Carrington."

"Charley's got a pretty good memory," Johnson said. "He even remembers our guests' names, especially if they give him a quarter."

"Is there a service elevator in the rear?" Dunand asked.

"Packages taken to apartments six to seven thirty, eleven to twelve, in morning," Charley said, as if repeating a ritual. "Six to seven thirty, I take up. Next time, porter take. Not yet next time. First time, nobody go up with me."

"Which is that," Wentworth said. "There's a fire escape, but even so—"

"The doors were locked, and the windows were locked, and the gun was his own, and it was in his hand," Captain Dunand growled. "We're a pair of fools, maybe, Jim. But… that scream! That may mean something."

"What do you suspect, gentlemen?" the retired merchant asked. When neither of the detectives replied, he added, "I had always thought that the police were well pleased if a death appeared to be a suicide."

"We like to make work for ourselves," grinned Jimmy.

"I wish the young men in my firm felt the same way. If you tire of the detective bureau, come and see us. Now, if you gentlemen are finished with me, I'll run along."

"May we ask Mrs. Johnson a few questions, later?"

"We're both at your service. All we knew about Carrington is that he was very quiet and kept to himself, and that he was apparently a man of means." Johnson waved a hand toward the furnishings of the apartment. "This cost a pretty penny," he commented. "My firm's in the importing business, and I can assure you that these paintings and ornaments are genuine. I've never seen finer, even in China."

When the talkative old merchant had gone, Jimmy said, "Got an offer of a job, anyhow, chief." And then, without warning, he turned on the elevator boy. "Who did you take up to this apartment this morning?" he snapped.

"Nobody."

Since the Chinese was startled, he said the single word in his native tongue, and was forced to repeat it in English. Wentworth was now satisfied that the elevator boy had spoken the truth.

2

CARRINGTON'S BODY WAS taken to the morgue. The apartment in which he had lived was searched from floor to ceiling. There were no finger-prints on the gun except those of Carrington. There were no finger-prints at all on the door of the safe. Every window fastening was examined, to make certain that none of the locks had been tampered with. The rear door—the service door, leading to a small hallway and the second elevator—was locked. Like the front door, it was fastened with a chain bolt. The chain of the front door had been ripped down, and the lock broken, when O'Malley had burst his way inside.

George Carrington had blown his brains out. He had been alone when he had done it. Suicide. But why was the safe empty? And what had made the dead man scream out in agony before he had fired the fatal shot?

Carrington had been alone when the trigger was pulled. Both Dunand and Wentworth were convinced of that fact. As they left the apartment at last Dunand said, "We haven't missed a bet, Jim. The circumstances are unusual, that's all. As far as the scream goes, he may have gone batty before he shot himself. And the empty safe only means that he'd destroyed all of his papers."

"Ever see the knob of a safe without finger-prints, chief?"

"Yes," said Dunand. "I know a man in the city here who

always opens and closes his safe with gloves on. Then if he's robbed, we'll be able to get the prints of the thief without the man's own marks being in the way. This fellow may have had the same habit, and did it that way this morning because he'd always done it that way before. May have been just nutty enough."

Carrington's out-going telephone calls revealed nothing out of the ordinary, and finally Dunand said, "Go down to your beat, Jim, or the Chinks will miss you. I'll have Carrington's past examined, but unless something unusual comes up, you might as well forget this."

The two men separated at the front door. Dunand went back to his office. Jimmy walked thoughtfully down the hill, and just as the clock of Grace Cathedral struck noon he started to pace his beat. Every so often a Chinese merchant bowed to him; here and there Jim stuck his head into the doorway of a bazaar and said good morning to the placid proprietor. When he finally came to the bowl shop of the Wangs, a father and son who had at times tipped him off to impending trouble in the Oriental district, he went leisurely inside.

Young Wang Chen-p'o, in American clothes, was smoking a cigarette behind the counter.

"James," he said immediately, "I think we've been put on the spot."

Wentworth knew the indomitable courage of the Wangs, who had been threatened before for being friendly with the police.

"I'll lock you up for sixty days for vagrancy," he said. "That'll keep you safe."

"Don't like your prison diet. Not enough rice. My honorable father has gone to see the priest, who is even more versed in Chinese lore. Perhaps when he comes back we will know what the trouble is."

"What happened?"

"An hour or so after we opened the store this morning, we found a little snake made out of paper fastened to the inside of the door. It is probably some sort of a warning. But we don't know what kind."

"Who put it there?"

Wang Chen-p'o shrugged. "It may have been stuck on the door yesterday, and we didn't see it until this morning, when the light was better. Who? Your best friend may be your worst enemy if sufficient gold is placed in his hand. I—here comes my honorable father, Jimmy."

Old Wang shuffled slowly into the shop. Behind him were two slender Chinese in black. Wentworth knew that both were hatchetmen hired for protection by the Wangs. The ancient Chinese bowed gravely to Jimmy, walked behind the counter and then drew himself painfully to a high stool.

"I learned nothing," he said in Cantonese to his son. "However, it will be well if you stay at home after dark."

"The priest knows nothing, honorable father?"

"He says he has never heard of a snake warning."

Silently, he forestalled Wentworth's request by drawing out a little paper snake from his coat and handing it to him.

"A cobra," Jimmy ejaculated.

"A king cobra," said old Wang. "The deadliest serpent in the world."

"And," said his son, "I have just observed a man walk past our miserable store. He looked inside. With interest.

If he saw you examining the snake, Jimmy, we are in for trouble, having shown it to you, and you are in danger for having seen it. Watch your step, James."

Wang the elder smiled for the first time. "Jimmy is now happy. Danger, to him, is food, shelter, temple and women. However, the little snake may have been a joke. Chinese humor is sometimes devious. It may mean any one of a thousand things. Or it may mean—"

"Death," said his son.

"Or Kong Gai," said Wentworth.

At the evil name, old Wang's head lowered. "The same thing," he muttered. "Kong Gai the deadly. In my unworthy opinion, I should say that the cobra would be the symbol Kong Gai would select with which to warn men of his displeasure."

The three were silent. Kong Gai, the mysterious and ferocious legendary figure of Chinatown, feared by all, who knew that Wentworth was more than a patrolman. About Kong Gai nothing was known. Jimmy had crossed his evil path several times, and each time had come away with one of Kong Gai's tongmen as a captive. But all Wentworth knew of Kong Gai was that the Chinese had a voice as sweet as a gentle summer breeze; a voice like a girl's. Whether Kong Gai were a dwarf or a giant, Jimmy had no idea.

Kong Gai was back of every evil happening in Chinatown. His tentacles were always reaching out. He controlled the opium importing, the opium smoking. He exacted tribute from respectable merchants. What was Kong Gai up to now?

"The king cobra," said Wang thoughtfully, "warns once

before he strikes. *He* never warns before striking. I think I will employ another hatchetman, Jimmy. I am too old to stand the excitement of an unhappy death."

"If you could tell me who might've put the warning on the door, I might be able to help."

Wang bowed courteously. "Chen-p'o and myself have talked over every visitor to our shop," he said. "All were honest men. All men are honest, until it is worth more to be the opposite. We have no idea who left the little snake."

"Let me know if you learn anything," Wentworth said. "I'll drop in later—"

"At twenty minutes past one," grinned young Wang. "We set our clocks by you, Jim. Well, don't take any money with holes in the middle."

Wentworth stepped boldly out of the shop, giving his uniform belt a hitch, but before he started northward along his beat he gave one swift look southward. So far as he could see, all was serene. The Wangs were in for something. Jimmy knew how useless it would be to report anything to headquarters. If the Wangs' lives were saved, he had to do it himself. How? He had no idea. If Wang and the priest did not know exactly what the snake warning meant, no white man—not even one who knew much of Chinese lore—could hope to solve the mystery.

As Jimmy passed the curious shops—in one a live octopus, with its suckery tentacles reaching up the glass water-filled tub in which it was kept, and where, under water, it would be butchered to provide feasts for wealthy Chinese—he dismissed the Wangs, and wondered if Dunand would discover anything about Carrington which would be interesting. No finger-prints on the safe. The scream of agony.

Because of the snake warning, Jimmy thought, "Not even a snake could have got into Carrington's apartment. The man committed suicide. That's all there was to it. I'll bet Dunand finds out Carrington lost his shirt in the market, and went haywire."

As he came to a corner of Dupont Street, and stood idly a moment watching two Chinese youngsters sidle up to a fruit stall, coaxing each other to get nearer to a tempting pile of lichee nuts, some one on the side street cried out wildly, in terror.

Wentworth's body tensed. He was running westward even before he actually saw what was happening.

In the street, halfway up the block, lay a Chinese. A second Asiatic was bending over the prostrate form. As Wentworth raced up the steep street, the second Oriental, seemingly warned, jumped up, and began to run. The fleeing Chinese was lame, and ran slowly. Wentworth had no need to shout, nor to draw his gun.

The narrow street, a moment ago filled with Chinese was emptied miraculously. Even the blind beggar propped against a sunny wall opened his eyes and scuttled away. There remained only the man lying in the street, the fugitive Chinese, and the detective.

Jimmy's long legs drew him nearer with every bound. The fleeing Oriental, perhaps warned by a confederate, turned. He saw how close the blue-clad officer was. With an instant's hesitation, he twisted sidewise and darted down the nearest dark cellar stairway, with Wentworth less than twenty feet behind him.

As the detective leaped down the rickety stairs, he jerked out his small electric torch. It was dark as the pit in the cellar. Wentworth, as he ran, pressed the button of the torch instantly, and light flashed. But not from the torch. Stars danced once before Jimmy's eyes, stars whirling and dazzling, and then everything went blacker than the silent cellar, and the detective, smashed over the head, fell to the dust of the floor, unconscious.

3

BEFORE JIMMY WENTWORTH opened his eyes, he knew several things. Firstly, he was bound. Secondly, he had been the biggest fool in the world, to have followed the Chinese into the cellar after Wang's warning to watch his step. Thirdly, his head felt as if somebody were hitting it with hammers. And lastly, he was in a room where lights were lit.

The thought, and the pain throbbing through him, must have made him blink, for a sweet, lovely voice said, "You are awake, detective? I was growing impatient. Your head aches. That I regret, but it was necessary to strike hard. If you will open your eyes, I promise a most unusual feast of beauty, which will make you forget the pain. In addition, you have wanted to see me. Here I am. The man who is rightly feared. Kong Gai."

The sweet, melodious voice trembled on the last word. Wentworth shivered, and then slowly opened his eyes.

Facing him was a wizened Chinese, seated on a teakwood stool. Kong Gai's evil eyes watched the white man with delighted content. On one silk clad knee was a thick writing pad. In the Chinese's right hand was a pencil studded with one blue jewel.

Strangest of all, kneeling at Kong Gai's slippered feet was a Chinese girl. Although Jimmy Wentworth knew only too well the sort of fate in store for him, he was unable to avoid staring at the exotic figure. The girl was dressed in magnificent brocaded silks, pale blue and orange. Her face was almost Caucasian. In her smooth black hair was a white gardenia, no paler than her cheeks. Her eyes, somber as pools of ink, were fixed on the bound detective.

Kong Gai's pencil moved. He handed a sheet of paper to the girl, and she read, softly, "How do you like my voice, Mr. Wentworth? If you thought to find me, by means of it, that would have been difficult, wouldn't it? It is a useful voice."

Did the girl hesitate an instant before she continued? Did Kong Gai's yellow eyes darken at the infinitesimal pause? "Since my daughter was educated in a mission, she speaks both English and Chinese. What do you think of the little idea of my mouthpiece?"

"I think," said Jimmy, "that in a few minutes you'll have a lot of police breaking in here when I don't report at headquarters."

The deadly face wrinkled with enjoyment as Kong Gai's fingers scrawled the next message.

"In where?" read the girl.

Jimmy knew that his feeble, obvious bluff hadn't worked. Where? He had not the slightest notion. After he had been slugged, Kong Gai's hatchetmen had probably carried him, through underground passages, to this room. And it was undoubtedly a long way from the cellar just off Dupont Street.

"Anyhow," Wentworth said coldly, "I wouldn't mind a cigarette."

Kong Gai scribbled a few words on his pad; the girl read them aloud—"Get the white man cigarettes"—and then, like a sleepwalker, went to an ivory box on a carved stand and brought Wentworth one of the paper tubes. She knelt beside him, put the cigarette between his lips, and lit it with a bit of twisted paper. Wentworth, when she was close, saw that her eyes were entirely blank.

A clap of Kong Gai's hands brought her back to him. She read what he had written on the pad.

"Those are very good cigarettes, detective. I bought them in India. There is a very little opium in them for flavoring." The girl puzzled over a word, and then continued, *"Papaver somniferum*—which is opium—is a boon to all Orientals, detective. In bringing much of it into this country, I am doing good. Don't you think so?"

Wentworth wondered how much Kong Gai would boast. Not that it made any difference now! Instead of answering the question, he said, "The cigarette tastes fine, Kong Gai. I suppose you learned about the little cobra you put on Wang's door in India, also?"

The ugly Chinese snarled a word, and then smiled. He wrote swiftly. The girl read, "I was afraid you had been told about the snake in the Wangs' shop. It is a warning from the King Cobra—Kong Gai! Soon you will see how it works."

"Just as soon die that way as any other," Wentworth told him. He knew that Kong Gai was amused, and that the Chinese had watched him when he looked about the room, searching in vain for some means of escape, some plan. "When it comes to a tough way to die, Kong Gai, you won't like the noose. We'll get you."

Wentworth was trying to anger the Chinese again, but couldn't do it.

Kong Gai had been writing, his eyes shining as his pencil moved. When he had finished the girl voiced his message.

"You are mistaken, detective. Since this is your last day to live, let me point out your error before you learn it yourself. I have seen a coolie bitten by a cobra. He felt burning pain at once. Within a minute he began to lose power over his legs. In a few minutes more his lower jaw began to fall. Froth and saliva ran from his mouth. He was in agony. He moaned and twisted his arms. Then they, also, became paralyzed. Only his brain was clear, to feel the pain, to know that death was coming. That is how the Wangs will die. It is how you will die."

Wentworth stared at him, as if Kong Gai were really the King Cobra. The evil snake-like eyes fascinated him, and it was a full minute before he was able to say, "If the police don't get you for killing me, they'll hang you for murdering the Wangs."

Again the horrible pause while Kong Gai scribbled his retort.

"I think I will leave the Wangs where your learned police can find them. The post-mortem appearance is not distinctive, detective. I do not believe your blundering surgeons will find out what really took place. It will amuse me to read your newspapers. 'Mysterious death dealt to Chinese merchants.' And who would expect a cobra bite in San Francisco?"

Jimmy supposed that once Kong Gai had ceased enjoying the situation, it would be his own finish. What a way to die! Bound! Caught by his own foolishness!

"Why, dear detective," the pale girl read, "the poison from a cobra is so terrible that when a white man, of any intelligence, knows what has happened, he blows out his brains rather than face the agony—"

"Like Carrington," Wentworth snapped.

Kong Gai himself, proof that he could talk, screamed, *"Hai!* How did you know?"

Jimmy hadn't known. Some strange intuition had forced him to say the words.

The wizened Chinese had slipped from the teakwood stool. He came directly in front of Wentworth.

"You know too much," he snarled. "It is a good thing I have you here! How much more do you know?" His eyes darted at the white man venomously. "Who have you told about the cobra poison—about the death of the snake?"

Wentworth spat out the end of the cigarette.

"If you do not answer, I will give you only a little cobra poison! Just enough so that your tongue becomes motionless, and grows large until your mouth is filled with it, and you choke to death—"

"That'll be a fine way to make me talk," said Jimmy.

Kong Gai struck him in the face.

"Bring on your snake," the white man suggested. "Let's get this monkey business over with, Kong Gai. I'm not going to tell you how much I know, nor who else knows about anything."

The Chinese fumbled in his coat and drew out a hypodermic. "Many a cobra has been killed to give me this poison," he boasted. "It is pure cobra venom. I can keep it for years, and by adding water, have something as poisonous as when the venom came from the cobra. The death is lingering, and very painful. I will thrust the needle into your vein—"

"Is that what you did to Carrington?"

Kong Gai rocked back on his heels. "So the great detective doesn't know so very much? No, that is not what I did to Carrington. It is not what I will do to the Wangs. You talk too much, detective. You give yourself away."

"So do you," said Wentworth. "You talk like a mission Chino who went to an American college—"

"And was laughed at! And saw the woman he loved stolen by a white man! But there has been revenge, my friend! Little Rose-blossom"—he waved his hand toward the girl—"should have been my child instead of Carrington's... and now she is indeed mine! To do with as I wish! She has no will but mine—"

"Or your drugs—"

"Her father finally discovered my trail. I was ready for him. His own hand spattered his brains on the walls, and you, oh, fool, thought he had killed himself. I was not there, but my hand pulled the trigger! Just as I will kill the Wangs, the father and the son! *Hai-ya!* To-morrow they will see a little spider, perhaps, that symbol of ill luck. One of them will squash it with his hand. And inside the spider, made so carefully from paper by a man I know, is a tiny bit of spun glass, and beneath the glass is a little capsule which breaks... and into the veins goes the venom of the king cobra!"

"Carrington wouldn't have hit a spider with his hand."

"Ah, no. A friend of mine went to see him. Yesterday! And when my friend departed, he carefully placed a capsule, and a bit of spun glass in it, on the door knob! And when Carrington went to open the door this morning he knew—within a fraction of a second, when his palm began to burn—that Kong Gai had found him! And you, white fool, thought he had committed suicide!"

Kong Gai laughed shortly.

"I have boasted," he said, "but it will not do you any good, Wentworth."

He clapped his hands loudly three times, and in a moment a thin, silent hatchetman padded into the magnificent chamber. Kong Gai scribbled on his pad, and handed the note to the blank-eyed, dazed girl.

"Drag the white dog before me," read Carrington's daughter. "We will put the serpent mark on his chest and listen to his screams." In the same lovely, monotonous voice, she went on, "Little Rose-blossom has been a good girl. She may stay and see the entertainment, after which she will be given the pale violet drink she loves so much."

For the first time the girl showed animation. She turned gratefully toward Kong Gai, as if thanking him for his kindness. Knowing the terrible drugs of the Orient, Wentworth was positive that the girl was kept under the influence of one of them, a mixture with opium as its base, which destroyed reason and senses.

The hatchetman jerked Wentworth to his knees, and dragged him directly before Kong Gai. Then he padded over to the brazier, and put a thin silver opium pipe into the red coals. He seemed happy. He hummed to himself as he watched the end of the pipe slowly turn bright.

When it was white hot, he stepped to Wentworth's side. A knife, delicately wielded, ripped through the white man's uniform and bared his chest.

Jimmy's arms strained against the thongs; they cut into

his wrists, but the soft, pliable leather did not give at all. If only his hands were in front of him!

One hand smoothing the girl's hair, Kong Gai, the girl kneeling at his feet close to Wentworth, leaned forward. His eyes shone brighter than the coals. He looked, and was, a king cobra ready to strike.

The hatchetman smiled at Wentworth, as if it were the greatest joke in the world, and, still humming, went to the stand, returning with brazier and pipe. He cut pieces of Wentworth's heavy blue uniform coat into strips, and made a handle for the pipe.

He said, "For your honor, oh king of all the cobras!" to Kong Gai, and then picked up the heated pipe.

"First trace the body, and last of all the hood," Kong Gai hissed. "And then, highest of all—near his throat, where the flesh is delicate—the symbol of Kong Gai!"

Wentworth felt sweat burst from his forehead as the heat of the pipe neared his skin. True to his nature, the hatchetman did not hurry. He, like his master, wanted this white dog to anticipate the pain. Jimmy's lips were a thin gray line. Every muscle from head to foot was as taut as steel. They wouldn't get a sound out of him. He wouldn't move. He wouldn't even shut his eyes against the agony. He'd grin. They couldn't wipe that grin from his face as long as he was alive.

Then, almost before he felt the pain sear his chest, the stench of burning human flesh—his own—rose to his nostrils. The torture had begun.

4

WHAT MADE JIMMY WENTWORTH, isolated and bound, drive his head into the hatchetman's middle he never knew. Escape was impossible. What the Chinese actually wanted most of all was to have him try escape; to have him beg and plead and writhe before them. Perhaps he saw, for a fraction of time, a flicker of intelligence in the girl's dazed eyes. Perhaps he hoped to make the hatchetman pick up his discarded knife and bring instant, painless death.

Into the thin hatchetman's belly Wentworth drove, with all the force of his long, powerful body. The unexpected assault, with no warning cry, no telltale movement of an eyelid, drove the Chinese back. He fell against the girl, against the high stool of Kong Gai. The three fell backward together in a heap, with Kong Gai and the hatchetman spitting anger.

Wentworth rolled to his side. Once his blind aim missed. Then welcome pain shot to his head from his wrists.

The hatchetman was on his knees struggling to free himself from Kong Gai's flowing robe. Instinctively, the Chinese sprawled forward toward the knife on the rug. Wentworth, half blind with pain, jerked his arms wide, and the thongs, burned partly by the coals, snapped.

The two men came together just as the Chinese reached his knife. Wentworth had no second to lose. Any instant

Kong Gai would clap his hands and bring men. If only the devil didn't want any one else to see what had happened! The knife was high in the air. Wentworth's fist swung with terrific force, and the hatchman's head was almost snapped from his body.

Kong Gai was swooping down now, his face a mask of demoniac rage. In his hand flashed a long, double-edged blade. On his knees, Wentworth had no possible chance to parry the blow. Death was close, and he had asked for it before. Now his hands were free, and he was ready to fight for life.

He snatched up the heavy, coal-filled brazier, caring nothing for the anguish the hot metal brought, and hurled the fiery weapon straight at Kong Gai's face. The Chinese screamed once, terribly. Before he could cry out a second time, to summon aid, the detective was all over him at once, and bore him to the floor.

With Kong Gai's own robe the detective bound and gagged him. The hatchetman was stirring; voices outside chattered and questioned. Wentworth glanced at the girl. There was a little pucker of doubt between her eyes, but she stood motionless beside the overturned stool. Here and there coals began to smolder on the rugs. Wentworth kicked them together swiftly, and then emptied a flower bowl over them.

He dragged the hatchetman beside Kong Gai, and bound them back to back. Then his face lit. He cast about the room until he found the pad of paper, and wrote on it rapidly.

When he handed it to the girl, she said aloud, clearly, "When I clap my hands, I desire that one of my servants secure an automobile. Have it wait for my honorable self at the door below."

Wentworth hoped the door was below! He listened to the girl's lovely voice sing the command in Chinese. He wished that he could take Kong Gai along with him, but that was impossible. Not only must he rescue the girl, but he must take no chances in doing it.

Beside Kong Gai Wentworth knelt.

"I'm going to borrow your clothes, oh, great Kong Gai," he said. "I do not suppose you will wait for me to return, or, if I did, your hatchetmen would let us in before you escaped. So I say good-by, oh, boaster! First"—releasing one of the makeshift bonds—"I am going to borrow your clothes." Expertly, Wentworth stripped the Chinese. "Probably you wear a different costume when you go riding," the white man said cheerfully. "If you lose face for appearing in the street in silks, I'm sorry. I'd ask you where your street clothes are, but I don't suppose you'd tell me. Thanks for your hospitality, Kong Gai. I'll return it just as soon as I can."

Gagged, Kong Gai could only make inarticulate noises, akin to the venomous hiss of a viper.

In Chinese attire, the lean white man seemed to have suddenly shrunk in size. He stooped. His shoulders bent forward. His knees, under the silks, bent also. He appeared no taller than Kong Gai. Last of all, he unlaced his shoes. After he had slit the heels of Kong Gai's slippers, he pulled them over his own feet.

Kong Gai and the hatchetman he dragged to a far corner, and covered them with a rug. He had a moment's hesitation: he could carry Kong Gai easily enough, but would Kong Gai ever carry anything—and Wentworth, to the servants outside, must be Kong Gai. No, it wouldn't work. The first job was to save the girl, if it could be done.

Wentworth padded Orient-fashion, over to her. He took her hand and patted it gently. Then he wrote on the pad again. There was a way he might be able to return! But that would mean bringing the girl with him. Out! He tore up the sheet, and wrote on it: "I expect several white men. If they return before I am back, bring them to this room without question." That would bring several of the Chinatown detail inside… and perhaps nab Kong Gai!

He wrote a few more words, and handed the paper to the girl, guiding her toward the spot where the hatchetmen had entered earlier. In her sweet voice, associated with Kong Gai's presence, she said, "Open the door. Kong Gai departs," and added the order concerning the admission of white men.

The door opened. Wentworth's head was hidden in the silks. Even this precaution was unnecessary. In the dim, sandalwood-scented hallway, servants bowed low. None dared lift their eyes to the dread figure of their master, Kong Gai, the cobra king, whose very touch was death. Even the half dozen slim hatchetmen lined against the far wall averted their eyes in superstitious fear. Kong Gai was a generous master. His commands, spoken through the white maid, were rewarded with gold and the juice of the poppy. But who could tell what might happen if the Evil One were addressed without permission? Hence it was considered wise to look the other way.

One cringing old Oriental shuffled ahead of Wentworth and the girl. The aged Chinese opened doors, and slid back secret panels, for the "master" and his white slave girl. The hall was long. There were stairs to be mounted. Lights were snapped on, and off, by the old man. Runways had to be carefully descended. For a full five minutes Wentworth and the girl followed the servant. Once the air grew cold, still, and damp, as if they must be underground. Once, when the lights were on, Wentworth saw an apparatus designed to collapse the walls. He guessed that they were in some deep tunnel, far below the streets. Up and down they followed the servant, around corners, sometimes doubling back on themselves.

At last, his hand on a great iron bolt, the servant bowed low, and said, "The hire-machine is outside, according to your command. I am your slave, Kong Gai. I live as you live. I dare your anger. Oh, Kong Gai, is it wise to go into the street in bright silk?"

"It is wise," Wentworth said in the same dialect.

He was ready to throttle the Chinese if the man detected the different voice, but all the servant said was, "Go in peace, oh, Kong Gai, and return safely. I will go to your room now, and pray to your great idol."

Wentworth wanted to keep the servant out of that room! So he said, in a husky tone, "Wait here for me. I return soon."

It was very dark where they were standing. Behind him, Jimmy caught the flicker of pale yellow light. He heard the thudding of feet in the passageway. Some one must have entered the room and found Kong Gai!

"Your blind servant hears something, oh, Kong Gai," muttered the old Oriental.

"Open the door!" Wentworth growled in Chinese.

"Perhaps it is a message for you—"

Wentworth shoved the servant away from the barrier. The Chinese, having guessed that something was amiss, screamed, "It is not the voice of the master! Come quickly, brothers!" The blind servant tried to push Wentworth back, clawing at him with long, jagged nails.

Thrusting the old man back, Jimmy fumbled for the bolt. Would it push back? Yes! But was there some other lock, to which the servant had the key? If the door didn't open, Kong Gai's horde would be on him in another minute. And then Wentworth, holding to the bolt, jerked the door open. The sunlight streamed in.

Hurrying the girl ahead of him, Wentworth saw a taxi waiting in the narrow alley. The driver jumped from his seat and opened the door.

"Get going," Wentworth snapped. "Step on it!"

"Say, what's this?" the driver asked belligerently as he saw the girl. "I ain't gonna get mixed up in no funny business."

"If you don't snap into it, you'll get a bullet in the back! Police headquarters on Kearny Street. Hall of Justice. Come on!"

The driver hesitated. He was behind the wheel now, trying to puzzle things out. Who was this Chink speaking like a white man? And what a swell looking jane he had with him, all dolled out in Chink clothes! "I don't want none of this," the driver growled. "The pair of you get out!"

Wentworth, knowing how every second counted, urged, "You can't go wrong taking us to the Hall of Justice, man! This's life or death! I'm on the detective bureau, hurry it up!"

The driver started to say that he himself was the chief

of police when the first shot roared in the narrow street. No car ever leaped forward any faster than the taxi. Wentworth, thrown back against the cushions as the machine swayed down the street, said to the girl, "You're safe, Miss Carrington."

She stared straight ahead as if she heard nothing. Jimmy looked directly into her sad, dazed eyes. "Damn Kong Gai!" he muttered.

5

EVEN OLD DENNY, seeing his last years of service as door-man in the Hall of Justice, who had seen many strange things in his long life, was startled when Wentworth and the girl passed through the door. A girl, white, beautiful, dressed in silks bright as the sun, with a flower in her black hair, with kingfisher-jade on her fingers—that was a sight to stare at! But Jimmy Wentworth! Old Denny could see the young Chinatown detective's blue patrolman uniform under a silk Chinese robe and, where the uniform was ripped apart, could see a long seared red mark on his chest.

A hundred thousand questions were in Denny's mouth, but all he said was, "Captain Dunand's in his office. An' there's a couple o' newspaper hounds waitin' to see him as usual."

"Thanks, Denny," Wentworth grinned. "I'll give 'em something to think about, won't I?"

The three newspaper men, waiting for a statement concerning a bootleg raid, stood in front of Dunand's door when they saw the pair approach. "What's up?" they chorused.

"Go outside and you'll see," Jimmy told them. They vanished toward the elevator before Jimmy opened the chief's door.

Dunand was alone. He turned, and then stood up when

he saw Jimmy's silent companion. Wentworth led the girl to a chair, and forced her gently to sit down. Then he walked close to Dunand.

"This slave raid business's bad, Jim," Dunand said quietly. "One of the missions tip you off? You'll find that she's the legal wife of somebody now, even if she wasn't when you rescued her. That's what always happens. Before you tell me about it, there's something doing on the Carrington case—"

"I know," Jimmy said. "She isn't a slave girl, captain. She's Carrington's daughter."

The grim captain of detectives leaned far back in his chair. He looked briefly at the lovely girl, sitting so silently, and then said to Wentworth, "There was mention of a daughter in Carrington's safe deposit box. But that isn't all. We've learned how Carrington died—"

"Cobra poison."

Dunand ejaculated, "How'd you know? The chemists just found out!"

"Kong Gai told me."

"Talk," Dunand ordered.

Swiftly, Wentworth explained.

"I told Dr. White he was crazy," said the captain. "Told him there was no cobra in the apartment, and no way one could've got in. What a fiend that man is!"

Dunand fingered some of the reports on his desk— charts of absorption bands from the police chemist in many colors: dark violet for codein, violet-red for caffein, a pure violet for strychnin; there was a full spectroscopic test which discovered the animal poison from the cobra venom; there was even a photograph of the venomous effect of the poison on the blood of the dead man. The customary mucous membrane of the stomach was missing, proving that the chemist had not been fooled for a minute.

"The blood'd turned black, and was very fluid," Dunand said quietly. "White was on the right track at once." Soberly, "I'll call a matron, and then I suppose she'd better take Miss Carrington to a hospital to rest up. Carrington was a very rich man. He's got a sister living in Oregon. We'll wait until she comes before deciding what to do." Dunand was all crisp decision now. "The taxi driver's waiting? Right. He'll remember the exact location. We'll rip Chinatown apart to get Kong Gai this time."

"I was five minutes walking out. There are walls which can be collapsed. You'll never find his real den. Even if you did, chief, you wouldn't find him there."

Dunand drummed on his desk. "Don't like bein' beaten!"

"Neither do I. And the longer I stay here the better chance there is of missing the actual murderer of Carrington."

"What?"

"Kong Gai 'll attempt to carry out his threat to kill the Wangs. That's where I'm going."

"Somebody'll be waiting to knife you—"

"Can I have a coat, chief? And a gun. Kong Gai got mine."

"Better have the nurse fix that burn."

"It doesn't hurt now." Jimmy grinned at Dunand. "Want to come, chief? We'll get into the Wangs' shop without being seen."

Dunand reached instantly into his drawer for his own

automatic. "If the newspaper boys get hard boiled, Jim, tell 'em we're goin' out for lunch."

"Sure," Jimmy agreed. "They saw me come in. That 'll satisfy 'em perfectly!"

The station nurse knocked. Inside, she took one look at the girl, saying shrewdly, "Drugged. Little doses all the time, probably. She's temporarily deaf, I think. It will be some time before she is better."

"Take her to a hospital. Send out for whatever things she needs," Dunand ordered. "I'm… going out to lunch."

Jimmy, buttoning his coat, went to the silent girl's side. "Everything's all right now," he smiled. He reached down and patted the lax hands lying on the silk of her gorgeous robe. The girl's eyes lifted slowly, and Wentworth thought he saw a flash of recognition in them. For some reason he did not understand this pleased him very much.

The newspaper men were waiting. "Look here, officer," one of them said. "You told us if we'd go outside we'd find out what was the matter."

Dunand yanked at his detective, but Jimmy stopped.

"No," he objected. "You asked what was up, and I told you if you went outside you'd see."

"We didn't see anything! What was up?"

"The American flag," Wentworth grinned, and hurried after Dunand to the elevator. The newspaper boys didn't think it was funny, and went downstairs to pump Denny, which did them no good at all.

Wentworth dismissed the taxi driver after the cab had taken them just to the shadow of old Grace Cathedral, on the edge of Chinatown. The Oriental district teemed with Chinese, with tourists; the windows of the bazaars displayed wares of the East; the guide on the corner prom-ised: "See the mysteries of Chinatown. Singsong girls. Tong men. Joss house"… and Wentworth, suddenly, drew Dunand toward a little stand where coconut candies and lichee nuts were sold; where china lilies bloomed in blue pots.

The old vendor murmured, "Peace to the friends of the house of Wang." He ducked aside. The two white men stepped past him. A door, seemingly a part of the wall, opened, and closed at once as the detectives went through it.

"We'll come out in the back of Wang's shop," Jimmy said. He reached, in the darkness, upward, and took down a flash light. "I don't see how we can be too late. I left Kong Gai pretty unhappy. It 'll take him time to get after the Wangs, but he'll do it as soon as he remembers he boasted to me about it. And then we ought to nab the actual murderer of Carrington—the man who did the deed—if not Kong Gai. And that will hurt him, and hurt his reputation."

As they walked along the damp passageway, Wentworth told his chief briefly of the reason for the Carrington girl's capture, of the other things he had learned about Kong Gai.

"The man is a fiend," Jimmy said. "He wants power. He hates white men. I think he controls the opium traffic now. And he has a finger in the pie of smuggling Chinese into this country. In a short time every merchant in Chinatown will be paying him tribute. We've got to get him before that happens."

"There were some letters in Carrington's safe deposit box

which bear out what you believe, Jim. Kong Gai thought to destroy all the evidence by having the little safe rifled. By the way, I jumped the Chink elevator boy; asked him— or had one of the men do it—who was in the apartment yesterday. He insists no Chinese went to Carrington's rooms at any time. He's lying—"

"Maybe. Kong Gai's wealthy now. No telling who he has working for him. Well, we'll see in a moment or two, if we're lucky."

A door, thick wood and steel, blocked the way. With a coin, Wentworth knocked against it, and metallic sound filled the tunnel. Four times Jimmy tapped on steel, then once, then four times again. A singsong voice, dim and muffled, said:

"How long a time is fixed for the life of man?"

Wentworth answered instantly, in the same tongue, "It is limited to the time that suffices to emit a breath."

The guard tapped twice on the door. Wentworth answered with two taps, and then with four and one, short and sharp. The barrier swung slowly open.

"Honorable younger brother," the detective said, "there is no time to be lost. Are the august Wang and his son Wang Chen-p'o above?"

The guard slid back the bolts. "Come," he invited.

The detectives followed the gaunt hatchetman around sharp turns, until they were in a simply furnished room. Here a relative of the Wangs, busy with writing brush, went into the shop to return with young Wang.

"Still alive?" Jimmy asked.

Wang Chen-p'o, dressed in American clothing, offered

cigarettes before replying. "So far, so good," he admitted. "Alive, James, but a trifle nervous."

"Why?"

Chen-p'o shrugged. "The warning of the snake."

Dunand was glancing curiously about the room. He guessed how valuable some of the simple bowls and ornaments must be; but what interested him more was the rack of rifles against a wall, and the three lean Chinese playing some game on the floor beneath the weapons.

"Anybody come in you're doubtful about this morning, Chen-p'o?"

"The usual tourists. That's all."

"You're sure?"

"Positive."

"Then all we need to do is wait."

Young Wang puffed deeply on his cigarette. "For... Kong Gai?" he asked slowly. "For his vengeance?"

"Correct."

"I suppose you don't care to tell me what's in the wind?"

"Not time, old man. Only this—and tell your father also—don't touch anything, anywhere. Especially not a spider. Got that right?"

"A spider should be instantly killed—"

"You'll be, if you smash it! Got it straight?"

The Chinese nodded soberly. "I suppose you want to get where you can look out into the shop, or did you just come to warn us?"

"We want to watch."

The younger Wang went to the wall, and slid back a small peephole. "In front of this, Jim, is a cupboard," he explained. "I'll open the cupboard when I return to the shop. There are some bowls on the shelves, so arranged that you can see the door, and most of the counter. My honorable father will sit where you can see him. That O.K.?"

"Fine. Remember, don't kill any spiders!"

"Not me. If there is any supplementary killing to be done, James, why not let one of our hatchetmen do it? The boys really need exercise. They'd enjoy a little recreation."

"We want to capture the man, or men, alive."

"It seems so silly; you want to catch a man alive, just to be able to hang him. It is not logical. However, I am your friend. Far be it from me to criticize your strange customs."

6

WHILE JIM WATCHED and listened, he and Dunand spoke together in whispers. They followed the curious trail which had started at Carrington's apartment; followed it step by step until it brought them again to Wang's shop. Dunand was positive that a trace of the cobra poison would be found on the door knob of Carrington's room. The police chemist has said that it dried to yellow crystals, and retained its deadly properties for a long time. If the Chinese came to play the same prank on the Wangs, with a poisoned artificial spider, the similarity of method should be sufficient to convict the murderous attendants of Kong Gai.

Wentworth knew Chinese habits and the Asiatic mind well enough to be certain that Kong Gai would attempt to carry out his boast. He hoped that the King Cobra would do it as speedily as possible. When he thought of Kong Gai's vengeance striking at the lovely, defenseless white girl, Carrington's daughter, his lips thinned to a white line. Kong Gai was a devil. He had really killed Carrington three times: once, by stealing his child, the second time by poisoning the white man, who knew the awful death in store for him, and thirdly when Carrington had blown out his brains rather than let the fire of the venom burn through his veins. Wentworth knew he would face Kong

Gai again. If only, when that time came, he had a gun in his hand!

Several customers, men and women, entered the shop—all Americans. Wentworth watched them all. They made their purchases, and departed. Two white men came in; they bought a Canton ginger jar. While one of them paid for the porcelain, a sedate Chinese merchant waddled in.

Wentworth, recognizing the Asiatic as a respected merchant, relaxed as the conversation began. The two white men, waiting for young Wang to wrap the jar, stood listening as if enjoying the—to them—unusual scene.

"On the tenth of this month, honorable Wang," the merchant said, "a feast is to be given in my poor house. We need new bowls for tea. Is it permitted for me to select from your admirable collection?"

"I have only miserable bowls, none suitable for a man of your taste, Po Ling. If I show them, I beg that you overlook their many defects."

Captain Dunand, peeping out, whispered to Wentworth, "That fellow in the gray suit. I've seen him. I know. He was mixed up in some robbery. We couldn't prove it on him."

Wentworth nodded, and watched closely. He slipped his gun from its holster, in case either of the white men made a motion toward the Wangs. The fact that the two Americans remained in the shop—young Wang had handed them the package—was now suspicious. Different patterns of porcelain were brought. Po Ling selected a design. The interminable argument about price began. Penny by penny Po Ling raised his offer, penny by penny Wang dropped his demands. Finally they met.

"It is agreed," Po Ling smiled, and stroked his face. Immediately one of the white men stepped away from the counter, and started to examine porcelains on the shelf opposite. On the counter, where his hand had rested, Jimmy saw a little brown spot. The spider. "I am a poor man," Po Ling grieved, "but my guests must have proper bowls."

He drew out a silken coin sack, and, in opening it, stared at the top of the counter. "Honorable Wang!" he cried, as if disturbed. "I see a spider! I cannot make a purchase where such an unlucky and evil insect lives!"

Old Wang said placidly, "I will kill this spider," and raised his hand.

Wentworth and Dunand rushed into the shop almost side by side. Although no word had passed between them, Dunand covered the white men, and Wentworth had his gun squarely at the Chinese merchant.

"Do not move," Jimmy commanded in Chinese.

Dunand's men were white as sheets, although both tried to laugh. The merchant's jaw dropped. He did not move. Instead, before Wentworth could cover his mouth, Po Ling wailed nasally, loudly, "Help! Help!"

Before he repeated the word, a shot ripped through the window of the shop. Jim fired instantly, over Po Ling's shoulder, as four hatchetmen, who had been lurking outside, slid like black shadows into the bowl shop. Captain Dunand whirled toward the door, and one of the white men smashed him with his fist behind the ear.

Old Wang, behind the counter, stroked his wrinkled face. Chen-p'o shouted a command in Chinese.

In the split second of time possible, Wentworth saw

everything happening before him. The merchant Po Ling was scuttling for the door. The two white men had both drawn guns, but did not seem to want to use them. But the four hatchetmen slipping forward had no such scruples. Three edged toward the detective; the fourth bent over Dunand's prostrate body.

Wentworth fired at him, his hand as steady as if he had been at pistol practice. The Chinese squealed, and fell half across Dunand's body. Two more Asiatics, both waving automatics as if they were knives, raced into the shop—the hatchetmen who had been acting as observers from the other side of the street.

"Do not kill the white dog! Kong Gai wants him alive!" one shouted.

Instead of backing away, Wentworth, his gun blazing, rushed forward. Some Chinese would knife Dunand at the first opportunity. A knife whirled at Jimmy as he fought to reach the prostrate captain. Hands clawed at him. Wentworth felt hot pain in his shoulder. He fired his last shot point blank into a snarling, spitting face.

"Drag him down!" some one screamed.

The hatchetmen forced Wentworth sidewise by sheer weight of bodies. A shelf of bowls crashed to the floor. Jimmy knew he could never hold them off. They'd rather take him back to Kong Gai than anything else. They'd rush him out of the shop, to a basement somewhere close, and that would be his finish!

From the rear of the room the Wang guards came. In their hands, swung like clubs, were heavy rifles. Skulls cracked. A guard cried aloud as a Kong Gai knife reached his heart. The bowl shop became a terrible place of battle, of blood and agonized screams and death.

Po Ling, the old merchant, had vanished. The two white men were moving cautiously doorward, intent on leaving. Kong Gai's hatchetmen now had their hands full. The detective managed to batter his way after the pair.

"Get 'em up!" he roared about the frightful tumult. "Drop your guns! Turn around! Face the wall!"

One of Kong Gai's men screeched, "Let us depart, brothers of the snake! This is no longer good!"

Nor was it. Although Kong Gai's two gunmen had shot three of the Wang guards, Captain Dunand, lying on the floor, was now up on one elbow. Very precisely he was crippling one after another of the hatchetmen. Considering that he had been knocked unconscious before, his aim was miraculous.

The place was a shambles. Only old Wang was a spectator. His son, Chen-p'o, had grappled with a Manchu hatchetman, a man with jagged fangs showing over his lower lip. The hatchetman bore the slight Chen-p'o toward the counter. Step by step, inch by inch, Chen-p'o resisted, but the hatchetman bore him back until Chen-p'o's hips were against the wood. Then, using his legs as levers, the Manchu began to exert real pressure. His jaws dripped. Backward went Chen-p'o. In another few seconds his back would be broken.

Old Wang, without unseeming haste, selected a pair of ivory chopsticks from beneath the counter. Dunand dare not fire, lest he kill Chen-p'o. Jimmy's gun was empty. The guards were too engrossed in their battle to see what was taking place. But old Wang deliberately picked up the artificial spider from the counter. He looked at it quizzically and then leaned forward. When the spider was on the cheek of the hatchetman, old Wang pressed it against the skin.

For one second more the Kong Gai hatchetman tried to snap Chen-p'o's back, and then his hand raked at his cheek.

"The cobra!" he wailed. "The cobra poison!"

"Exactly," said old Wang, and smiled.

Two of Kong Gai's men were dead, and two of the Wang guards. The Manchu was going to die. He dropped to the floor, and was reciting as many prayers as he could remember. There were bloody shoulders from Dunand's shots. The two white men kept their hands high. Captain Dunand, sitting up, was now complete master of the situation.

"Jim," he said contentedly, "this was great! Have young Wang call the wagon. It's a grand haul."

Wentworth lined up the wounded hatchetmen, and, taking no chances, ordered the Wang guards to watch the door, lest a rescue be attempted. Jimmy did not think it would occur. Kong Gai must have figured that he had sent enough men for a simple task. Also, the King Cobra was probably either fortifying his own lair, or finding a new one.

The street outside remained still as death. Only a few white tourists walked along it, gazing into the windows, and wondering why there were so few Chinese about. Chinatown knew what was happening. At such a time a man hid deep in his own cellar.

"Turn around, you two," Dunand commanded the pair of white men, after Chen-p'o had called the Hall of Justice. "A pair of rats," he decided.

"Hop-heads," Wentworth said shortly.

"It's gettin' pretty tough when a man can't go into a store an' buy somethin' without havin' the cops pull a gat on him," one of the men blurted.

"Sure. It's a rotten shame," Jimmy agreed. "In a minute I'm going to start crying."

"You got nothin' on us," the second whimpered, appealing to Dunand. His hands were shaking. It was obvious that Kong Gai's hold on him was through opium. "You gotta leave us go."

"Concealed weapon," Dunand reminded him. "And you can't deny you cracked me on the jaw."

"I was scared, cap. Honest, I was scared. Suppose you was buyin' a cup in a Chink store, and th' bulls come rushin' in. You'd be scared, too, cap. I ask you. Wouldn't you be scared?"

"I would, if I were you," Dunand said. His voice became colder. "Cuff 'em, Jim."

Wentworth did it. "We are holding you," the captain of detectives said grimly, "for the murder of one Walter Carrington."

The second man began to tremble violently. "We… We… I…"

"Shut up," snarled his companion. "That's all boloney, and you know it. Carrington blowed off his dome. I read it in th' papers—"

"You just went to Carrington's apartment to see the view out of his windows," Dunand suggested.

"Who says we was there?"

"The elevator boy'll say so," Dunand snapped. "Don't talk. Anything you say will be used against you."

The patrol wagon roared down the street. The shop filled with blue-coats.

"Careful with that Chink," Dunand said, pointing to the man inoculated with cobra venom, who was writhing on the floor. "Doc says he's got a fancy serum, and he wants to try it out. If only Carrington had known there is a way to save life after a cobra bite!"

"Is that true, chief?" Wentworth asked. "I didn't know it."

"Doc says so. He used a lot of fancy words. Sometimes the serum works. Say, Jim, what's the matter with old Wang? What's he waving his arms about?"

"He's telling his son that when he himself was young, he could have killed all of the hatchetmen single-handed," Jimmy grinned.

DEATH ROCK

Chinese Rum Runners Were a Novelty, but
Wentworth Knew Only Kong Gai Could
Have Stolen the Rum Ship Margarita

1

"KONG GAI"

THE AMBULANCE DOCTOR rose from his knees stiffly, having just lost a round in his endless battle with a tireless enemy.

"Well, he's gone," the physician said soberly, glancing down at the silent figure lying on the wharf. "Somebody shut that thing off!" The noise of a throbbing pulmotor was stilled. To Jimmy Wentworth the doctor growled, "What a terrific fight he must have put up, eh?"

The dead man was a terrible sight. His face was hidden in a blanket spread on the planks of pier 144C, but the back of his blond head, which could be seen was battered, bloody and bruised. The dead man's singlet was almost ripped from the powerful shoulders. It was stained with sea water and blood. The skin beneath was lacerated. Even the coarse blue trousers were hacked as if by many knives. One great hand, stretched forward, seemed to have every knuckle broken. It, also, was cut and bruised badly.

"There wasn't a chance to save him, detective," the doctor said. "The miracle is that he became partially conscious for a second. Matter of fact, he was practically dead when he was fished out of the bay. What d'you suppose happened?

Row on a tramp ship? Or a booze boat battle with hijack-ers out there in the fog?"

"Take your choice," Wentworth returned. "You're abso-lutely positive as to what the man said, doctor?"

"Absolutely. He said, 'Cohn's gay.' I remember it perfectly. At the time I thought 'gay' wasn't the word a sailor would use. He'd say 'lit' or 'happy' or 'full' or some-thing like that. Now, I imagine that your first job will be to look for this man named Cohn. That will set you on the right track, won't it?"

Jimmy said, "In your opinion, did the sailor drown, or did he die as the result of the beating?"

"Can't say until we examine his lungs." The doctor chuckled, realizing that Wentworth had answered ques-tion with question. "I didn't mean to tell you your business, detective," he said frankly. "We all like to try and figure out how a crime was committed, and some way to catch the criminal."

Nodding, Jimmy faced toward the city, as if turning to

meet the invisible foe. Under the steady coaxing of the sun, the fog about San Francisco was dispersing. Wentworth could see the gleaming tiled roofs of Chinatown. What mysterious things took place under them few white men— save the young Chinatown detective himself—could even guess. Jimmy's conjecture now was that the sailor had been slugged to death in some opium joint, and his body brought to the bay and thrown into the water. Had the tide been going out, through the Gate, the sailor would have been swept to sea. And the body never recovered.

"By the way," Jimmy suggested, "please don't repeat that sentence about Cohn feeling happy."

"Of course not."

" 'Cohn's gay,' " Wentworth repeated softly. That wasn't

"The white dog of a detective!" a Chinese voice screamed. "Kill him!"

what the sailor had said at all. It sounded like that, but the man had really said… Kong Gai! The name of the horribly evil master of Chinatown! Another death at Kong Gai's already bloodstained door!

Idlers had been kept from the end of pier 144C. While the doctor watched his assistant close the case of the pulmotor, Wentworth walked over to Officer O'Toole, who had been summoned when the body was seen floating shoreward, and who had directed the rescue.

"Anything on him to show who he was?" Jimmy asked.

"I was too busy givin' him first aid, until th' ambulance come. I never looked. But I see plenty of Svenskas like him on the water front. Just a good, hard-workin' squarehead, maybe come ashore for a good time."

Wentworth clung to his single clew. The sailor might have been bringing tins of opium smuggled into San Francisco up to one of Kong Gai's places. After the sailor had delivered his contraband, the Chinese had beaten him to death instead of making payment. Only the sailor's tremendous strength and recuperative powers had kept him alive long enough to float, somehow, ashore. Of course Kong Gai's men had thrown the sailor into the bay.

Gently, the detective turned the dead man over on the sodden blanket. A pair of wide, questioning blue eyes stared up at him. Wentworth shivered as he saw the newly battered nose, the gashed cheeks, the great circles of purple about each eye. The sailor must have sold his life dearly!

"I better call th' dead wagon," O'Toole said. In a hushed voice he added, "I bet th' Swede left his mark on th' guys which slugged him."

The doctor, ready to go, said thoughtfully, "I don't believe he was a Swede, officer."

"Why not?" Wentworth demanded.

"Cheekbones aren't high enough. The nose, if it weren't smashed, would be aquiline. His hair's faded by the sun. You can see how it is browner near the scalp. I'd say the man was English. And—" lifting up a dead hand, and indicating the unbroken finger nails—"hardly a common sailor."

The nails were clean, well shaped, and obviously had been carefully kept.

"Adventurer," Wentworth said. "He was around thirty-five. Maybe he was in the war, and couldn't settle down. Poor devil. Would you say, from the man's appearance, that he used drugs?" he asked the doctor abruptly.

"Not with eyes as clear as his. Absolutely not, detective. No. He was in perfect physical condition."

Wentworth slipped his hand in to the cold, wet trousers pocket, and found it, as he expected, empty. Kong Gai would never leave a scrap of identifying paper, even though the evil Chinese ruler of Chinatown was sure the body would never be recovered. But in the other pocket a soggy, wet mass met the detective's searching fingers. Even before Jimmy drew the discovery out, slowly, he knew what it was going to be. A roll of currency. The slippery elastic band told him beyond any doubt.

"And who'd of expected that?" O'Toole demanded thickly, his eyes as wide as the dead man's. "Look at that roll!"

The outside bill had forced the patrolman to blurt out his question. It was a gold back. It was marked $1000. Wentworth put the soaked roll of money on the blanket, and began to open it with expert fingers. The doctor began to rub his chin as he counted the bills when Wentworth separated them.

But it was O'Toole who finally said huskily, "Fifty thousand! An' me thinkin' him nothin' but a water front Swede! No wonder they sent you down, Jim! Fifty grand, an' him in a old pair of dungarees!"

"New ones," Jimmy said automatically. He placed the currency in his handkerchief and put it in his own pocket. "Forget you saw the money, Mike. And you, too, doctor."

So the man dressed like a sailor had managed to get away from Kong Gai with the payment intact. Fifty thousand dollars, in large bills. Jimmy's eyes shone. He had something to work on now, not only to find the sailor's murderer, but to ferret out another of Kong Gai's lieutenants. Thousand dollar bills could—and would—be traced.

The fog, over the city, was lifting swiftly, although the ferries on the bay hooted and blared as they felt their way toward the city. For a hundred feet from the end of pier 144C the water was visible, but farther out the curtain of heavy tide fog clung to the gray bay.

Wentworth said to O'Toole, "You've got the name of whoever found the body?"

"He's waitin' down at the wharfinger's shack, Jim. A longshoreman. He was sleepin' off a drunk. Want to talk to him? I'll—"

"Might as well drive down with the ambulance," Wentworth said, as the driver started his machine. "You wait here, O'Toole."

The longshoreman had little to tell the young Chinatown detective. He had been sitting on the end of a pile, wondering how to get breakfast. Then he had seen a body moving toward the wharf. At first he thought it was the woman who had disappeared, and for whom a reward was offered, and then he saw that the body was floating face downward, so it couldn't be a woman's. He insisted that the sailor had been trying feebly to swim, because his arms moved. Looking into the bleared eyes of the longshoreman, Wentworth discounted the testimony.

"You get ten dollars for sighting a body," he told the man. "There's your breakfast. All you've got to do is to go to the Hall of Justice. I'm phoning there; I'll tell 'em you're coming."

"Can I have four bits now?" the man requested.

When Wentworth gave it to him, he shuffled off. Using the wharfinger's telephone, Wentworth called head-quarters, and asked for Captain Dunand. He was given Dunand's office, but the sergeant in charge said, "The chief's out, Jim. He told me to tell you that there are three tramps anchored in the fairway. We've sent the police boat around to pier 144C. Go out with the tug, Jim, and see if there was a fight on one of 'em. That's what Dunand says."

"I've picked up something here," Wentworth said guardedly.

"On this case?"

"Right." Wentworth thought a moment, and decided that nothing would be lost by going out to the tramp steamers. The sailor probably had been on one of them. If so, some one aboard was mixed up with the opium smuggling, if opium had actually been delivered to Kong Gai. Glancing hastily about, Jimmy saw that the wharfinger had gone outside with the driver of the hearse.

"While I'm out on the bay, sergeant, I wish you'd have some bills traced. The numbers run consecutively. From 217499MX to 217549NX." Lowering his voice, Wentworth added: "And they are all thousand dollar bills, Keegan!"

"On a sailor?"

"In his pocket. An elastic around 'em. They'd been in the water for some time. The currency wadded up the minute I touched it. Five, six hours in salt water. The sailor was alive when he was pulled out. But he'd been beaten to a pulp. We've got something!"

"Thousand dollar bills—that's a front page story!"

"Keep it under cover," Wentworth pleaded. "We've got to have time. I've got the money. It won't come in with the body."

"Sure, Jimmy. I'll just tell the news hounds that a sailor was fished out, and give 'em the usual description—"

"Don't say a word, or they'll keep at it until we're wrecked! If only the mere fact that a sailor was found is printed, we'll never learn another thing. Don't let a word get out, Keegan. And," he finished softly, "if Captain Dunand comes in before I get back, tell him the man was murdered by Kong Gai!"

Wentworth heard the sergeant swear once, and then Keegan said grimly, "Good luck to you, boy. We'll give you a good funeral, anyhow."

"Thanks," Wentworth chuckled, and hung up the receiver. The grin was still on his lips as he went outside.

2

BULLETS IN THE FOG

THE POLICE TUG Mayor Eben Prentice nosed her way through the fog until she swung cautiously under the stern of a rusty old tramp anchored westward of the ferry lanes. The bow of the steamer was headed toward the Gate, although she was beginning to move slowly on her chain in a sluggish circle. The tide was changing. Soon it would again be running strongly out to the Pacific between Fort Point and Bonita Light.

Wentworth could read the squat vessel's name:

GALATEA—MANCHESTER

When the tugboat captain inched his sturdy little craft alongside, the detective was able to see the British flag flying. Was the ambulance doctor correct? Did the dead sailor come from a British ship? Was the murdered man an Englishman, and not a common sailor at all?

The tugboat captain hailed the ship and made fast. It was several minutes before Wentworth and two men from the Harbor Station climbed the ladder and were on deck— plenty of time for the Galatea to be prepared for questioning. And the greeting given the police was hardly jovial.

"Come aboard us," the captain of the Galatea protested bitterly. "We're a very desperate craft. Full of hemp from Calcutta. But we've got a bottle of whisky in my cabin, perhaps. Or a few cases of beer. My mate undoubtedly keeps some Hollands in his locker—"

"Bangin' aboard like a lot o' ruddy pirates," the little cockney mate sputtered. "I never hear o' such a thing. Nice way t' welcome us, I says. Bad 'nough t' fight into th' rotten port with a mean wind an' lie out here shiverin' in th' fog, without no constables wantin' t' search us—"

"Why this fuss, captain?" Wentworth asked pleasantly. "Don't you want to be searched?"

"Search away," the captain snapped. "If you Yanks wanted to do your duty so badly, why not go outside the Heads? I saw a five hundred tonner lying outside. If she isn't laden with whisky I'll eat her. But that's work. You don't want any of that! No, you come aboard me, and rip my cabin apart to find a few bottles of King William! You—"

"What you're carrying is none of my business," the detective said quietly. "I'm a policeman, not a Federal officer. But you've a man missing, captain."

"Not from the Galatea, mister." The captain cheered up instantly. "Why, I haven't been ashore myself. That's why I'm a little out of patience. I'm waiting for your port doctor to pass us—if he ever gets out of bed and comes out to examine us. Hmm. Man ashore, eh, and in trouble with the police? Not from my ship."

"A man might have swam ashore?"

"If'c'as," the relieved mate snarled, "I'll break 'is blasted 'ead!" His voice rose shrilly, and the crew of the Galatea straggled on deck. "Where's that long-nosed cook? Don't tell me 'e's jumped ship! Flies 'e 'ad in my oatmeal this morning! If 'e's jumped ship, I'll fly 'im, I will! I'll—oh, there you are, cook! 'Urryin', too. An' a good thing!"

The sour-faced engineer groaned, " 'Tis bad enough not to be able to buy whusky on shore, wi'oot losin' a mon's own property, captain. Is there no protest can be made aboot it?"

"These aren't prohibition officials, McGregor," the captain said. He turned to Wentworth. "They are all here. Want to see my papers? Not a man missing."

"How about a tall, well built Englishman, captain?"

"An Englishman? A sailor? Mister, I've got Finns and Swedes and Danes and Portagees and a lascar fireman, but an Englishman?" The captain laughed shortly. "I haven't seen an English sailor for ten years!"

" 'Ow about me?" the mate expostulated.

Wentworth turned to one of the Harbor officers. "The other tramps anchored out here—where'd they come from?"

"Erricson, mixed cargo, from Copenhagen, and Molly Peters, Glasgow, with camphor, tea, and hardwood from Formosa," the policeman said. "Both carry wireless. We've been in touch with them, Wentworth, but both report no man missing. Which," he said, lowering his voice, "may not mean a thing, under the circumstances. They'd cover up, if for no better reason than not to be delayed in sailing."

The Harbor men, Jimmy knew, considered the case nothing more than a drunken fight aboard ship. Until the affair was explained to Dunand at headquarters, it was not the detective's place to talk.

"We coaled alongside o' them, in Honolulu," the mate said. "No Britisher on them ships, orficer!"

"The vury engineers are foreigners," the dour engineer of the Galatea grumbled. He scratched his chin, and then tried to smile. "Detective," he said, "as mon to mon and between friends, should your rum boat be caught, what are the chances for a poor engineer to buy a case o' Scots, perhaps at a leetle reeduction? We'd be gone within the week, and nothing said. It's a grand opportunity for you to make a few dollars!"

Grinning, Jimmy said, "The police haven't anything to do with catching rum runners. That's up to the Coast Guard boats, and the Federals."

"She was only a mile outside, waitin' for fog to run in," the engineer announced. "You c'd catch her as easy as easy. I had the glasses on her. Cases o' Scots. Bushmill's. King George. The tarps were off. From Vancouver, she was. If I try to buy one bottle ashore, the price'll be shameful—"

Wentworth, addressing the captain, said abruptly, "A man's been murdered, captain. Slugged to death. Could he have floated in from this rum runner?"

"With a tide running as she has, I'd say it was possible."

Wentworth took the captain to one side. He said earnestly, "I'm taking your word that there was no fight on this ship, and that no man is missing. I need help. Tell me: there are three ships anchored off the north piers. You know the other two. Which would be apt to carry opium?"

"Any of us, mister. We've all been in the Orient."

The detective felt the reticence of the ship's officer. "Look here, captain," he urged, "a man's been done to death. An Englishman—a white man. If you will only tell me what I've asked, I may be able to get the murderer."

"The Molly Peters loaded in Formosa. Of the three,

potentially she's the most guilty. The Erricson's completely manned by Danes. We ourselves may have a tin or so aboard. We've searched for it ourselves. No captain wants his vessel confiscated, nor to lose his ticket. My mate didn't find any, and he's a good ferret. But the Peters is a dirty ship, with a dirty crew."

The bay was booming with sound. The siren on Goat Island bleated; the raucous bell-buoy on Alcatraz clanged—bang-bang, bang-bang; the distant hoot of the Bonita Point lighthouse's horn howled through the fog. To the eastward, in the ferry lanes, the white boats proceeded at half speed in the tule fog, now a belt across the fairway. San Francisco and the Marin shore were both free of the mist, but the middle of the bay was still thick.

Captain Mitchell seemed listening. Wentworth was about to leave the ship when the captain said, "Power boat. Not using her siren. 'Bout half speed. If she isn't careful, she'll smash into us."

Stepping to the rail, above the Prentice, the captain leaned over the side. The two Harbor men were climbing down. Wentworth waited to thank the intent captain.

"Too fast," Mitchell muttered. "Hear her, detective? Putt-putt-putt. Pretty fair sized craft. Powerful engines… she ought to come out of the fog," he said, pointing, "just about there. In a minute."

"Thanks, captain," Wentworth said, eager to get on with the search. "If any of your men get hilarious ashore, let us know. Maybe we can square it in return for your information."

Jimmy was halfway down the ladder when he heard a

bellow above him: "Port, you fools! Port! You're running me down! Port!"

Out of the fog a power boat raced, a long gray craft as mysterious and deadly as the thick mist from which it had emerged. The power boat shot toward the helplessly anchored Galatea and the old Prentice beside her. The police tug's captain, a pilot retired from the sea, must have seen the gray craft just as Captain Mitchell yelled, for he snatched at his whistle, and the tremendous blare of it almost tumbled Wentworth from the swaying ladder.

On rushed the gray craft, in a straight course from the ocean. Not until it was a bare, dangerous fifteen feet from the Galatea's bows did the lean power boat swerve. Wentworth had twisted about on the ladder, watching. He braced himself for a possible crash.

Some one on the gray craft screamed in a high-pitched Chinese voice: "The dog! The white dog of a detective! Kill him!" In the same split second, bullets thudded against the steel sides of the Galatea.

Jimmy dropped to the deck of the tug.

"Kong Gai!" he cried. "After that boat! Don't lose a second!"

The sturdy Eben Prentice churned the gray water to a white foam as she fought her way out from the tramp. By the time she was clear, the gray power boat was out of sight.

"Swung about," Captain Harris growled in his beard. "Saw you. Saw us. Gone back into the fog. It's clear, toward the city. See? Never find her now—"

"Until she lands?"

"Where'll that be? She'll get a new coat of paint. Or

duck out of the Gate again. Spotted you, eh? Some of your Chink friends, boy?"

Kong Gai, in a power boat! Why? The answer still seemed obvious to the young Chinatown detective. There was a large shipment of opium in the bay, important enough for Kong Gai to supervise its smuggling into the city. And the opium would come from the tramp on which the Englishman was murdered. Only one fact bothered Wentworth. Why had the British sailor's body been in the water for five or more hours? He dismissed this by deciding that the desperately wounded man had been unable in the fog, to find his way easily to shore.

"We'll board the Peters," Wentworth said. "That is, if you are absolutely sure it is useless to look for that power boat."

"Not a chance to pick her up out here," the captain grumbled. He called, "Hey, Sparks!" only to find the radio operator just outside the wheelhouse, an automatic in his hand.

"Put that gun away," Harris ordered. "The fight's over. Before it commenced. Better luck next time, Sparks. Now, call headquarters. Tell 'em we were fired on. They're to watch for a gray power boat. Fifty footer. Brasswork bright. Corliss engined. Code that, d'ye hear? Anything to add, Wentworth?"

"Not until we've been on the Molly Peters," Jimmy frowned. "What chance is there to catch that gray boat when she lands? We want a man on her."

"A hundred miles of docks around the bay, Wentworth! She can slide her nose in anywhere. Or transfer her passengers. Headquarters 'll telephone everywhere, but they won't find that boat!"

Wentworth strained to catch sight of the Peters as the captain inched his way through the thicker fog. He was staring into the wall of mist when Sparks brought the word from headquarters. "Have Wentworth return immediately. Important developments." The message was signed by Captain Dunand.

Jimmy instantly scrawled a reply on Sparks's pad: "Want to go on another tramp steamer. Things are hot out here now."

The Prentice was edging toward the rusty Formosa-loaded tramp flying the gay Peruvian flag when Sparks, with a grin on his face, brought Dunand's answer. It was entirely to the point.

"I'll make it hot for you if you aren't in my office in an hour," the captain had radioed in police code. Which left Jimmy Wentworth no choice as to what he must do.

3

THE LOST MARGARITA

"THOSE BILLS," THE gray haired captain of detectives stated quietly, "were all drawn two days ago from the account of Cohn, Crawford & Company, at the Sierra Pacific Bank, Jim. Numbered from 217499MX to 217549NX. Cohn, Crawford are supposed to be manufacturers' agents, but the department of justice tell me they're mixed up in rum running ventures, both from Mexico and Canada. Which makes your Kong Gai guess all wet."

"The ambulance M.D. did say the dead man whispered, 'Cohn's gay,'" Jimmy admitted. "But how do you account for that boat cruising in the bay? Kong Gai was certainly on it. He took a couple of shots at me."

"He has plenty of reasons for wanting you dead. Coincidence. Anyhow, Crawford is here, waiting to be questioned. He's mighty nervous, Jim. He must know something. I had him kept waiting until you showed up."

Crawford was a thin, sandy haired man, who spoke with a slight Canadian accent. Dunand wasted no time.

"Mr. Crawford," he said, "I regret the circumstance, but we must ask you to explain what was done with the fifty thousand dollars your firm drew from the Sierra Pacific.

Specifically, why was it withdrawn, and who received the bills?"

"I must consult my attorneys before replying, sir," Crawford said uneasily. He cleared his throat. "May I ask what interest the police have in the matter?"

"Murder," Dunand said laconically.

The nervous man struggled to pull himself together. "Please lay your cards on the table," he pleaded. "Murder? In which the thousand dollar notes are involved? Impossible!"

"They were found in the dead man's pocket, Mr. Crawford."

"In what way," the sandy haired man asked, "am I, or my firm, connected with the death of a Chinese?"

Dunand's eyes flicked over toward Wentworth, and then he said, "Let my detective tell you. He's working on the case."

The death of a Chinese! So the gray power boat in the bay did mean something. Alert, Wentworth said easily, for all his excitement, "If the bills were drawn by your firm from the bank, sir, and were later discovered in a murdered man's pocket, don't you think it's fair for us to request an explanation?"

"I suppose it is," Crawford said. "However, I can say nothing until I consult my attorneys. That is final, gentlemen." He smiled vaguely. "The strangest part of it is, whether or not you believe it, that I haven't the slightest idea how the Chinaman was killed, nor why."

Wentworth leaned forward in his chair.

"What makes you think it was a Chinese, Mr. Crawford?"

The sandy haired man was startled. "Wasn't it?" he demanded.

"No," Jimmy told him.

"A white man?"

"Yes."

Crawford's sallow face became paler. His hands worked together, and his lips twitched. Would he talk now? He would!

"I wonder if you'd give me a description of the man?" he said, licking his lips. And, before Wentworth could speak, he went on rapidly. "He wasn't quite a tall man, was he? Fair? Very well built. Blue eyes. A powerful chap?"

"Beaten to death," Wentworth said sharply.

"Harry!" Crawford covered his face with his hands. Both detectives sat silently. Both kept their eyes glued to the despondent merchant. It was a full minute before Crawford looked up. "Gentlemen," he said, in a calmer voice, "it must be my brother. I—I don't understand it!"

"If you will tell us what you know, we can bring his murderer to justice," the captain of detectives said.

"I'll help you all I can, gentlemen. That may not be very much. You tell me that Harry was, poor lad, beaten to death? I can hardly believe it! He had the strength of a bull. And the Margarita had a picked crew. There is something very terrible about this. Poor Harry."

The doubt in Dunand's mind about the whole affair come out as he asked, "Was there ever bad blood between your partner and your brother?"

Crawford said, "Harry didn't know my partner, sir. He'd never seen him."

"They were on a party together," Dunand disagreed. "Your brother said, 'Cohn's gay,' just before he died."

Laughing shortly, unhappily, Crawford said, "That isn't possible. Cohn is a man in his eighties. His money started our firm. He is bed-ridden; hasn't been out of his house for years. I can swear to that. His doctor will tell you that Cohn couldn't walk if he tried. And Harry doesn't know him at all. You talk in riddles, captain."

"If he'd never seen Mr. Cohn," Wentworth said softly, "had he ever seen… Kong Gai?"

"I had hoped it was Kong Gai who was dead," Crawford said, shivering.

Wentworth and Dunand exchanged glances.

"I think," Dunand suggested, "that you had better tell us all you know. We, also, would like to see Kong Gai dead. At the end of a noose."

Crawford pulled himself together.

"This is a terrible shock to me, gentlemen," he said. "I'll do my best. Our firm was organized long before the war, when Mr. Cohn was a well man. We dealt exclusively in articles imported from the Orient. Just how, or when, it was decided to deal in illicit liquors I have never been certain. However, it was done within the law, as we see it. Shipments are made from Canada and from Mexico, and sold by us outside the cruising limit.

"Harry had never come down with one of our vessels. He pleaded to throw up his job—he hated it—and join the Margarita. Like a fool, I agreed.

"The Margarita carried a full cargo of spirits. A valuable cargo, the largest we have ever shipped. It was to be delivered, twelve miles out, to men employed by a Chinese named Kong Gai. Who is Kong Gai? Gentlemen, I have never seen him, although we have done business with him many times. He is a myth. An evil myth. Kong Gai was to take the liquor, at an exceptional price. And I feel that in some way he is connected with Harry's death. He—"

"The fifty thousand dollars," Dunand broke in. "What about it?"

"I sent a boat out to the Margarita yesterday, with orders, and the money. The cargo was to be turned over to Kong Gai's representatives in the usual manner, but I wanted to tell the Margarita's captain, Jerrold, that all payment had already been made to us, here, in advance. The fifty thousand dollars was—I will be frank, gentlemen—to pay for another shipment to be loaded in Mexico and brought to the States."

"You say Kong Gai has paid for the stuff already?"

"He has. In cash."

Wentworth said thoughtfully, "Could Kong Gai have known your brother carried that amount of money?"

"Perhaps." Crawford's hands twitched. "He knows everything, that devil!"

"And tried to rob him, and your brother put up a fight?"

"I can't believe any one was able to knock Harry out! Not only was my brother a brave man, but he was a fighter. And the crew of the Margarita can hold their own anywhere. She is heavily manned, and, I will admit, heavily armed." Excitedly, Crawford added, "Where was this fight? Where was Harry's… body… found?"

"Floating off pier 144C." Gently, Wentworth added, "Do you wish to see him?"

"I understand everything less and less," Crawford

muttered. "Harry in the city! Why?" At last his shoulders squared. "If you think it advisable, I'd like to telephone my office. The Margarita is equipped with wireless, although we never use it when near a States port. But her captain might shed some light on the affair, and he may have got in touch. Or we can try to get him."

Dunand gave him permission instantly.

After Crawford had finished his telephone conversation, he turned again to the detectives. "It is stranger than ever," he said. "My office manager tells me that the customary code word from the Margarita, telling us that she was unloaded and departed, has not been received at all. A representative of Kong Gai has been to see us. He tells us that the Margarita is not lying at the appointed place, and demands repayment of Kong Gai's money! Could she have gone ashore? Is that how Harry met his death?"

"He said 'Kong Gai!' before he died," Jimmy Wentworth said.

Crawford slumped in his chair. "I can tell you nothing more," he groaned. "It is all dark to me."

There was complete silence, and then Dunand said, "It's your case, Jim. Handle it the way you want."

"How is the money to be repaid Kong Gai for the unreceived liquor?"

"In the customary untraceable manner," Crawford told them. "A draft to be paid in Canton."

Wentworth drummed on the desk. Nothing there! Except that it proved that Kong Gai was not only careful, but that his tentacles reached clear back to China. "Who are your dealings with here?" he asked. "Who makes the arrangements with you? How is it done?"

"Always by telephone. When money is paid us, it is by cash being deposited at the Anglo-Chinese Bank, either at Canton or Shanghai. The bank cables us that the amount has been deposited to our credit. I tell you," he said vehemently, "I know no more about Kong Gai, and who are his men, than you do!"

Another blank. A third time Jimmy tried for an opening. "When you telephone Kong Gai, what number do you call? Wouldn't some one in your office know?"

"We never call him. He calls us." Flushing, Crawford said, "Once, we wanted to learn, out of curiosity, where Kong Gai's headquarters were. We investigated his call. It was made from a pay station in Chinatown.

Jimmy remembered something suddenly. "Was your Margarita a five hundred ton ship, sir?"

"She was! How did you know?"

"The captain of a tramp steamer saw her lying outside. I don't know when. Yesterday, I suppose."

"Of course she was outside," Crawford said querulously. "Didn't we send fifty thousand out to her? And our launch returned with a message from Harry, saying he was feeling fit. What's that got to do with this, detective?"

"Ships don't disappear," Wentworth said. "But I'll bet that sometimes they're hijacked, just like the trucks."

"Nobody stole the cargo of the Margarita! She's manned with ex-Royal Navy men. They stand watch. She's armed with machine guns. And when a cargo's delivered to another vessel, not more than two men at a time are allowed on board. Our crew stand guard every moment, and the other craft is kept under our guns!"

"Who's the person to ask about missing ships?" Wentworth asked Captain Dunand. "She's still there, or she's left, or she's sunk. And we ought to know."

Dunand picked up his telephone. "Get a report on the Margarita, supposed to have sailed for San Francisco from Canada," he said. "And tell 'em we'd like it as soon as possible."

The three men sat without speaking. Crawford had recovered his courage; Dunand was completely at sea; Wentworth didn't see where to start on the case. Kong Gai's hand was clearly shown. The obvious thing was that the Chinese had hijacked the Margarita. The presence of the power boat returning through the heads indicated the possibility. However, the gray craft might have returned after failing to find the rum runner. Against this was the presence of the money in Harry Crawford's pocket, and the well armed and alert Margarita.

The telephone buzzed. Dunand listened, and then said, "Thanks. That's all." He turned to the other two. "The Margarita," he said gravely, "has been reported as lying outside the twelve-mile limit. A coast guard boat has been watching her, but lost her in the fog. Now, however, she is reported as being ninety miles south of the Gate, apparently on the way to Mexico."

Crawford blurted, "Impossible!"

"Your brother might have had a fight with some one on board, and rather than tell you of it, the captain sailed south with the cargo."

"Captain Jerrold's Harry's friend. And mine. I beg of you, gentlemen, not to leave the matter as it is!"

"We won't," Jimmy Wentworth said. "Your brother whispered 'Kong Gai!' and we're going to get to the bottom of this, somehow."

"You can count on my help."

"Thank you, sir. We will." Under his breath Jimmy added, "When we can think of something to ask."

4

THE BRANDY TRAIL

WITH CRAWFORD'S CONSENT, the police department merely gave out that a body had been found floating in the bay, and that it was without identification. An exact description, however, was given to the newspapers, which made Wentworth positive that somewhere in his secret chambers in Chinatown Kong Gai would be chuckling with delight.

Two days passed without event, but on the third Crawford hurried into Dunand's office. Despite constant efforts, the merchant had been unable at any time to get in touch with the vanished Margarita, nor had her captain wirelessed his employer.

Crawford was excited.

"I had promised a very good friend a case of special brandy," he said to Captain Dunand. "Last night I was at his house. After dinner, he twigged me about my failure to deliver, and I told him that we had one more shipment coming, and that I would try and get it for him. One more shipment—and my last, captain! I'm through. After Harry's death... But to return to the brandy. My friend said, 'Don't bother, I picked up a case of it this afternoon. Taste it, and see if you don't agree it is authentic.' I tasted it. My friend had decanted the bottle, but I asked to see it anyhow. Captain, he did buy a case, and I am absolutely convinced that it was the case which was on the Margarita!"

"Who'd he buy it from?"

"His regular bootlegger."

Dunand nodded, and then said, "Excuse me a moment." He told the operator, "I want Wentworth here. Take him off his beat." Then: "Let's have the man's name—the bootlegger."

"I wouldn't—"

"Do you want your brother's murderer found?"

Crawford's lips tightened. "I do," he snapped. "The bootlegger who sold the brandy is named Brusanari—"

"Know him," Dunand said. He lifted the receiver, and said, "Send some one out to round up Angelo Brusanari. Bring him here. Vagrancy, if he argues. He's not to get in touch with any one about anything."

"You think there is something to this?"

"We'll find out where he bought his stuff. Trace the shipment up to the time he received it, if we can. Get the Federals' help if we need it. It's a clew. We haven't had much to work on. Now, any word from your ship?"

"Not a sound!"

Crawford was gone, but Jimmy Wentworth had arrived before the bootlegger, Brusanari, was brought in, all protests.

"Say, what d' hell you tryin'?" he demanded. "Where you get dis vagrancy stuff, huh? What you t'ink I am, cap? A bum or somet'in'?"

"I'd hate to tell you, Angelo," Dunand grinned. "You'd

get mad. But all we want is a little mouth music from you, then you can beat it and peddle your bathtub gin—"

"Say, my stuff's all imported!"

"Sure. Like the Penguin brandy. Where'd you buy it, Angie?"

"Same guy I buy from all d' time. It come high, chief! You want some? Maybe I can pick up a case nex' mont'. I dunno. I buys it from Joe Ferrara? Why, cap?"

"You just answer questions, Angie, and don't ask 'em. Joe Ferrara? Old Juicy Joe, eh? Well, unless you want us to get tough, Angie, forget I asked you about it. Stay and have dinner with us, anyhow, just to show we're friends."

"I'm pinched?"

"No. I just want to make sure—" Dunand winked at Wentworth, who knew that the bootlegger would be held until Ferrara was brought in, lest he scare the other into hiding—"make sure that you get a good feed on the city to-night, Angie."

"I keep my mout' shut."

"That's a good boy. Only open it to eat and drink, Angie, and you'll live to have stomach ulcers from your own booze."

Step by step the department traced the case of Penguin brandy, clear down to a fishing boat owned by one Peter Gonzales. There the trail ended. Gonzales said that his boat had been hired to go a few miles or so up the coast, outside the heads, and bring a cargo of liquor in through the Gate.

"*Sangre d' Dios,*" Gonzales told Wentworth, "I go, I find place, I see men. In black. Masks on face. Me, I am scared, I tell you! But I am beached, I cannot run away. In my boat is loaded whisky from Canada, *sí.* Was brandy, there? Me,

I do not know. Perhaps. You say so. Who were the men? I do not know!"

Were the men Americans?

How, countered the owner of the fishing smack, could he tell what they were? Could he look through the masks? "All I know is that I was very frightened," he insisted.

"Look here," Jimmy demanded, "did you see a rum runner lying farther out?"

"No, *señor* policeman. But I saw one close in, anchored."

"How close?"

"A quarter mile."

"The Margarita?" Wentworth snapped out.

"*Si, señor* captain. That was her name."

Wentworth said to Dunand, "We've made only one mistake. We should have kept every one locked up, from Angelo Brusanari right on down the line—"

Without seeing what Jimmy was driving at, Dunand retorted, "Sure; that'd be fine. Attorneys raising Cain. Newspaper boys yelping at us to find out what was up. We'd have had as much secrecy as an olive in a bottle."

Gonzales was held for further questioning. What Jimmy Wentworth meant when he said the chain of liquor sellers should have been kept in jail was explained by his discussion with his chief.

"If Crawford means what he says—that he's willing to do anything to catch his brother's murderer—we've got one chance in a million. Shall I ask him?"

"Ask him what, Jim?"

"To have that last ship of his come down to San Francisco, and arrange to have the cargo of booze delivered to Kong Gai. Just the same as the Margarita's liquor."

"You think Kong Gai hijacked it?"

"I do, chief. Here're my reasons. The first is the dead man. The second is that the Margarita hasn't been heard from. The third is that the booze has shown up for sale. The fourth," he added very quietly, "is the fact that I've picked up rumors of a big party given in Chinatown, at which a very fine brand of Scotch whisky was served. And the last reason, chief, is what the dead man said in his last moment. 'Kong Gai!'"

Dunand rubbed his chin. "I don't want to let Crawford in for more trouble. It's a ticklish business. We'd be forced to work with the Federals. How do we know that the Margarita's crew weren't working with the hijackers? And don't forget that Kong Gai demanded repayment for the booze he said he didn't get."

"Which is the devil all over! Chief, he's like all crooks. He's got to boast."

Wentworth quietly unbuttoned his coat, and showed Dunand a slash on his shoulder. "I was separating a couple of fighting porter-coolies this morning," he said. "One of 'em turned on me, and when he struck out with his knife said something about laughing at white men. One of those ambiguous remarks, but the sort that means something in Chinatown."

"What'd he say?"

"He said, 'We kill you all, policemen and sailors alike!'"

"Make your arrangements!" Captain Dunand snapped. "You'll be working in a different county. When you go, I'll have a Marin County deputy with you. And you'd better be sworn in as a deputy marshal, in case you make an arrest at sea. We don't want to be beaten in the courts if you make an arrest."

Nodding, Wentworth said, "Fix it so I can have all the dope on tide and that sort of thing, chief. I'd like permission to take a day off, too. I want a look-see at the coast where the Margarita transferred her cargo."

5

THE ROCK OF DEATH

THE YOUNG MAN in linen knickers who jumped from the small roadster at the gas station in Bolinas looked like anything except the stereotype picture of a detective. In the little machine was a girl. It would have been difficult, now, to recognize her as Lucile Carrington, whom Jimmy had rescued from Kong Gai some time before. The girl's father had crossed the fiendish master of Chinatown. In vengeance, Kong Gai had stolen the white woman, and kept her under the influence of drugs. She had indeed become the "voice" of Kong Gai. After Wentworth had escaped with her from Kong Gai's torture, a month in a hospital, and another month of rest, had brought about complete recovery.

Jimmy almost wished that the excursion to the ocean, just north and west of San Francisco, were only a pleasure journey, although he knew that the only reason Lucile Carrington had been willing to come was because Kong Gai was mixed in the case.

She sat quietly in the roadster while the tank was being filled with gasoline, and Wentworth talked with the service station man.

"How's the road down to the ocean?" Jimmy asked.

"Ain't none," the man said. He pointed to the hills between Boliness and the sea. "You can get up there's far as Tony Mendoza's ranch," he said, "an' if you want a drink, Tony's th' boy who can give it to you. Tell him I said you was O.K. But from Tony's to the 'bandoned pier there ain't nothin' but a cow trail. Don't try it, mister. Get stuck in th' sand. It ain't much of a walk; mebbe three-quarter of a mile all down hill. Goin' on a picnic?"

"Not to-day," Jimmy grinned.

"Yeah," the service station man said vaguely, glancing at the girl. He grew confidential, which pleased Wentworth, since it proved that not even a suspicious man would take him for a detective. "If you want a li'l drink here in town, you can get one at Chung Kee's Laundry. You go to th' side door, an' tell 'em Joe de Borba—that's me—sent you. Good stuff, too."

Again Jimmy said, "Not to-day," and then added casually, "What's this abandoned pier you were talking about? I thought the coast was too rough here for that sort of thing."

"It is. Th' bozos who started to make it only got as far as blastin' rock. I dunno what they was goin' to use it for."

"Landing booze, maybe?"

The service station man shook his head. "Naw," he said, and spat at the young detective's ignorance. "When you land booze, you don' want no pier, mister. You land it on th' beach somewheres." He grinned broadly. "I bet Tony Mendoza's seen a thing or two, although he can't see right down to th' ocean except through th' cypress trees… Well, have a good time, mister."

Jimmy climbed back in the roadster, and drove slowly through the little town's main street. Huddled between a garage and a grocery store was an old shack, with a sign Chung Kee—Laundry painted on a dirty glass window. Wentworth drove past it rapidly. Here, he felt, was one of Kong Gai's outposts. His observant eye caught the fact that a telephone wire ran into the laundry. That in itself was incriminating. It showed also how safe Kong Gai felt— how sure he was that his outpost was unknown to the police, and that the Federals, working through the coast guard at sea, would pay no attention to a dirty Chink laundry. Who ever heard of Chinese rum runners? No wonder the wily Kong Gai had decided upon such a safe and lucrative business!

Lucile Carrington stood up when Wentworth finally stopped the roadster at the top of the long row of hills. She looked at the ocean; Jimmy looked at her.

"It's so lovely—so free and clean," the girl breathed. "I'm glad I came, Mr. Wentworth."

"So'm I," Jimmy said fervently. "If you'll wait out here, I'll only be gone a sec'. Then we'll walk down to the shore."

"I hope you brought something to eat," the girl smiled. "I'm starved!"

Jimmy's face fell. "Never thought of it," he mourned. "But maybe I can get some chow from this Mendoza. It's as good a way as any to talk to him."

The kitchen of the Mendoza house was filthy. Jimmy came to the point at once. "Joe de Borba told me I could get a drink here," he said. "But how about fixing me up a lunch for two? Sandwiches. And," he added, grinning, "if you think I'm safe, let me have a bottle of wine to go with them."

Swarthy Mendoza grunted, "I never see no prohi dressed

like you, mistaire. Ice cream pants ain't what prohis wear, nor cops, neither. Sure I feex you up!"

Jimmy sat on a broken-backed chair while Mendoza poured red wine into a bottle, and while his slatternly wife cut bread and put meat or cheese between the slices. As Mendoza wrapped the bottle in newspaper, Jimmy said, "Where's the best place for us to eat, Tony? Somewhere on the beach where it'll be protected."

Tony shrugged. "Anywhere," he said. "What's a difference? Anywhere on d' sand. Not on rocks, mistaire."

Maria Mendoza hastily crossed herself. Wentworth did not miss her sign of fear and reverence. He followed the lead instantly.

"Why not on the rocks, in a nice sunny spot, Tony? That's what I'd thought of."

Tony handed him the bottle, and took the money before he said, in a low voice: "Keep off rocks, mistaire! Or... you die!"

Laughing, Wentworth said, "Go on! I've climbed a lot of mountains. I won't fall into the sea, Tony."

Mendoza shook his finger in the detective's face. "You are young," he said. "You t'ink you are smart? Well, when you go to ocean, you find one, two, t'ree li'l rock, all togadder by cypress tree. Below, you see rock very big. Fifty feet from water. It is very smooth water below. Very deep. I tell you, you watch rock! You stand at top. You count waves. One li'l one, two li'l one, one more big. T'ree time you count! An' then, mistaire, you see something! Mebbe so, mebbe not. Anyhow, you keep count! One, two, t'ree! An'—"

His wife broke in, "You keep 'way from rock! Or you weel be dead, an' gone, an' crabs eat you in ocean!"

"Sure, I'll keep away," Wentworth said soberly. "We're just here for a picnic. I only wanted to find a good place to eat. You don't have many people come here?"

"It is deserted spot," Tony Mendoza agreed. "You are first in weeks… goo'-by, mistaire. For the sake of Maria, my wife, stop on way back an' show yourself, eh? Have a good time. That is fine wine!"

With his two parcels under his arm, Wentworth ran back to the car. "Let's go," he said happily. "Tony promises us the eighth wonder of the world, all free of charge, and with the added incentive of danger."

As they walked down the almost invisible path, sinking deeper and deeper into the sand dunes as they advanced, Lucile Carrington said, "You like danger."

"Part of the job," Jimmy said. "Let's talk about something more pleasant."

"I don't mind," Lucile smiled. "What do you suggest, Mr. Wentworth?"

"As a start, we'll discuss the matter of my christening. I was christened James, you know, so my friends could call me Jimmy." Wentworth grinned. "And now that we've decided that, let's talk about what makes your eyes so blue."

The sandwiches were eaten to the last crumb when the pair went in search of the three rocks at the base of a cypress tree on the cliffs. When they discovered the place, it was at the top of a little cove, with a long sweep of rock reaching down to the black water below—water still and deep and inky. It seemed a good landing place, for the rock, at the bottom, shelved to the water. There were signs of blasting and a few holes, as if this were the place where the pier had been contemplated.

"Now, all we've got to do is count," Jimmy said, "and, according to Tony, we'll see something. Come to think of it, the service station man didn't want us to come here, either."

Far out in the ocean there was the black smudge of a steamer's smoke; nearer, a lumber schooner plowed its way toward the Golden Gate. Jimmy estimated the Gate's distance as not over a mile or so, although it, and San Francisco, were both concealed by a jutting point, beyond which was Bonita Light.

Together, the man and girl began counting. They started when a small wave dashed a few feet up the rock. One, two, three… four, five, six… every third wave was larger than the two intervening ones. The twenty-seventh wave flung itself a few feet higher than the others.

"We'll try it once more," Jimmy said, "but I can't get very excited over this display. Any one knows that waves run in threes… let's count them again."

When they had counted to twenty-five, the water below seemed to suddenly turn to a deep green, with flecks of foam dotting the surface. At the twenty-sixth, the water began to boil. A moment later, as Lucile's lips formed "Twenty-seven," a long, heavy roller appeared as if by magic from the calm sea. Up to the rock it swelled, slowly, inexorably. It gained height as it advanced. Up and up it swept, higher and higher. With a mighty roar it swept upon the rock, a full thirty feet from the bottom!

Spray covered man and girl. Lucile's hand went to Wentworth's arm, and he held her tightly to him. The giant wave smothered the rock below, licking at every crevice and then it slowly receded leaving the deep pool as black and silent as before.

"Horrible," Lucile whispered.

"So that's what killed Harry Crawford," Wentworth said aloud. His arm kept the girl against his side instinctively. "That's what happened!" In his heart he was saying, "Oh, damn Kong Gai! Damn that devil's mind!" But all he said to Lucile was, "I think we'd better wait for another big wave, hadn't we?"

The girl slipped away from him. She was shaken, but she managed to smile. "So that's why you brought me here, Jimmy?" she said. "You're a fast worker!"

"Angry?" Jim Wentworth asked.

"Certainly I am," Lucile announced, but she was smiling as she said it.

6

THE BATTLE OF THE ROCK

CROUCHED IN THE cypress hedge beyond the Mendoza ranch on the headlands, Jimmy Wentworth could think of no detail which had been neglected. A dozen feet away from him was a Federal officer. Every ten feet or so, circling Death Rock, was either a deputy or a coast guard. They had gone silently over the hills during the night, and had waited, blanket wrapped, through the cold, foggy morning. San Francisco was covered with the white mist, but here and there in the ocean a slight wind whipped the concealing fog to shreds.

And, now and again, Wentworth could catch a glimpse of the Santa Ygnacia, of Crawford's fleet, as she nosed her way gently shoreward.

Kong Gai, through his system of daily telephone calls, had kept in touch with Crawford, and with the coming of the liquor craft. He had made his agreed advance payment, not haggling at the price. What he did not know was that Crawford, directed by the detective bureau, had changed the code messages used to keep in touch with the rum runner.

"Want captain come ashore immediately" no longer meant "Land cargo where next directed." But that was the message the operator on the Santa Ygnacia had received, just as the Margarita must have been wirelessed! To land the cargo where directed… by Kong Gai!

At Death Rock.

Where not all the machine guns, nor all the powerful and loyal men, could save either their ship or themselves. It was all too clear what had happened to the Margarita now. Her crew, acting under Kong Gai's orders—how Kong Gai obtained the code Wentworth guessed. Crawford had a Chinese cook, who by now was probably on his way to headquarters—her crew had come close inshore, and started unloading the cargo. Timing the arrival of one of the great waves, Kong Gai's hatchetmen had come up in the power boat, on the seaward side of the Margarita, and killed every one on board. The captain, and the machine gunner were undoubtedly stunned by the catastrophe on the rock, and had fallen easy prey to the highbinders' knives…

But this time, it would be different. The Santa Ygnacia's crew knew, ahead of time, what to expect. However, they would seem to fall for the plan of Kong Gai. And the deputies and coast guard, ashore, would prevent the escape of a single man, including Kong Gai. That was Wentworth's plan.

The Santa Ygnacia was nearer, creeping as close as she dared to the cliffs. It was dangerous work, but rum running was a dangerous trade.

Like black shadows, men appeared at the top of Death Rock. A pole was fitted together; in a moment a white flag appeared, held by two of the men. Another pressed an automatic automobile horn at quarter-minute intervals, directing the Santa Ygnacia's course to the shelving rock.

The rum runner, not over a dozen lengths off shore, dropped anchor; the rattle of her chains echoed a moment, and then all was still. Her screw moved slowly, as her captain turned her head toward the sea, in case he was forced to run from an unexpected visit of the coast guard.

The leader of the Chinese on the rock began to wigwag with the flag, using international code.

Wentworth was unable to read the wigwagging, but a coast guard man crawled up to him and said, "Here's what they've sent: 'Land cargo. We will watch. Hurry.'"

"That means the gray power boat's in position on the other side of the Santa Ygnacia," Wentworth muttered. "Here's where we get action!"

"All set for 'em," the coast guard man grinned. "We want Kong Gai as bad as you, detective, but this is your party."

To have caught the Chinese—there were seven of them—at the top of Death Rock, would have been simple. But every one concerned wanted the Chinese in the power boat. And the gray craft would not approach until the sailors were on the rock, and the big surge coming shoreward.

A boat was lowered from the Santa Ygnacia, and case after case dropped to her. Kong Gai must have figured—wisely enough—that every one on the rum runner would be too busy to pay attention to the sea, with the exception of the sailor peering out in the fog toward the ocean and the Gate, watching for the possible approach of a coast guard vessel. When there were cries on shipboard, this sailor would certainly run to see what was happening, and the Santa Ygnacia could be boarded just as her sister ship was boarded and captured.

Had there just been a fight ashore, the sailor would not have left his post. He would expect shots, and watch all the more closely. Kong Gai's plan was demoniac in its perfection.

The boat, heavily laden, from the Santa Ygnacia, was rowed slowly ashore. The sailor in the bow leaped to the shelving rock, and dragged the prow up. Swiftly and silently, with never a look about them, the other two sailors began to unload the cases.

The circle of men hidden on the cliff kept eyes only seaward. Each man was counting to himself, counting in multiples of threes. Twenty-seven was reached. Nothing happened. And twenty-seven again. The sea grew murky below Death Rock, but there was no sign of surge.

The boat was nearly unloaded. Wentworth's heart leaped. Suppose the sailors were caught trying to return to the Santa Ygnacia just as the wave roared in! And then, at twenty-five, he saw the sea at the base of the rock turn to bright, horrible serpent green. He waited a second more. His eyes went to the Chinese, who were now jabbering together excitedly, having seen what Wentworth saw.

The detective did not waste another instant. Between his teeth had been a whistle; the blast from it, as he blew swiftly, sent gulls from their perches. The Chinese on the rock turned, every one of them. Some had guns in hand, others knives. Below them, the three sailors raced upward on Death Rock, raced for their lives, falling, stumbling, clawing upward to safety, away from the tremendous surge of the mysterious swell from the Pacific.

The circle of men surrounding Death Rock from above tore forward. A gun cracked as one of the Chinese fired. Marshals and coast guards, with a long score to settle, and mates to be avenged, pulled trigger instantly.

From below came the terrifying boom of the giant wave. Wentworth dashed toward one of the Chinese, who, wiser than his fellows, was attempting to escape the cordon. As Wentworth dived for him, trying to knock him out rather than kill him, he could hear the quick crackling sound of the machine gun on the Santa Ygnacia. Which meant that the power boat had attacked!

The Chinese was a tall, wiry Manchu. For a moment Jimmy had his hands more than full. But the hatchet-man was more intent upon escaping than anything else, and when he tried to squirm away, Wentworth expertly smashed him over the head with his gun. The man dropped, and lay still. Wentworth paused and handcuffed him before rushing over to the edge of Death Rock.

Two of the Chinese were dead. The others on the rock were standing close together in a sullen group. One of the Chinese, however, had leaped or been thrust into the upward surge of the great wave.

Fascinated, every one on the rock—coast guard men, deputies, the three sailors from the rum runner, drenched with spray, but safe after their race with death, even the terrified Orientals—stared down at the tragedy below.

The hatchetman who had stumbled from the rock was trying, frantically, to swim out of the seemingly innocent pool below. The green water sucked at his feet. He was swirled round and round, battered against the sharp ledge terribly. Rescue, as the coast guard men knew, was impossible, although one of them was already on his knees at the base of the cliff, trying to snatch at the drowning man, while a mate, arms about the coast guard man's middle, sat braced against the cliff.

Once a case floated past the Chinese, and as he grabbed at it, the case was sucked down to the bottom of the pool. Again the Chinese was smashed against rock, a dozen feet from where the coast guards tried to save him, and then, suddenly, without a cry, he vanished.

In the dead silence a highbinder shrilled in Cantonese, "Ho Mu'y is gone forever! He will never be seen again!"

Although all stared down, there was no sign of the Chinese's black-clad body, either in the pool or in the sea beyond.

Wentworth, waiting for the arrival of Captain Dunand, wondered how Harry Crawford had managed to swim out of the pool, battered as he must have been. And yet that was what must have happened. Crawford had been beaten, but not by fists—he had been hammered and lacerated by the rocks. Instead of having been sucked down to death, the white man's powerful swimming and great heart had, in some way, taken him to the open sea. Just how would never be known. Whether he had found a piece of driftwood or a plank from some lumber schooner, or actually floated in unaided, helped by the swift incoming tide through the Gate, to be found off Pier 144C, was another mystery of the sea.

What desperate fight was going on aboard the Santa Ygnacia the men on shore could only guess. Above the rat-tat-tat of the gun came the screams of dying men, and then, suddenly, the ship's gun ceased firing. The action was all on the far, invisible side of the ship, and it was several moments before a man with a white flag appeared on the ship's bridge.

As Captain Dunand, from his vantage point higher up the hill, arrived, the sailor signalled.

"All well. Killed six. Power boat escaped with old Chink at wheel. Two caught alive."

"Kong Gai, gone again!" Wentworth muttered.

"We'll be waiting if he tries to get through the Gate," a guardsman said. "Although, in any kind of fog, with a fast boat, the odds are all in his favor."

Kong Gai, vanished, when they were positive they'd have him! The wily old master of Chinatown took no chances. When his men had boarded the rum runner, he must have stayed on the power boat, and backed off until he was positive the decks had been cleared of all the white men.

It had been decided in advance that to have a coast guard vessel standing out to sea would have frightened off Kong Gai entirely; there was no way to prevent escape in the power boat.

Dunand drew Wentworth aside. "The department's been working, Jim. Didn't have time to tell you before. Death Rock was O.K. until this year. The natives are all scared of it. Bodies washed off, never recovered. And why? It's a man made death trap!"

"What?"

"Absolutely. The smoother the sea, the more dangerous it is. Some one, employed by Kong Gai, had construction started for a pier. I had a look at the plans last night. Work was stopped when 'it proved too expensive' was the tale

Kong Gai's men told the engineers. They weren't a marine firm; Kong Gai had his own plans.

"And what plans! A V-shaped formation was made in the ledge, under water. Like a funnel. It forms an unusual wave current, forcing the water to back up in the pool. And the continued thrust of just the right number of waves causes the sudden rise. A rise of thirty feet—"

"What happens to the bodies?" Wentworth was unable to get the vision of the Chinese being sucked to death in the green caldron of water from his mind.

"There are jagged rocks—the teeth of the sea—at the bottom of the pool. The grind of the water tears the battered bodies and then winds them up in the kelp. It's horrible." He put his hand on his detective's shoulder. "You've done good work, boy. Kong Gai is crippled for a while. The chief himself wants to thank you to-night."

Wentworth flushed with pleasure. "That's great," he said. "Will he keep me long? I'm… well, I'm going to be busy to-night, captain."

The gray-haired captain of detectives glanced shrewdly at Jimmy, and then he laughed.

"Hmm," he said. "So that's it, eh? If she says 'yes,' Jim, we might stretch a point or two and make a sergeant out of you."

THE BLOODY EMERALD

*A Girl Murdered and a Gem Stolen—
and Only to Jimmy Wentworth Do
These Crimes Spell "Kong Gai!"*

1

THE MAN IN THE STRAW HAT

THERE IS ALWAYS a tremendous and awed hush in Kent-Giddings, as if customers and clerks are completely aware of the fabulous value of the merchandise contained in the famous jewelry store.

Under the plate glass of the display counters are gem-studded wrist watches, rings of platinum set with the usual precious stones. There are necklaces as fine as any possessed by Indian potentates. In the rear of the store is a gigantic safe, where the finer jewels are kept in a series of shallow drawers, each gem in its wrapping of cotton and tissue. Here are star rubies and alexandrites from Ceylon, black opals from New South Wales and fire opals from Queretera; here also are the finest diamonds, sapphires, emeralds, all waiting to be shown to the clients of the establishment.

Kent-Giddings surrounds this wealth with every possible protection. A keen-eyed house detective sits on a concealed balcony. There is a direct wire to the Protective Association, and another to Headquarters. Under every counter is a buzzer. The door to the street, the only door from the sales floor, can be closed electrically. The doorman is a former police officer with a record for courage.

The very position of the jewelry store is a preventative against robbery. It is on a corner, a principal intersection, of San Francisco's shopping district. The traffic officer in the middle of the street, without turning his head, can see inside through the wide windows. A hundred people every minute, many of them tourists on their way to Chinatown,

Jimmy lashed out with his fist as the Chinese swarmed over him

three blocks distant, gaze inside as they pass. The slightest commotion would cause a crowd to gather instantly.

Outside, on this summer day, Kent-Giddings felt as impregnable as the Mint or the sub-treasury. Most of the passers-by were intent on going to lunch. Inside, the shop was normally busy, since a third of the clerks were taking their own noon-hour off. The house detective, his lunch on a tray, watched automatically as he ate. In front of him was a button. If he were to press it (not once in all his service had the button been touched) a signal would flash in Headquarters, and the riot squad would come roaring up the street.

At the other end of the wire, Captain Dunand, of the detective bureau, was thinking that things were too quiet. Even in Chinatown, that seething pot of intrigue, where young Jimmy Wentworth paced his beat (up toward the Stockton Street tunnel) alertly, everything was peaceful. The captain of detectives thought uneasily that storms always broke out of clear skies.

As each customer entered Kent-Giddings, the house detective examined the newcomer with practiced eye. A woman. Another woman. A man. Next a girl. The detec-

tive decided that he had seen her photograph in a Sunday paper; probably she was coming in to look at wedding announcements. A man entered; the house detective classified him at once as a business man, or possibly a successful attorney. Custom-made shoes. Good clothing, well tailored. A slight air of nervousness, such as men in a jewel shop always have when they contemplate an important purchase. The watcher on the balcony lifted his coffee cup and drank as the middle-aged customer stepped up to a counter… everything was quiet and as it should be in the store.

"I'd like to see an emerald ring," the middle-aged man said to one of the clerks. "A good one."

"We have some fine ones, sir. Do you want a square-cut stone?"

"It's for my wife," the man said. "I don't know. Only I want a good one."

The clerk drew out a tray from his counter, in which every ring was set with an emerald, some surrounded by diamonds, others plain. Once the customer picked up one of the handsome platinum circles, and then, after looking at it closely, put it down as if uncertain. "They all look alike to me," he said. "What is the difference in the emeralds?"

"All are good, sir. Well cut, and proper color. The regulation emerald. If you wish, I can show you some unset stones. They are very fine. Many people prefer to select a gem, and have it set for them."

"Are they better emeralds?"

"They are. Or perhaps I should say, they are more unusual in size or shape or color. These, of course," the clerk explained swiftly, not intending to lose a sale, "are as fine as can be sold for the price."

"Let's see 'em," the middle-aged customer suggested. "I want a good one. Only I haven't a lot of time. Got to meet my wife for lunch."

As the clerk slid his tray of ordinary emerald rings away, he ventured, "You are from the East, sir?"

"Straw hat gives me away, eh? Or is it the way I talk?"

The clerk was well trained and polite. "The hat," he smiled. "As to your voice, I thought possibly you had a cold."

"All down-Easters talk through their noses," the customer said. He added, confidentially, "You know, this is our first trip to the Pacific Coast. We come from Portland, Maine."

"I trust you have a good visit. Now I'll go and bring some finer emeralds. If you find one you like, I'll show you a variety of settings for it."

The man in the straw hat stood at ease while the clerk went to the rear of the store. The house detective glanced at him, and saw that he was doing what almost every Kent-Giddings customer did while waiting: the man glanced about at the opulence of the jewel shop. When the customer lit a long black cigar and fumes of it drifted up to the balcony, the house detective, Simmons, almost reached for his stubby black pipe. He envied the man below, who undoubtedly had also eaten lunch, and was now topping the meal off with a good heavy smoke. Only Simmons could not smoke while he was on duty.

In the rear of the store, as the clerk requested an assortment of fine emeralds, he said to the man in charge there,

"Visitor. Buying a ring for his wife. First trip West. New Englander. He talks through his nose. He'll probably look at some of the gems, and then ask his wife about 'em."

"Maybe it's a peace offering," the other man suggested. "He may've been partying, and has to square himself."

"Hope so," the clerk grinned. "Then I'm sure of a sale… put in the Charlton emerald, too, Richards. He might buy it."

As the man at the safe brought out a small envelope, and gave the clerk the enclosed tissue, he said, "Twenty-five thousand dollar emerald buyers don't grow on bushes, Jordan. It makes the others look pretty ordinary."

"You never can tell," Jordan said. "Every man who has seen it falls for the red cast… and this fellow may have sold out a chain of grocery stores… it's worth showing."

With the gems, each in its tissue wrapper, on a small tray, Jordan returned to his counter. Up on the balcony Simmons saw that he was bringing something from the safe—something valuable, for an instant later a light flashed where the house detective could not miss it. This was the warning to him that extremely valuable merchandise had been withdrawn from the safe, and was now on the sales floor. Being a thorough man, Simmons now divided his attention between the outer door and the customer in the center aisle—the man with the straw hat. He would let his eyes stray away from the middle-aged man for a moment or so, but never longer.

Kent-Giddings took no chances. Although the store was surrounded with every possible mechanical device, although every jewel was insured, yet Kent-Giddings did not intend to have ruined its reputation for never having been robbed. One robbery always meant that another would be tried, for the impregnability of the shop would be in question. Nothing had ever been stolen from the store— not even a semiprecious ornament palmed by a shoplifter.

Simmons, when his eyes would return to the center aisle, was never the least bit disturbed. He could not hear the conversation below, but he saw that everything was progressing quietly. The customer continued to smoke his long cigar. No crook, no nervous man planning trouble, could possibly smoke so naturally. Simmons was satisfied with everything except the smell of the heavy tobacco smoke. That made him wish for a pipe himself.

With a dozen emeralds before him, the customer was obviously undecided. He picked up first one, then another, of the gems. He looked at the rare red-green Charlton emerald.

Finally, he drew out his watch. It was an old-fashioned affair, very large, and when it was opened so the face could be seen, the man in the straw hat held it before him. What he saw, as in a mirror, in the burnished gold of the case, must have been everything behind him: the clerks, the customers, probably even Simmons's balcony above the sales floor. The man looked at the watch for a considerable time, as if trying to make up his mind.

In his nasal twang, he said at last, "I suppose I'd better ask my wife. Yes, sir, I'd better ask her. You know how women are. Four thousand dollars is a sight of money. And that big funny colored one! Twenty-five thousand, eh? I'd never thought it. Looks like a piece of glass."

"I brought it out to show you, sir. As a curiosity." Jordan picked up one of the emeralds. "This one—the four thousand dollar one you like—is a very fine gem. By all means have your wife see it. Only I thought you wished to surprise her. We could have the stone set by five to-night if you wish."

"A lot of money," the customer said, still staring into his watch. Suddenly he bent forward, at exactly the time Simmons had turned away, at a moment also when the clerks in the store were all busy, as if the man had seen all this in the polished surface of his watch case, and said thinly, more nasally than ever, "Here's Matilda's photograph. Married thirty-seven years this August. This picture is older than you are, eh?"

The clerk leaned over his counter; his customer, half shielding the watch in his hands, bent close, until the brim of his straw hat almost touched the gem salesman's forehead. If any one had been looking at them, it would have seemed as if the two men were examining something—probably one of the emeralds—very intently.

Jordan's lips formed the words, "I don't see any picture!" as the man in the straw hat opened another cover to the watch; the second movement may have stopped the words. As it was, he said nothing, but remained leaning forward.

And the man, well dressed, middle-aged, with a straw hat on his head and custom-built shoes on his feet, walked away, and out of the door to the street!

Simmons, on his balcony, actually glanced once at the clerk, leaning forward on his counter, before he saw the gem salesman's hand suddenly lower to the glass of the counter itself. Simmons pressed a button as he stood up, and the outer door locked mechanically, with a click that made the doorman swing about, hand going under his plum-colored uniform coat.

Only a moment Simmons hesitated pressing the buzzer which led by direct wire to Headquarters. Hesitated because he knew how Kent-Giddings would frown on publicity. The man in the straw hat was gone; Simmons knew that. And in that tiny fraction of time while the house detective summoned his wits, Jordan's head jerked upward. Froth was on his lips, now that the previous stupefaction was over. His face was livid, his eyes glassy and bulging.

Simmons's finger went forcibly against the button, the button to the Association, and to Headquarters, where Captain Dunand was figuring on the best place to go for lunch. Simmons leaped to his feet. He saw Jordan's body sway, saw the horribly contorted, convulsed face, with death plainly written in the eyes.

As the house detective thundered down from the balcony as fast as he could tear, another odor drifted nauseatingly, terrifyingly, through the stench of the strong cigar the man in the straw hat had been smoking so contentedly. An odor which almost made Simmons's faithful heart stand still… bitter almonds! The house detective knew only too well the significance of that smell; even rookie patrolmen are taught to fear and recognize it. Hydrocyanic acid gas. Cyanogen. One whiff—death.

Simmons knew also, while he rushed up the broad center aisle, through the confusion of excited clerks and alarmed customers, that there would be no jewels on top of the plate glass counter. Every emerald would be gone… and every emerald was gone! The marvelous Charlton jewel, with the bloody color streaked through the emerald green, had vanished with the other precious gems.

And Jordan was dead. Artificial respiration, inhalations of ammonia, the use of external and internal stimulants from Kent-Giddings's emergency cabinet, were all useless. The unfortunate gem salesman had been killed by a gas which allowed no time for remedies.

The man in the straw hat was gone. The emeralds, a hundred thousand dollars' worth, were gone. A trusted clerk was murdered. Kent-Giddings had been robbed at last, carefully, cleverly, by a man who left not one single worthwhile clew to be followed.

2

WENTWORTH IS ATTACKED

THE RIOT CAR roared past Jimmy Wentworth, although, standing almost directly in its path, he did his best to force the driver to stop. Wentworth was in the exact middle of the Stockton Street tunnel, where his beat ended; here, at the call box, he had been accustomed to send in his "Everything's O.K." where listening Oriental ears couldn't hear every word he said, as they would in Chinatown proper. The Stockton Street tunnel, dimly lighted, connects Chinatown with the retail shopping district; automobiles and street cars use it, but few pedestrians. In Chinatown all was quiet. No red placards pasted on blank walls announced impending *kim chong p'at*, the vengeance of the hatchet. Even Kong Gai, the evil influence of the Asiatic district, a fiendish Chinese who had instigated many crimes which Wentworth had solved, seemed to be under cover.

The riot car flashed past the Chinatown detective, leaving the tunnel blacker than before. Wentworth bent down, electric torch in hand, to verify what he had discovered before telephoning Headquarters.

The body, propped against the tunnel wall near the call box, was that of a young Chinese woman. Even to the Occidental eye, she had been lovely. She was taller than most of the Asiatics, and very slender; the lashes of her closed eyes were long and black as ink. Her skin was creamy, and not yellow. She was dressed in black street garments, but either she had been hastily reattired from the usual house costume of pale silks, or her clothing had been disarranged when she was taken into the tunnel. There was a faint perfume about her, and the young detective identified it as coming from the extract of *chu-sha-kih*, a rare Chinese flower.

How the girl had died was clear. The knife, which had reached her heart, remained thrust into her breast.

Attached to the hilt of the knife was a twisted bit of red silk, which, to Wentworth, meant that whoever had murdered the girl had done it because of "love." That was the sign of the silken cord. Wentworth, easing the body back to the pavement, wondered just what had happened, without ever expecting to find out. Had the girl been untrue to her master? She was too lovely to have been a Chinese wife. If the truth were ever learned, they would probably find out that the girl had been smuggled into the States as a slave girl. Or had she been killed by a jealous "first wife?"

Her fingers had been stripped of rings. There was not even one engraved with the fortunate signs of the sun-and-moon on kingfisher jade. Wentworth supposed that was to prevent discovery of her identity, and yet, if that was the reason, why hadn't the body been slid into the bay, where it would float out to the ocean?

Placing the body near his call box was like saying to him, "I have killed this woman. What are you going to do about it?" Wentworth believed suddenly that only old Kong Gai, the king cobra back of every evil happening in Chinatown, had engineered the murder. It was like Kong Gai to kill, and then to display what he had done. But why would the Evil One drive a knife into a lovely girl's heart? Jealousy... unfaithfulness... if that were the case, the body of a dead Chinese man would be found before long, as a warning to Chinatown to keep away from Kong Gai's slave girls.

As Jimmy unlocked the call box, he thought, "That's all wet. Kong Gai'd keep his women—one as handsome as this girl—well hidden. There's something behind all this."

Wentworth reported directly to Captain Dunand. "I've found a dead woman in the tunnel," he said. "Chinese. Knifed. Young, well-dressed and pretty. She... what did you say, sir?"

"I said," Captain Dunand's voice came over the wire, "that you talk like a newspaper reporter." His chief was angry. "Send for the wagon," he snapped. "What do you want me to do?"

"Yes, sir," Wentworth said, wondering. "I thought it looks like Kong Gai's work again—"

"Bah!" the captain of detectives shouted. "You've got Kong Gai on the brain. I suppose you have a hunch he robbed Kent-Giddings, too! If—"

Excitedly, Jimmy broke in, "The riot car went through the tunnel—"

"Sure. They were going fast. They thought maybe your Kong Gai was going to waylay 'em." His voice dropped as he added, "It's going to be one of those mean cases, Jim. Planned in advance. No clews. I'm positive. Something was due to break."

Wentworth asked, "What'd they get at Kent-Giddings?"

"Plenty. Look here, Jimmy, you walk down there, after the wagon comes. Nobody'll expect a cop in uniform to be from the bureau. You might pick up something. You can work on the dead woman afterward."

"It was murder," Wentworth said soberly. "A nasty one—"

"There's murder at Kent-Giddings also," said his chief. "A cyanide gas. A clerk is dead. Talk to Simmons. He's the house dick at the store. And"—a little less soberly—"don't try to mix Kong Gai and Chinatown up with a jewel robbery, Jim. The man we want is a white man. You tell me anything about a Chinaman and I'll put you out in the Sunset district to walk a beat, boy!"

When the dead wagon came to a stop, Wentworth asked the driver, "See anybody at the mouth of the tunnel when you came in?"

"Couple of Chinks smokin' cigarettes."

"I'll hang on the back of the wagon and you slow up a bit when you come to 'em. Then I'll drop off." Wentworth decided that Kent-Giddings could wait a few minutes, despite his chief's order. Chinatown was his real assignment. Dunand had told him to go to the jewelry store out of sheer desperation, and Wentworth knew he would not be kept on the case, but sent back to the Oriental district. "And don't tell the chief what I'm doing, either!"

"He's upset," the driver's assistant grinned, as the body was placed in the morgue car. "Cheney's on vacation, and so's Riordan. They're the jewel crime boys. I hear"—all the assistant actually knew was that there had been a robbery—"that a gang went into Kent-Giddings, with shotguns, and cleaned the place… gee, but this girl must've been pretty, when she was dolled out, huh?"

"Lift, and don't talk so much," grunted the driver. "All set, Wentworth?"

"Let's go," said Jimmy. "Just slow up a little when you see the Chinos. I'll hop off. You keep on going."

Wentworth wondered if he might be able to surprise the Orientals into saying something, perhaps in Chinese, which might be helpful. The men might be hatchetmen, or spies, or lookouts, or they might be simply standing around in the sun and smoking. Anyhow, it was worth a try, and it would only take a minute. He would never have another chance to question any one near the scene of the crime, or where the body had been found. Wentworth was pretty certain that the murder had not been committed in the tunnel.

While the morgue car was being driven northward through the underground thoroughfare, Wentworth was thinking, "The detective who solves the Kent-Giddings robbery and murder will get plenty of credit. It won't be me. And if I get anywhere with this case of the dead girl, nobody'll care."

Jimmy wasn't sorry for himself. To be exact, he was more concerned with the murdered woman than with the jewel robbery. Had Kong Gai a hand in the girl's death? There was something funny about it. The knife had been driven clear through her coat. That wasn't right. The coat and everything beneath should have been pulled aside, so, if death were because of unfaithfulness, the blade could "kiss flesh." That was the Cantonese method.

The only other possibility was that the knife had been

plunged into the throbbing heart in a moment of terrible passion, when the proper way of killing had been forgotten.

The car slowed imperceptibly. Wentworth dropped off. He walked swiftly to the three Chinese who stood idly at the tunnel's mouth. One smoked a cigarette, the second ate an orange, the third was reading *Chung Sai Yat Po* as if very interested in the news. Jimmy's quick glance saw that it was yesterday's paper.

He said at once, "You see China girl go inside here? When you see?"

"No see," the orange-eating Chinese said, spitting out a seed.

"How long you be here?"

The Asiatic scratched his chin, and asked impassively of one of his dawdling companions, *"Ki tim chong ah?"*

There was certainly nothing in that simple question, "What time is it?" to make the cigarette-smoking Oriental addressed take a deep puff and blow it skyward. Nor was there any reason why the pock-marked Chinese reading the old newspaper should have struggled to refrain from smiling. Jimmy Wentworth, on edge and observant, could only suppose that the insolent trio were laughing at him, as Chinese laugh at white men who expect an answer to any forthright question. It was also possible that the trio were endeavoring to learn if he understood what was said in Cantonese, by asking something which might have made the detective turn his head automatically and look up at the old cathedral clock.

Wentworth stood silently, as if waiting for an answer to his question. Finally the cigarette smoker himself glanced toward the clock tower, and said droningly, *"Yat tim chong lok.* It is one o'clock." After which he said something under his breath which made the other two grin.

Jimmy could not catch the singsong Cantonese, but the man behind the newspaper said, in an almost inaudible whisper, *"Ho siu yan yau yat pak soi meng."*

"Few men live to be a hundred years old," was what the pockmarked Chinese had said. So far as Jimmy could see, there was no sense to it, except as an answer to whatever the other Asiatic might have remarked, which Wentworth had not heard. But the Chinatown detective felt that if the three were spies, waiting to report the discovery of the body by the police to whoever had committed the murder, they would have acted very differently.

These were probably smart-aleck mission-educated Chinese, having some fun with a policeman. No sense wasting time on them. Playing his part as the Chinatown patrolman, Wentworth said gruffly, "Well, don't stand around here, boys."

As Jimmy turned to start back through the tunnel leading toward the shopping district and his assignment at Kent-Giddings store, he knew that one of the Cantonese spoke softly, almost eagerly, and that one of the others seemed to object to whatever the words implied. In the same split second the third Oriental—Wentworth could not tell which speaker was which—snapped a whispered command in Mandarin. Only the word, "Yes!" but spoken in the classical language of China, it was sufficient to make the detective stop instantly.

He had no chance to turn, not even his head. One of the Asiatics dove at his legs, catching him expertly just below the knees, and knocking him to the pavement, in the

very shadow of the tunnel's mouth. As Jimmy Wentworth
fell, he managed to twist partially about. Every second he
expected to feel the sear of a long knife as it was driven to
his heart.

It came to him in that moment that these three might
actually be the murderers of the beautiful Chinese girl, but
that the knowledge would never do him a particle of good.

The three Chinese swarmed all over him at once. Hands
raked at him. Wentworth, head clear, knew that one of
the Asiatics was pawing under his uniform coat, trying
to find his gun. A thumb pressed at his neck, numbing
every sense and muscle. To be killed by his own weapon!
That was a joke worthy of Kong Gai, and yet Wentworth
did not believe that the archfiend of Chinatown would be
satisfied with any death in which the King Cobra himself
did not have a hand.

Wentworth thrust an elbow fiercely upward. His knees
worked viciously as he tried to get the three clinging, clawing bodies away so he could use his fists. All he needed was
time. An automobile would pass, or a street car, if he could
only keep alive that long, there in the shadow.

In his ear he heard, explosively, "Kong Gai will laugh at
this, oh, white fool!" Then horrible pain tore at his face.

In desperation, Wentworth managed to jerk one hand
from the clawed talon holding it. The pressure on his lean
body lessened suddenly. Jimmy lashed out with his fist.
The blind blow brought a grunt of pain from one of the
assailants, who hissed venomously as he must have reached
for his knife.

The thin voice of the pock-marked Chinese protested
vehemently, "No! Enough! It is done. Now, run!"

The final words were almost obliterated by the clanging of a street car as it emerged from the tunnel's mouth,
northbound toward Chinatown and the bay shore.

Dizzy with pain, Jimmy Wentworth struggled to his
feet. Up the street he saw the three hatchetmen fleeing.
As his hand went automatically for his gun—which was
gone—the trio vanished around the first corner. No matter
how swiftly Wentworth could race after them, they would
be out of sight when he reached the corner, and no one
would tell him where they had gone. Chinatown had seen,
but would say nothing. Knowledge is a dangerous thing.

The motorman swung from the forward platform of the
car: "I seen 'em run," he shouted to the detective in the blue
patrolman's uniform. "A whole gang of Chinks. Maybe
twenty. Up that way!"

One of the men passengers asked hastily, "What's
happened, officer? Tong war?"

"Had a little disturbance, that's all," said Jimmy Wentworth.

"Hmm," growled the conductor. "Maybe that's all, but
you better get your face fixed. Somebody's about cut off
your ear."

"It couldn't have been Chinese," a woman from the street
car objected. "They are so peaceful. Right in broad daylight!
A bootlegger cut your ear, officer. That is what happened.
Isn't it?"

Jimmy Wentworth almost smiled, despite the pain. He
thought of saying, "Madam, I wasn't cut. I was bitten by a
mad Chinese dog owned by a fiend named Kong Gai, who
rules Chinatown's underworld. I don't know why it was
done, either." Instead, quietly, he said, "You may be right,"

and, with his handkerchief wiped blood from his cheek. He hoped that somebody in the drug store on the far side of the tunnel would be able to slap adhesive over the wound after disinfecting it. A chewed ear was all in the day's work. Jimmy Wentworth knew that he was lucky to be alive.

As he walked away, with plenty to think about as he headed toward Kent-Giddings, he heard the woman say, "You'd think he'd be courteous enough to explain what happened! He's probably paid by the bootleggers himself. That's why he didn't dare go after them, and wants to blame it on the poor Chinese. It was a drunken brawl. *I* have an idea that the officer was intoxicated himself."

"Some pretty funny things happen in Chinatown," a male passenger said soberly. "Things we don't dream about. Why, a judge at the City Hall told me—"

"Nonsense," sniffed the woman. "I've a friend whose cook, a faithful old Chinese, has a son who is a professional man in Chinatown. He makes more money than many white men, but he never misses church, and teaches the proverbs in the most beautiful classical Chinese language. And he had to overcome a great handicap. My friend says her cook's son had smallpox when he was a child, and is terribly marked. Let me tell you this: you don't hear of any Chinaman robbing stores, the way Kent-Giddings was robbed this noon! If the police want to *do* something, why don't they catch the robbers? Only"—she sniffed again, although she was almost out of breath, "only they won't!"

"Hmm," the male passenger groaned to a friend. "Now I know what lethal gas is. The cop was wise! He didn't stop to argue with her."

3

JIMMY TALKS WITH HEADQUARTERS

THE FRONT ENTRANCE to Kent-Giddings was open when Jimmy Wentworth walked past; inside, business continued much as usual, although Wentworth's one glance told him that the clerks were keyed up and nervous. The Chinatown detective, on his assignment, went around to the rear delivery door, and found a special officer from the Protective Association standing there.

"I'm from Headquarters," Wentworth said, as the officer blocked his way.

"Yeah? Well, I got no orders to let even a cop inside. If you got a message, give it to me."

Wentworth showed his shield. "Can I go in now?" he grinned.

"I never heard of no cop bein' a dick," the special officer muttered. "That's a new one on me... sure, go on in. They're all upstairs," he volunteered. "An' gettin' no place. My boss's there, too. An' mad. It's a swell job some crook done. Got away clean."

"Thanks," Jimmy said, and went inside.

He knew that Captain Dunand expected him to stand around, listen, and, if possible, learn something. The astute captain of detectives did not intend that Jimmy should act as if he had been put on the case.

And so when he entered a room upstairs—a room paneled in walnut, where customers were taken to view designs for precious ornaments—he said to the uneasy manager of the store, who was talking with two women, "I've been sent here in case the detectives need a policeman."

The manager nodded, saying, "Very good. The detectives are now questioning the people who were in the store."

Jimmy stood quietly in a corner. Apparently the two women had already been asked for what they knew by the detectives who had accompanied the riot squad, and the manager was explaining that he was very sorry that they must remain until the others were questioned. What Captain Dunand, and the special officer also, had intimated was being borne out by the conversation. Summed up, it meant that Kent-Giddings had not the slightest idea how the crime had been committed, nor who had done it.

It was a full ten minutes before the door opened, and a half-dozen men, followed by the men from the bureau and Simmons, the house detective, returned to the room. Hearne, from Headquarters, was obviously in charge, and Jimmy remembered that the jewel-expert men were on vacation—another reason why Captain Dunand had grasped at every straw, and why he had been sent on the case.

Hearne nodded to Jimmy, who said swiftly, "I'm just here in case you want anything."

The plain-clothes man nodded again, to show he understood, and, after one shrewd look at Wentworth, said to the manager, as much for his fellow detective's benefit as for the jewelry executive, "None of these people have anything to tell, Mr. Hammond. This gentleman"—indicating a young man—"was buying a diamond ring, and he says that he thinks he saw the crook look at his watch just before the trouble began… but that doesn't help any."

"These ladies would like to get away," Hammond suggested. "Isn't there some way they may be excused—"

"Everybody can go," Hearne decided. He turned to the young man, saying, "You are the only one who noticed the man at all. We've got your name and address. If we want you, will you come down to the Hall of Justice?"

"Glad to. But I don't see where I can help much."

"Neither do I," said Hearne glumly.

When every one had filed out, Hearne said to Jimmy Wentworth, "I'm going to stay here. Got a report to make, and no time to write it. Come here, and I'll tell you what I want done."

Going to a long table, Hearne sat down, and Wentworth sat close beside him. In a low voice Hearne began to talk.

"It's lousy, Jimmy," he whispered. "Not a clew. Not a trace. Here's what's happened. A man comes in—the crook. Middle-aged, well dressed, wearing a straw hat. That's all, except that he's supposed to come from the East. New England. The dead clerk told that to the man who has charge of the safe. The devil was smoking a big, heavy cigar. Simmons knows that, and verifies the description. The cigar fumes must have covered up the first hint of cyanide gas. I don't know which gas it was, but the clerk passed out in a hurry."

Remembering his training, Jimmy said softly, "It only

takes a whiff or two of some of the cyanides. But how'd he generate gas here—in plain sight, with the clerk able to watch him?"

"Search me," Hearne muttered. "That's what Dunand'll want to know."

"What'd he get away with?"

"Nearly a hundred thousand dollars' worth of emeralds, Jimmy! And one stone worth twenty-five grand in the bunch! Called the Charlton emerald. Has a reddish tinge." As Wentworth's eyes lit, the detective added: "No... you're wrong. That's what I thought, too. But I've learned that the clerk showed the Charlton emerald without hoping the crook would buy it. Just brought it out to show off Kent-Giddings's stock. There's only one funny thing—"

"Why he wanted to see emeralds?" Jimmy asked.

"Right. Why not diamonds? Easier to sell."

"Funny," Wentworth admitted.

"Yeah," said Hearne. "Dunand'll just laugh his head off! Well... that's all there is, Jimmy. How come Dunand sent you? Any of my business? The crook wasn't a Chink. That's positive."

"Happened to call in. Dead girl in the Stockton Street tunnel. Dunand said he wasn't a Chino. Sent me here on the long chance I might pick up something to help you boys. Which I haven't. If you don't want me, I'll get back to my beat."

"That's where I'll be—poundin' one," Hearne growled. "Not a clew!" He added in a friendly voice to the younger detective: "Good luck with your dead girl, Jimmy. Who was she?"

"Chinese," Jimmy Wentworth said. "Nobody cares about her."

As he stood up to go—he saw nothing for him to do, and nothing at all to be gained by talking with the cigar-chewing Simmons—the telephone rang. The manager answered it, and said to Hearne, "It is for you, detective."

Hearne took the instrument, said, "This's Hearne," and then listened. Jimmy Wentworth, waiting for a word with his fellow detective, heard: "It was, eh? The doctor said... yes, that's the way the clerk died. It only takes a little of th' gas? Did I... no, we don't know how it was done... that is" (for the benefit of the manager) "not yet." Hearne must have heard something not to his liking, for he began to flush. Drearily, he said at last, "Yes, captain, he's here." To Jimmy he grunted, "Wants you."

Wentworth heard Dunand's quick, rasping voice: "You, Wentworth? Found the Chink who robbed Kent-Giddings yet?"

Jimmy knew only too well how feverishly Dunand had been waiting, hoping that Hearne would pick up some clew; knew how the department would be pressed for a solution of the crime and the capture of the criminal by the papers; knew exactly how Dunand must be feeling.

What trace had Hearne missed? There must be something. No crook ever was able to cover a crime completely. Thinking of Hearne, whom every one in the department liked, Wentworth said quietly, "Give us time, sir."

"Got a clew?" Dunand snapped.

"Give us time," Jimmy Wentworth repeated.

He knew what Dunand must be thinking: that his detectives must have some tiny notion they were working on.

Dunand's voice was actually more cheerful—which made Wentworth ashamed of himself—as he said, "Well… can't expect too much in the first hour. Go ahead, Jimmy. Do what you like. Er… by the way, they brought the woman's body in. She was killed instantly, Jim. And I can tell you why."

Jimmy thought, "Now Dunand is going to spring the old triangle-jealousy stuff. Some fool reporter's suggested it, and the dead girl's story will be fluffed up in the newspapers. Which will make me look like a fool in Chinatown. That's not so bad. The more the Chinos laugh at me, the better off I am." It came to him that Chinatown was laughing already, about the brave white man who had his gun taken from him. Aloud, Wentworth said, "Tell me why, captain."

Dunand's voice was low, as if he found the relating rather distressing. "Her man killed her, Jimmy. All you've got to do is find whose slave girl she was. You see"—the gray-haired captain of detectives' voice went lower than ever, as he whispered, "She was a leper, Jimmy. First stages. Hard to tell. The M.D. here just told me. No doubt about it. That's why she was killed."

Involuntarily, Jimmy Wentworth shivered. He had picked up the beautiful dead Chinese girl, had handled her, examining the body for evidence, for anything to show her identity and caste.

His face was white as he said, "You're right. That explains it. The Chinese are in deadly fear of—"

"Don't say the word," Dunand cried over the telephone. "You didn't touch her, did you, Jimmy? If you did report here. Right away. To the M.D. He'll disinfect you, or whatever they do." In a more natural voice he continued: "Now that I've solved your crime for you, boy, get us something on this Kent-Giddings robbery! Otherwise the same stunt 'll be pulled in a dozen stores all over the State."

In a voice as low as Dunand's had been, Jimmy Wentworth said grimly, "I think I can, sir."

"What? You mean it?"

"I do," said Jimmy.

The young Chinatown detective's eyes were bright again as he hung up the receiver. Without an instant's hesitation he demanded of Kent-Giddings's manager: "I want a list of every Chinese customer of the store. Names and addresses. Every Oriental that you have done business with for a year. Can you go through your files in any way and get the names of any Chinese who have written you about anything? I want that also." In explanation of this swift outburst, Jimmy Wentworth added soberly: "That is, Headquarters have requested this data. I don't know what for."

"We can get it," Hammond promised. "It may take a half hour or so—"

"Telephone whatever you find to Captain Dunand," Jimmy asked.

"No Chink pulled this job," blurted Simmons. "I got a good look at the guy. He was as white as you." Parrot-like, the old store detective clung to the only visible facts in the case: "He was middle-aged, smoked a good strong cigar, wore a straw hat and good clothes, and comes from New England—"

Aware that he was overstepping the bounds of a patrolman, nevertheless Wentworth asked, "How do you know that?"

"The clerk said so before he was killed—when he went back to get th' emeralds. He told one of our men. 'He comes from New England,' he said—

"How'd the clerk know?"

"Because the dirty murderer talked that way! Through his nose."

Jimmy Wentworth waited for Hearne to say something; when his fellow detective was silent, Wentworth said, "He had his nose stuffed with cotton. That's why he talked that way."

Hearne said sharply, angry with himself for falling in with Simmons's earlier "clew": "Right, Jim! Kept him from bein' killed by the fumes."

The manager was telephoning for the data Wentworth had asked for. In a low voice Jimmy said to Hearne, "Go to the window, Bob. See if you can see any Chinos standing around anywhere."

Hearne's eyes opened wide, but he did as his companion suggested. His practiced eyes swept up and down the street.

"No," he said. "None I can tell, anyhow. But a Chink in white man's clothes is hard to see."

"Sure," agreed Jimmy. "I've got a fool notion Kent-Giddings is being watched by Chinese. If not from the street, then from an office building window. Hope nobody recognized me when I came along."

Hearne asked softly, "What's up?"

"Just a hunch. For lack of a better one, I'm going to follow it."

Mr. Hammond, having finished his orders for the requested information, said curiously, "Officer, what makes you think a Chinese is involved? We have Chinese people on our books, and think highly of them. Frankly, I feel that the man who robbed us, and killed poor Jordan, is a clever jewel crook. I fail to see where the Chinese come into the picture."

Jimmy Wentworth said slowly, "We mustn't neglect to follow every indication, no matter how ridiculous it may seem, sir."

"There is an indication that Chinese are connected with this crime?"

Cautiously, Wentworth said, "I must ask that you say nothing about this to any one, sir. Not a single word. If you do, we will get nowhere—granted there is something to what I think—and, besides—"

Jimmy stopped, and then shrugged.

"What he means," Hearne explained jovially, elated that Wentworth had obviously uncovered some hidden angle to the robbery and murder, "is that if anything gets out, he'll get bitten in the other ear."

"Go ahead and laugh," Jimmy Wentworth grinned. In the excitement of the affair, he had momentarily forgotten touching the Chinese girl. "Just the same, when you say 'bitten,' it isn't any joke!"

While Hearne stared at him, Wentworth was not forced to explain further, for Kent-Giddings's manager said, "Personally, I fear you gentlemen are not looking in the right direction. I feel strongly that the criminal is a jewel thief—"

"He was a middle-aged man, well dressed, like all our customers, and he wore a straw hat," old Simmons repeated, "and he come from New England... or maybe he had cotton stuffed up his nose, I dunno."

Wentworth went to the telephone, and when he was given his number began to crackle into Cantonese: *"Sin sang h'la ni kam man ho'la! Chi chong n'go kin ko ni'chi han ni!"* It sounded as if a tong warfare were about to break out, but all Jimmy was doing was greeting his friends the Wangs and inquiring into the state of their health, before requesting that young Wang Chen-p'o, ally of the police, meet him as soon as possible in Captain Dunand's office.

When the Chinatown detective had made his arrangements, he said to Hearne, Hammond and Simmons, "We may all be right. Simmons's description is undoubtedly correct, Mr. Hammond's guess that the criminal is a jewel thief is perfectly possible, and your guess, Hearne, that there isn't a clew, may be the wisest thing that's been said. Anyhow, we'll find out before very long."

"It don't make sense to me," Simmons grumbled, when Wentworth had left. Puffing out his lips, he growled, "Chinks! Pooh!"

Hearne grinned. "That's the way I used to feel about Wentworth," he said. "But the kid's a wonder... have a cigar, Simmons?"

4

THE DEADLY WATCH

ALTHOUGH JIMMY WENTWORTH had planned to lay his facts—and his guesses—directly before Captain Dunand, the head of the detective bureau would hear nothing, and rushed his Chinatown detective to the Headquarters physician. And so it was a full hour before Wentworth, in plain clothes, reappeared in Dunand's office. He had been scrubbed and disinfected. Every inch of his lean body had been first rubbed with a burning solution, and then suave, sweet oils had been applied. Even his hair and his eyebrows had come in for special treatment, and his eyes ached from the liquid which the doctor had dropped in them. The inside of his mouth and his throat were raw from gargling. The bitten ear's temporary adhesive had been removed, and it had been properly bandaged.

As Wentworth, fuming at the delay, at last returned to Dunand's office, he was greeted instantly by Wang Chen-p'o: "You smell like a Chinese orchestra," the young Oriental merchant laughed. "More exactly, Jim, you stink. What've you been doing? Crawling in sewers looking for clews?"

"I didn't ask you to come here to laugh at me," Jimmy retorted to the American-educated Chinese who had

helped the police several times in their search for the elusive
Kong Gai who held the reins to Chinatown's underworld.

"Some of these days," Chen-p'o smiled, "you will not ask
me anything, old man, because your nose will lead you into
danger once too often. Now, what's up? Captain Dunand's
been talking about the weather and the baseball scores. Is
that why you want me here, Jim?"

Dunand grunted, "He hasn't told me, either, Chen-
p'o. That's why I couldn't tell you. But"—the gray-haired
captain drummed on his desk—"if he says anything about
a dead girl in the tunnel, instead of about the Kent-Giddings robbery, I'm going to send him out to the sticks
again. Now, talk, Jimmy!"

Wentworth took one of young Wang's Turkish cigarettes
and lit it. Then, blowing smoke high into the air, he said
suddenly to his Chinese friend, "And what did that mean?"

"Blowing smoke up? That somebody's going to die."

"That's what I thought," Jimmy remarked. "Now, in
Chinatown there's a fellow who's pock-marked, Wang.
Slender, and not bad-looking. His father's a cook for some
white people. Who is he?"

"Many of our countrymen have had smallpox, Jimmy.
I'm afraid I don't know."

"This chap has two buddies." Briefly, as well as he could,
Wentworth described the other two Chinese. "Does that
help you any?"

Young Wang shook his head. "Not much," he admitted.
"I'll inquire at the tongs for you. Are they the boys who
did the things to your ear, Jim? Kong Gai's hatchetmen?"

"Umm," Wentworth agreed shortly. "They did more
than that, the dirty pups! They took my gun away from me,

and they stole my watch." To Dunand he explained, "It was dad's watch. The one the department gave him when he saved those women. Dad gave it to me in Peking, before he died." In a grim voice Jimmy added. "That's what you call adding insult to injury."

"We're on an important case," Captain Dunand groaned, "and the dumbest dick in the department lets a couple of cheap crooks steal his watch and take his gun! That's the damnedest thing I ever heard in my life!"

"You're going to hear worse," Jimmy told him. "Now we're going to start in with the dead girl."

"If you begin any of that nonsense, or anything about Kong Gai—"

"Maybe not Kong Gai," the Chinatown detective admitted, "but the girl, yes." He faced Wang Chen-p'o, and spoke directly to him. "Wang, who's got the prettiest slave girl in Chinatown? Beautiful, slender, almond-eyed." He shifted to Chinese: "Voice like the *fung-hoang*, eyes like black jewels under brows curved like the wings of the swallow. Who is she?"

Wang Chen-p'o shrugged.

"It sounds," he admitted uneasily, "like one of Kong Gai's slave girls. He imports the finest women. I heard that he had a new one brought across the border a few weeks ago. It might be the new slave girl. Why, Jim?"

"She's the one who was found in the tunnel—with a knife in her heart. The cut," Jimmy said soberly, "was made clear through her garments, Wang. Whoever did it was pretty angry. That isn't the way a Chinese kills a woman."

"Unless he is maddened."

"What's all that got to do with the Kent-Giddings

emeralds?" Dunand shouted, losing patience. "I want action, Jim!"

"You'll have it," Wentworth promised. "Only, where the Oriental races are concerned, you've got to look closely and step softly." His voice low, Jimmy said, "I think I'll let you explain this to the captain, Wang."

"Explain what?"

"A fine emerald—the finest in the State, perhaps— has been stolen. A Chinese woman has been murdered, a young and lovely slave girl. You can tell Captain Dunand the connection very simply, Wang, when you know"—soft-ly—"that the slave girl was a leper."

Wang's eyes widened. He said, "Ah, is it so?" and then turned to the gray-haired chief of the bureau. "My friend Jimmy has made a wise guess," he told Dunand. "The connection exists. An emerald, worn in a ring on the index finger of the right hand, is considered protection against leprosy, captain. Nothing else will ward off the fatal disease. And "—gravely—" the emerald must be stolen, otherwise the charm will not work."

Dunand was sitting straight up now.

"Not only that," Jimmy Wentworth said, "but, according to my old nurse—every one in China is afraid of leprosy, captain—if the one who steals the emeralds is caught while the crime is committed, the leper himself will surely die."

Dunand stared from Chen-p'o to his own detective. He sighed once, and then he said, "Your theory, Wentworth, is that some one—Kong Gai, perhaps—discovered that his woman was a leper. In order to stop the disease making inroads on his own person, Kent-Giddings was robbed of the Charlton emerald? I... damn it, Jimmy, I don't believe it! If it were the case, only one emerald would have been stolen. As it was, a dozen or more were taken. You've got a pretty theory, but it's bunk."

Wentworth lit another cigarette, and remained silent. Up to the captain's office, high in the Hall of Justice, drifted the noises from Kearny Street. The great bell of the old cathedral suddenly boomed four times—*bong! bong! bong! bong!*—like the thunder of a Chinese temple gong.

"Even if it is true," Dunand muttered, "what are we going to do about it?"

"Try to grab the pock-marked Chinese and his two companions, first off—if we can. Get the man who stole the emeralds, and killed the clerk in Kent-Giddings, which ought to be fairly easy—"

"*What?*"

"Absolutely, if my theory is correct."

"How, Jim?"

Eagerly, Wentworth explained. "First, we telephone San Quentin and Folsom for the photographs of every jewel crook—"

"And get a couple of hundred pictures! Simmons couldn't identify a man from that lot if he tried! You've seen it attempted before, Jimmy."

"No, chief; we'll only get a very few photos. Because we're going to ask for those of jewel crooks who've been released who have been marked as being D.U.'s—that's dope users, Wang—while in prison. That's how Kong Gai, if it is Kong Gai, or any one else would be able to force a white man to work for him. If we haven't luck in the State prisons, we'll wire Washington and Oregon. The crook comes from a State penitentiary where there are Chinese. You can bet on that."

"And after he grabbed the Charlton emerald, he took the rest for himself," Dunand cried.

"Probably, chief. Now do you think I'm all wet?"

"I think it's the craziest thing I ever heard," Dunand told him briefly. "So crazy that it may be true. I'll phone the prisons, anyhow. But where does your being assaulted fit into the picture, Jim? It seems to me that if the pock-marked fellow were in the know, he'd want to keep out of sight. Why would he jump you? Why steal your gat and watch? It don't make sense."

"I don't get it either," admitted Wentworth. "The three could have finished me right there, except that it isn't Kong Gai's way to get revenge. He'd want to have a hand in it himself. They were Kong Gai's hatchetmen, all right. They told me so... and that's funny, too! They'd know I'd go after 'em as soon as I could."

"Which means," Wang Chen-p'o suggested amiably, "that they don't expect you to go after them, Jim."

Uneasily, Captain Dunand said, "That's sense. You've got to be careful, Jimmy. It's like putting you on the spot. They are sure they're going to get you before you can get them."

Wentworth thought the same thing. His fist clenched instinctively. He knew the deadly brain of Kong Gai, who directed the opium dens and the tong killers, and who hated Wentworth with a venomous hatred.

"Either that, or they are sure I can't find them," he said slowly. "Think, Wang! A pock-marked Chinese, tall and slender—"

"The only one I can recall, offhand, is a chap who teaches

in the mission Sunday school," Chen-p'o told them. "He's too saintly for words, and he's pretty wealthy, too. Never heard of his being mixed up with Kong Gai or any one else."

"How'd he get his money?" Jimmy demanded.

Wang Chen-p'o smiled. "That," he said, "is never healthy to ask, in Chinatown."

"Well, I'm going to find out," Wentworth snapped.

"I believe he is a lawyer," Wang remarked. "Leases, contracts, that sort of thing. Nothing shady, so far as I know."

"I want my watch back," grinned Wentworth. "He might be the man. You never know. I'm going to ask him—"

"You stick on this case first," Captain Dunand insisted. "I'll get the photos, and we'll see if Simmons can identify any of the crooks. Maybe you want your watch, and I'm willing to help you get it, but first of all we're going after the man who killed Kent-Giddings's clerk and got away with one hundred thousand dollars' worth of emeralds in broad daylight—"

"Which means the man who is Kong Gai's tool," Wentworth interrupted.

"A murderer's murderer. You've got Kong Gai on the brain. Next thing I know, you'll be thinking this Kong Gai can get into my office here and kill you—"

With the words, there was a knock on the door.

The three men looked up. Captain Dunand's hand went like a flash toward the top drawer of his desk, then he cursed softly as he realized that he had been trapped into admitting the possibility of the very thing for which he had chided his detective. Young Wang shrank in his chair. Wentworth's eyes grew cold and very bright. As if he smelled danger.

It was only old Denny, the department messenger.

"A Chink kid gimme this, cap," he said, saluting grandly. "Th' other Chink kids with him was all eatin' Chink candy, I dunno why. The biggest of 'em, he gimme this li'l bundle. He says, talkin' like my laundryman, says he, bold-like, 'You go give this Captain Dunand velly quick. Not give it to nobody else.' An' here"—offering a small package—"is what he gimme."

"Lay it on the desk, Denny," said Dunand. "Thanks."

When the messenger was gone, Dunand picked up the package. It was some five inches long and an inch thick. Wrapped in paper, carefully tied with string, whoever had sent it took no chance that the youthful delivery boy might make a mistake. On the paper was written, in precise slanting letters:

> A.M. Dunand,
> Captain of Detectives,
> Hall of Justice,
> San Francisco.

There was a small dot on either side of the upright line of every "t."

Wentworth studied the handwriting as Dunand said, "What d'you boys make of my little present?"

"I do not care to make anything of it," Wang said instantly. "If you intend opening the package, I am going for a walk, far from here. Chinese funerals are very grand. However, I do not want one just yet."

"This's too small for a bomb," Dunand said jovially, "and too light." As he looked steadily at the package, a puzzled expression came into his face He lifted the oblong parcel swiftly to his ear. "Clockwork," he ejaculated sharply. "You're not so dumb, Wang."

"I go to my house," Wang Chen-p'o said simply, and without a moment's hesitation slid from his chair and left Dunand's office.

When the two detectives were alone, Dunand remarked, "If this had been sent to you, Jim, from some Chinese admirer, I could understand it. But who wants to get me? I haven't crossed any Chink lately."

Jimmy picked up the packet, and ran his fingers lightly over it. Then he pressed down more firmly, endeavoring to identify by touch whatever was inside. After he had done this, he grinned, without humor.

"Chinos do not use bombs, chief. I think this is what you'd call a Chinese joke. Unless I'm all wrong, my watch is inside. It has been sent to you just to show what a boob I am."

"So I'll take you off the Chinatown beat, eh?" Dunand's eyebrows bristled. He said angrily, "Well, let's open it and see if we get blown up. Here… I'll do it myself."

Wentworth already had the wrapping off. Under it, held by an elastic to a thin cardboard box, was a note, addressed to Dunand in the same handwriting as the outside. Only the dots under the crossmarks of the "t's" were like twin circles, joined together, like miniature spectacles. Like the marks on a cobra's hood.

Dunand read the note aloud.

"To the Important and Honorable Captain of Detectives
Dunand, Kong Gai sends greetings. He also sends the idiot
Wentworth's watch, taken by error by some thief. Let it be
buried with him when he dies. He has become a nuisance.
He is to die very soon. At the instant of death many things
may become clear to him, but it will be too late for him to
tell you about them."

"Short and to the point," Jimmy said. "Sweet soul, Kong
Gai is."

"Anyhow," his superior grunted, opening the box itself
only when he was positive that nothing was holding the
cover which might release a spring, "anyhow, you've got
your watch again. Now maybe you'll concentrate on the
Kent-Giddings murder and robbery. Take your watch,
Jim."

Wentworth took it, and then said strangely, alertly,
"What's the first thing I ought to do with the watch?"

"Why, examine it and see if it's O.K."

"Right! Have you any cotton?" Without waiting for an
answer, and while Dunand stared at him, Jimmy Wentworth went to the emergency case in the corner. He took
from it a roll of medicated cotton, and made four small balls.
Two of these he stuffed into his nostrils, two he handed to
Dunand. Then he said, "A customer at Kent-Giddings said
that the thief who got the emeralds looked at his watch
just before the murder was committed. And the murderer
talked through his nose—"

Dunand filled his nostrils quickly.

"Be sure and keep your mouth closed, too," Wentworth

commanded, and, when Dunand nodded, Jimmy opened the old-fashioned watch.

Despite the cotton stuffed in his nostrils, despite his holding the watch as far from his face as possible, the deadly odor of bitter almonds penetrated to his nose. Without the cotton, one or both of the detectives would have been instantly killed.

Side by side the two detectives rushed from the office, closing the door behind them. In the hall, Dunand snapped, "So that's how it was done!"

"That's how. And, chief, you're talking through your nose, just as the murderer talked in the store."

"Hydrocyanic gas, generated inside the watch somehow. Our chemist 'll learn how it was done." Taking the cotton from his nostrils, Dunand went on, "Nice work, Jim. It sounded like a fairy tale, until now, all this stuff about emeralds and lepers and Kong Gai. I… why, I damn' near believe it myself! I'll see what I can do about getting information on discharged dope users—jewel crooks—from the prisons. There may be something to it all!"

"There will be," Wentworth returned. "A dope user would naturally buy stuff Kong Gai controls, and then Kong Gai would control him, also. This crime was committed hastily. Kong Gai—or whoever owned the slave girl, and I think it was Kong Gai—had to work fast, to get his stolen emerald. He went after me as a sort of afterthought, or because somebody suggested killing two birds with one stone."

"What're you going to do next?" Dunand asked.

"Get the pock-marked Chino."

"How?"

Wentworth grinned. "If there's one thing an Oriental will do, it is to keep up whatever he's been doing in the past. And maybe it was teaching the proverbs in Mandarin Chinese, captain. To-morrow's Sunday. I'm going to Sunday school."

"What makes you think he's the right one?"

"Because ordinarily no Chink would send youngsters on an errand, chief; They'd send an old man instead. That's the proper way. But it was youngsters who brought the package here… and I'll bet they've all been taught their proverbs in the mission!"

Dunand saw the chase closing in. "I'll call up the warden himself," he said.

5

THE POCK-MARKED
MAN'S FALSE FINGER

THE MORNING SUN gleamed on the curved, bright-tiled roofs of Chinatown on Sunday morning. The great bazaars had not yet opened their doors for the usual tourist trade, although deeper in the Oriental district the heavy wooden shutters were down, to permit Chinese matrons to make their purchases before white men were abroad.

In the Chinese temple, staid merchants bowed before the image of Pou-t'ai, god of misfortune, praying that no trouble come to them during the day. Children thrust sticks of incense in the bowl of sand standing on a pedestal in front of Ch'ou-lao, lord of long life, that their fathers live to a full hundred years.

A block away, in a red brick building, mission youngsters listened to a harangue: *"On hai tan hai! mui lai pai kok! yan ch'sin ying'iu hü yat!* Everybody ought to go to church at least once on Sunday! I go three times, four times. It is a good thing to do."

The Chinese who was speaking so fervently was a slender, pock-marked Oriental, well thought of by the mission people.

The pock-marked Chinese was not as completely

absorbed in his task as usual. He knew that across the street from the mission stood a stooped, old-looking lily-vendor—who was really a capable hatchetman; he knew that leaning against the mission itself was another highbinder, who did nothing but stand in the sun as if waiting for his child to come out from Sunday school. He knew also that there was a rear door to the room.

Nevertheless he was uneasy. This Wentworth—even Kong Gai feared the white man a little, and Kong Gai was fearless!

In the pock-marked man's pocket was a thick roll of greenbacks, paid to him that morning. At first Kong Gai had been angered because his spies had exceeded their orders—to watch and see what became of the dead slave girl—but afterward he had become genial, as witness the payment of good American money!

When the pock-marked man had almost completed his morning lesson to the yawning children, two white women came into the mission and sat down.

The pock-marked man watched them shrewdly, and decided that they were what they seemed—patronesses of the mission, although he had never seen them before. However, if anything had been wrong, Quong Mi, outside, would have signalled him. Then the pock-marked Chinese would have ended his discourse abruptly, and left by the rear door.

But Quong Mi, the hatchetman, saw nothing wrong. True, a great automobile, such as wealthy white people drive in, arrived before the mission. Missing nothing, Quong Mi saw the chauffeur leave his seat and open the rear door of the limousine, helping the two white ladies to alight. Then the chauffeur returned to his compartment, and, after his mistress was inside the mission, began to read a newspaper.

Quong Mi, for all his good eyesight, missed one thing. Jimmy Wentworth had been crouched on the floor of the automobile. And the driver's rear-vision mirror was arranged so that it covered the entrance to the mission, and the driver—Hearne, from Headquarters—could see what was going on even while he had the newspaper in front of him.

Wentworth, through Wang Chen-p'o, had learned that the pock-marked man always came to the door with visitors, especially when they might make contributions to the mission, and often helped them into their machines politely.

Which was exactly what the pock-marked man did this bright Sunday morning. When the session inside was over, the pock-marked man went down the aisle—patting a child here and there as he walked—to the two women, who expressed their interest in the mission, and hinted that they might care to add money for the cause. Lueng Chau, the pock-marked man, smiled all over his face, and in excellent English admitted that contributions were welcome.

He walked to the door with the women, and, seeing the expensive machine waiting outside, toward which the white women went, he hurried forward to open the door for them. The chauffeur stepped out also, and Leung Chau gave him one look, deciding that all was well. What could possibly happen on this street, outside the mission, on a bright Sunday morning? Indeed, save for the two hatchetmen, the street was deserted. Leung Chau had forgotten that things had happened on another street!

He opened the rear door of the automobile.

And then something happened. The driver of the car, Hearne, gave Leung Chau a terrific push, hands reached out to grab the pock-marked man, the door of the car was slammed behind him. Wentworth's arms wound about the writhing body of the Chinese. The car lurched forward, flashing into high gear. The two women—police matrons—had jumped in ahead of Hearne.

Alert as he had been, the hatchetman's gun was not even out until the machine was a half block down the hill, gaining speed every instant. Quong Mi stood leaning against the building. Across the street, the other hatchetman stared at his bunches of lilies. Then, without a word passing, both disappeared.

The street, now, was silent and deserted.

Inside the automobile, the pockmarked man twisted about like a cat. He had no chance to go for his knife. With his jagged, long finger nails he tried for Jimmy Wentworth's face, but Wentworth, taking no chances, had Leung Chau pinioned at the elbow, and in another moment had the cuffs snapped on.

Then Wentworth shoved the Asiatic to the floor, and himself sat up on the seat. Hearne called, "All O.K., Jimmy?"

"Right," Wentworth said. Glancing down at Leung Chau, he added, "Few men live to be a hundred years."

"What does this mean?" Leung Chau snarled. "Do you know who I am?"

"Whatever you say," Jimmy Wentworth told him grimly,

"will be used against you. Do I know who you are? No, and I don't care. Now, shut up!"

Sometimes there is no better way to make a man talk than to tell him to keep silent, but Leung Chau did not open his thin lips again until he was standing before Captain Dunand's desk.

The gray-haired captain of detectives was in wonderful humor. Simmons had identified, from five photographs sent from the State prison, the man who had stolen the famous bloody-hued Charlton emerald. The drag-net was already out. As Wentworth had said, the middle-aged man was a jewel thief, and had been registered at the prison as a user of drugs. Had Simmons, or any one else, been shown a thousand photographs—the customary procedure—it would have been impossible to have identified the criminal. Given only five pictures, the task had been simple.

Wentworth had not believed that the thief and murderer would be harbored in Chinatown. The King Cobra did not care what suspicions pointed toward him, but with the leprosy "cure" involved, Kong Gai would take no chance at a failure in the "treatment" even if the thief were caught. This would probably suit Kong Gai, and remove a man who had a possible hold over the villainous Chinese master of Chinatown. If the thief—Gregory Petersen, alias Wilson, alias Hendricks—were in the city, the detective bureau would find him—find him anywhere, save in the tunnels and caverns of Chinatown itself.

And so Dunand was in a contented frame of mind. He said to Simmons, who was in his office when Wentworth and Leung Chau came in, "Here he is now. With his man. Got the right one, Jimmy?"

"This is an outrage," Leung Chau said. "I was escorting two ladies, whom I believed to be interested in my Sunday school, to a machine. This man throws me into the car, and brings me here. I am a Chinese attorney, captain, and I demand to know what all this means."

"You tell him, Jim," Captain Dunand said.

Soberly, Wentworth said, "You are under arrest for assaulting an officer."

"What officer, might I ask?"

"Me."

Leung Chau laughed. "Impossible! Why, I wouldn't think of doing anything like that, officer. When was all this supposed to have happened,"

"The day the emeralds were stolen from Kent-Giddings," said Wentworth.

The pock-marked man smiled broadly. "I hope you don't think I stole the jewels, too. Why, I can account for every moment of my time for several days—"

"Crooks always can," Simmons growled.

"Why did I assault you?" Leung Chau asked, as if highly amused.

Wentworth looked at him squarely. "You, and two other Chinese, were standing outside the Stockton Street tunnel, Leung Chau. You were waiting to see when I, or somebody else, would discover the body of a slave girl. After the discovery, you were to return to Kong Gai, and tell him what happened. And," Wentworth continued coldly, following his theory, "when the thief left Kent-Giddings, he walked a little way, and then got into a machine. When the machine left the tunnel, the thief threw you a little sack, filled with cotton—and an emerald. You were to take this to Kong Gai, after seeing what happened about the slave girl.

"Then I came along. I was in the tunnel before you were at its mouth. When I walked back on my beat, you saw a chance to curry additional favor with Kong Gai by beating me up, taking my watch, and then killing me just as the jewel clerk was killed. That's why you jumped me, Leung Chau."

"A fairy tale," the Chinese laughed. "Utterly nonsensical. Do *you* believe that rubbish, captain?"

"Yes," said Dunand shortly. Unseen, he pressed a button under his desk. Almost at once the telephone rang, and he answered it. "Oh, you want Wentworth, eh?" he said. Handing the telephone to Jimmy, and carrying out their plan, he continued, "I think it's a Chink, Jim. Sounds like it. Funny high-pitched voice."

Leung Chau was not laughing now. His face was yellow-gray, and had become impassive as stone.

Wentworth listened, as if some one were talking. He said slowly, "Thanks for the tip, Wang." (At the moment Chen-p'o was at family prayers; Jimmy was connected only with the officer in charge of the switchboard.) "You say somebody's found two bodies? Both of'em stabbed? Knife with a hilt shaped like a cobra's hood? Yes, that's Kong Gai's work. What was the message? Only 'One more bungler is to die'? No, that doesn't make sense. I suppose he means me, maybe. Oh, well, thanks anyhow, Wang. See you soon."

"More murders?" Dunand rasped, acting his part well.

"Two. Wang says he thinks they're hatchetmen. And a promise of another death."

Leung Chau said, in a queer, tight voice, "I am very tired,

captain. Are you through with me? If so, is there a place here I may rest?"

"Thought you were all for gettin' out of here," Dunand said.

Leung Chau's eyes darted about the room once. He looked like a man who had received his death sentence. Wentworth knew exactly what the pockmarked man was thinking. And then the Chinese said the very last thing Jimmy Wentworth expected:

"You have told me a tale," said Leung Chau. "One thing you have forgotten. Why did Kong Gai want the emerald?"

"To save himself from a horrible death," Wentworth said softly.

"You are a devil," Leung Chau screamed. His thin voice ran up the scale as he cried, "Outside, there is Kong Gai's vengeance! Here, there is you, an all-seeing devil! Gods of heaven, hell and earth, protect me!"

Before any one could stop him, Leung Chau's hand went to his mouth. When it fell limply to his side, all saw that the last joint of his little linger was gone, and that it must have been false.

Fanatically, Leung Chau shouted, "Oh, King Cobra, seller of the poppy-juice, and companion of fiends, I have told nothing!" Specks of foam began to gather on his lips. In a wild voice he shrilled, "I am as silent as the knife with which you stabbed the tainted slave girl!"

Wentworth, catching the stricken man as he fell, said quietly, "Call the M.D. if you want, chief, but it won't do any good. He had poison in that false finger. He was searched, or I wouldn't have let it go this far—"

Nodding, Dunand answered the summons of the telephone again. "Bring him up," he ordered briefly. To the other two men he said, "Final act, boys. They've caught Petersen, or whatever he calls himself now. Full of hop."

Leung Chau's body was laid gently on the floor. When a middle-aged, well-dressed white man, with shaking hands, was brought into the office, his first vision was the dead Chinese.

"You are under arrest for the murder of Jordan, and for the theft of Kent-Giddings's emeralds," Dunand said sharply.

The jewel thief was trembling. The boldness with which he had entered the jewel shop was all gone.

For a full minute he said nothing, and then words cascaded from his white lips. "Cap," he pleaded, "all I was told was that the watch had some gas in it which would put the clerk to sleep! I never knew it would kill him! Kong Gai had me where he wanted me. He wouldn't come across with any more hop unless I pulled this job for him." There was no courage, nothing but raving fear in the broken man. "I'll take the rap for robbery, cap. But… it isn't first degree murder, is it?"

Dunand's powerful fingers rapped ceaselessly against his desk. He could not look at the wrecked wretch of a white man before him. Once he glanced up at Jimmy Wentworth, who nodded. Very slowly, the captain of detectives said, "I'll suggest manslaughter to the district attorney, Petersen. That's the best I can do. Now"—to the officers—"take him away, boys. Tell doc to keep an eye on him."

"I've hidden all the stones but one," Petersen whimpered. "All but the biggest one. That went to Kong Gai—"

"That will help you," Dunand said soothingly. "Tell the boys where you hid 'em."

Alone with Simmons and Wentworth, the captain, said almost wearily, "I believe all he said. Kong Gai is the actual murderer. Jimmy, can't we get our hands on him?"

"Some day, chief," said Jimmy Wentworth. "If he doesn't get me first. I want him as badly as you do. I haven't forgotten what he did to Lucile Carrington—"

"Neither have I," Dunand retorted. The gray-haired captain began to smile. "How is she, Jimmy? Able to stand the shock of thinking she knows a lad named Detective Sergeant Wentworth?"

"Have I your permission to tell her that, chief?"

"Can if you want to," Dunand growled. He seized Jimmy's hand, and shook it. "You have earned it, Jimmy. This was wonderful work. Now, run along and tell her, boy."

As Wentworth was closing the door behind him, blinking to get the sight of dead Leung Chau from his eyes and mind, he heard old Simmons say, "I never seen no dick like that kid. He talks an' acts like one of our customers." Simmons could think of no higher praise. "The store'll be satisfied, cap, and the insurance company'll be tickled, even if this Chink murderer has got the red colored emerald. It was a grand piece of work, gettin' the crooks and the other gems. What gets me is that boy! I never seen no dick like him before!"

"He's a *detective*," Dunand smiled, offering Simmons a big, black cigar. "And what's more, one of these days he'll get Kong Gai—and the Charlton emerald. You wait and see. Why"—blowing smoke grandly—"I trained that boy myself!"

THE HORNS OF THE DRAGON

Down Along the Waterfront Crept Black-Clad Men with Staring Eyes—Kong Gai's Killers...

1

THE KNIVES OF THE HIP LEUNG

JIMMY WENTWORTH, IN his blue patrolman's uniform, knew as he swung swiftly off the steps of the California Street cable car to the pavement of Chinatown that something was wrong. The Oriental district was deserted; it should have been teeming with life.

The young detective walked rapidly down the street, heading for the blank wall where the Chinese post their signs. He was almost positive of what he was going to see, and he was not mistaken. On the wall of the corner building was the dreaded red placard announcing tong vengeance. The edges of the blood-colored paper were limp. The paste had not yet been dried by the morning sun.

Jimmy read Chinese as well as the Asiatics themselves; he walked past the wall without appearing to so much as glance at it. The Chinese considered him no more than the emblem of the white man's idiotic law; they did not know how much the China-born detective understood of their customs and language. Nevertheless, Jimmy Wentworth missed no word of the gaudy sign, pasted over announcements of steamship sailings, of weddings, of the birth of a firstborn male child. It read:

VENGEANCE!

DEATH!

Beware, Yee Yick Sun Tong! We swear vengeance! Hide.
We will find you. Run. We will catch you. Tremble. The knives
of the Hip Leung Tong will end your shivering with

DEATH!

The announcement of tong war between the powerful
Yee Yick Suns and the equally influential Hip Leungs
would mean horrible wholesale killings, with the police

The guns of the deadly assassins chattered

completely baffled, and the anti-administration newspapers demanding arrests which would be practically impossible to make. Not until many members of the two tongs had been murdered would peace be declared. Before that time, the tong war would spread from San Francisco to the other Coast cities, and work its murderous way eastward through every Chinatown until it reached New York.

As he walked along his beat, determining what action was possible, the young detective sergeant saw that some of the shops were already closed, and the heavy wooden shutters in place. The Yee Yicks had seen the warning and were going into hiding. Here and there, sauntering aimlessly in pairs, Wentworth noticed lean, grim-visaged Chinese dressed in black silk—Hip Leung hatchetmen, ready to kill any member of the Yee Yick Sun tong they saw.

Jimmy Wentworth knew that these hired highbinders

would kill on sight, without warning. No Yee Yick, young student or old merchant, could expect mercy from them. It would not do the slightest good to round up all of them he could find. Members of the Hip Leung tong, tradesmen, bankers, doctors, would come to the Hall of Justice and swear that the hatchetmen were honest, worthy Chinese. Wentworth knew that this had been tried before, and had not worked. After their release, the hatchetmen had been more venomous than ever, and the killings had continued.

The Hip Leungs had announced vengeance and declared war. Why? It was up to the Chinatown detective to learn, although he felt it would help little.

HE STEPPED QUIETLY into the bowl shop of the Wangs; old Wang Yu was a wise Chinese, young Wang Chen-p'o, his son, had often helped Jimmy Wentworth and the police. The old man was apparently drowsing on his stool behind the counter. Without opening his eyes he said, in a singsong monotone:

"*Cho san san t'ai hola.* Good morning. How is your health?"

Answering in excellent Cantonese, Wentworth said, "*Yau sam yat…* very good, honorable father."

"You feel better than the Yee Yick Sun tong members this morning?"

Smiling in agreement, Jimmy Wentworth asked bluntly, "Why are the Hip Leungs demanding vengeance?"

The old Chinese merchant opened his eyes, blinked, fingered his abacus, and when he closed his eyes, continued to move the little colored heads back and forth on the wires. He said gravely, "A Hip Leung has been killed by a Yee Yick Sun. The crime must be washed out with blood."

Although no report of any death had been made, Wentworth had realized from the moment he had seen that red placard what must have happened in Chinatown. "The Hip Leung was killed this morning?" he questioned.

"This morning," old Wang agreed. He raised his voice, calling nasally for his son. "Wang Chen-p'o knows more of the matter than my miserable self. He will tell you what he has heard."

Young Wang, dressed in American clothes, was grinning slyly as he hurried into the shop. He bowed to his father before addressing the white detective. "Now you'll earn your pay, James," he said, chuckling. "When the Yee Yicks and the Hip Leungs fall out, the police department is in for a hot time. This'll make you forget all about Kong Gai, James, my boy. Even the King Cobra can't compete with a tong war for murder, riot, and sudden death."

"Who killed who, and why?" Jimmy demanded.

"You know Sam Kee, the fellow who sells shrimp baskets at wholesale? Well, he's dead as a shrimp that's dried and shipped back to China, and the Yee Yicks killed him this morning."

"Why?"

Chen-p'o shrugged. "Two years ago, it seems, a Yee Yick was killed by a Hip Leung, and they've just learned about it."

"Rot," Jimmy Wentworth said.

"That's straight dope, Jimmy. Two years ago a Yee Yick died from a broken neck. Every one supposed that he had fallen down his own cellar stairs, being well filled with nice warm *ng ki po* and good cheer, but the Yee Yicks have learned that he was hurled into the basement by a Hip

Leung, and so they went out early this morning and killed Sam Kee, who was so unfortunate as to be the first Hip Leung they met. Now, of course, the Hip Leungs want a lot of blood and vengeance. The Yee Yicks, being one up, will try to keep ahead of the Hip Leungs by killing more of them. Say, Jimmy, how'd you like to have a nice quiet beat out in the sticks?"

Wentworth ignored Chen-p'o's laughter. He said, "About this man with the broken neck—how'd the Yee Yicks find out about it?"

"No idea, Jimmy. I don't belong to the tong. I'm not in on their secrets."

"You're sure Sam Kee was murdered by a Yee Yick Sun?"

"I'm sure he's dead, and I'm equally positive that the Hip Leungs are going to do plenty about it."

Wentworth said angrily, "It's so foolish, Chen-p'o. The tongs have been fighting off and on for years, usually about nothing. There's some flare-up, and before it is over a dozen or more fine men are dead. You know how hatchetmen are, even if white men and women are in their line of fire; they blaze away just the same. Look here, Chen-p'o, how well do you know the heads of the two tongs?"

"Jimmy the Peacemaker," Chen-p'o jeered. "Go ahead, if you want. The Chinese don't expect anything more sensible from a cop. Only I won't go with you. It isn't healthy to mix up in a tong war. I'd just as soon play around with Kong Gai and his cobra. Not me!"

WENTWORTH DIDN'T BLAME his Chinese friend; what he intended asking Chen-p'o was merely the kind of men the tong leaders were. Under no circumstances would he have asked Chen-p'o to go with him.

Old Wang Yu answered his unuttered question quietly, "Even if the tong heads desire peace, it is impossible. The families of Sam Kee and the Yee Yick who died two years ago will insist on war. The hatchetmen of both tongs will demand it, for gold will come to them for every killing."

"I've got to try," Jimmy Wentworth said stubbornly. "You know what a tong war means."

"I am surprised that we have not already heard the guns," the old merchant said. "That is because the tongs are now meeting to decide how many lives must be taken before vengeance is satisfied. Yes, my son, I know what it means. To-night, or to-morrow, the streets will run red."

"You think it is useless for me to appeal to the tong heads?"

"There have been wars between the tongs when your great grandfather was a baby. There will be bloodshed for Chinese vengeance when you yourself have great grand-children," said old Wang.

"Let him go and see the Yee Yicks and the Hip Leungs," Chen-p'o suggested. "It will take his mind away from Kong Gai. By the way, Jimmy, isn't it time that Kong Gai started something again?"

"One trouble's enough at a time," the detective grinned. "Well, I'll go and tackle the Yee Yicks first, and you can have a laugh at me."

"Speak softly to them," said old Wang. "Do not incur the anger of the tongs. Or a stray bullet may kill you as dead as one of Kong Gai's knives."

"James will speak to them about love and flowers," Chen-p'o laughed. "You ought to've been a missionary, Jimmy. Then you could say to the Yee Yicks, '*Ni kam yat yau hü lai pai t'ong lai ma,'* and they'd tell you to go jump in the lake. As a matter of fact, they probably won't let you inside the tong chambers… but go ahead and try."

"I will." Jimmy Wentworth lowered his voice. "It looks funny to me, Chen-p'o. Just avenging a murder which was committed two years ago. I want to find out about it."

"We have memories as sharp as our knives, we Chinese," said old Wang. "My advice to you is—"

"Yes, honorable Wang the Elder?"

"That you see the Yee Yicks. Ask how they learned that their brother was killed two years ago by a Hip Leung, instead of meeting death accidentally. *I* had never heard that it was murder; I hear many things in Chinatown."

"And shall I see the Hip Leungs, and ask them why they didn't boast of the killing when it was made?" Jimmy Wentworth knew that such was the customary practice.

"No. They may have been waiting all these two years to see if the Yee Yicks would discover what happened."

"And have your gun handy," Chen-p'o said urgently. "There will be guards at the Yee Yick chambers, and some of them may be the very hatchetmen who murdered Sam Kee. They know if they're caught, they'll hang. So be careful, Jimmy."

"They think I'm too dumb to bother with," grinned the young Chinatown detective.

2

SAM KEE'S BODY

IT WAS ONLY two blocks to the building which housed, on the third story, the chambers of the Yee Yick Sun tong. Wentworth opened the lower door on the street, and instantly three slender Chinese in black silk, barred his way. Jimmy Wentworth knew them for what they were—hired killers, hatchetmen, highbinders. Under each silken jacket was a heavy automatic, in each right hand, now inserted in the left sleeve, was a keen, straight-bladed knife.

Wentworth knew, even without Wang's information, that any or all of the three might have killed Sam Kee, and that if they believed he knew it, would knife him without compunction.

For a full minute the detective, dressed as a patrolman, and the beady-eyed Orientals stood face to face. From above, Wentworth heard the mournful wailing of a flute, and the minor jangle of a snake-bellied *san-hien*. Then one of the three hatchetmen said in broken English:

"What you want?"

"I wantchee go upstairs," Wentworth said sharply.

"No can do."

His mind made up, the Chinatown detective did exactly what the hatchetmen would expect of a blundering white policeman. He pushed one of them out of the way with his hands, as if he did not know that all three were holding knives, and began stolidly to march up the dark stairway.

One of the hatchetmen must have restrained the other two, for Wentworth heard him say in singsong Cantonese, "He is too big a fool to know anything. And even if he does, he will not come down alive. Ko Fan'chi has said we are to kill none but Hip Leungs. Let Ko Fan'chi talk to the white ape."

Wentworth walked up to the first landing; he knew that from behind peepholes other guarding hatchetmen were watching him. Without hesitation he continued up to the third floor.

Here two Chinese in black silk robes marked with the insignia of the Yee Yick Sun tong stopped him. One was a highbinder, probably the head of the paid killers, the other was a respectable merchant of Chinatown. The second man smiled, rather unhappily, Wentworth thought, and said, "Goo' morning, officer. Who you like see?"

"I want to see Mr. Fan'chi," Wentworth said. "Ain't he the president of the tong?"

"Why-so you want see him?"

Jimmy Wentworth answered heavily, "I gotta see him, and nobody else."

"He is very busy man."

"I gotta see him."

The merchant considered a moment, and then said, "Allo light. You come alongside me."

A door, iron-studded, was pushed slowly open, moving noiselessly on its hinges. Wentworth knew that between the outer layers of innocent-appearing wood there must be heavy sheet steel.

The Chinatown detective followed the tongman into a room, and instantly left America behind. On the walls were the sacred banners, yellow silk embroidered with the green and black characters of the tong. Wooden panels of carved gods ornamented with pure gold leaf leered down at him. At the far end of the room was a collection of swords, curved blades, straight blades, blades with jagged teeth cut in the blue steel. There were four rows of knives, also, of every variety, some of them having jeweled hilts. Jimmy Wentworth, with his knowledge of things Chinese, realized that every one of the murderous weapons had taken the life of some enemy of the powerful Yee Yick tong.

In the next chamber, separated only by a crimson silk hanging drawn back in the middle, Wentworth could see many members of the Yee Yick Sun gathered about a vermilion-painted coffin, in which was a little male Chinese doll, emblematic of the dead tong member, whose actual body had been shipped two years ago to China. In the Hip Leung rooms, elsewhere in Chinatown, other Orientals would be standing about the "body" of Sam Kee, and, as the Yee Yicks were doing here, promising terrible and immediate vengeance.

THE FLUTE WAILED, the three-stringed instrument made from snakeskin made tiny sounds which brought gooseflesh to Wentworth's arms and legs. This was no ordinary gathering. The speech he was hearing, made in whining Cantonese, was more than the customary demand for vengeance. Wholesale destruction of the Hip Leungs was being suggested! Old Wang had spoken truly. The streets were going to run with blood by the next morning.

Finally a venerable, pleasant-faced Chinese shuffled into the room. In the best of English, Ko Fan'chi asked, "What is the trouble, officer? I am very busy to-day. As you see we are performing a ceremony."

Wentworth, maintaining his supposed lack of knowledge about anything Chinese, said glumly, "Somebody's been telling headquarters that a tong war's going to start. I been ordered to see about it."

The head of the Yee Yicks asked, "Is that so, officer? Which tongs are to be involved in this war?"

"The Hip Leungs and the Yee Yicks, we been told."

Ko Fan'chi patted the tips of his fingers together; he smiled, and did not even trouble to lie to this stupid policeman. He said, "You may tell your superiors that there is a small matter requiring adjustment. Of course"—virtuously—"*our* tong will not sanction anything out of the way. You may assure your superior of that fact. We will be very circumspect."

"Sure, I'll tell him all that," Jimmy Wentworth said, trying to look as if impressed by the long words. "Now, mister, if you can tell me what's the trouble, we gotta have that for our records."

"Very proper," Fan'chi nodded gravely, contemptuous of this white policeman. "I see you are an intelligent officer. Say to your chief that a Yee Yick, by the name of Mok Mo, was killed two years ago by the Hip Leungs, and now we are meeting to—restrain our young men from doing anything about it."

The wily Chinese smiled slightly. Wentworth said, as stupidly as before, "Yeah. Sure. My chief'll be glad there ain't gonna be no trouble. Say, mister, how'd you find out some guy was killed two years ago, anyhow? We got a report about that at headquarters?"

"Hardly, officer. We only learned it yesterday; it was thought to be an accident. Yesterday, the gentleman you can see standing beside the red—box—in the next room, informed us of the truth."

Jimmy Wentworth's swift glance went to the man Ko Fan'chi indicated. The detective's keen eyes caught the fierce expression on the man's face, caught also the spasmodic twitching of the fellow's mouth. Opium smoker. At the same moment, the informer, having doubtless heard Ko Fan'chi's words, looked up also, and then began to harangue the others in Cantonese.

"We must make haste, oh, brothers of the hatchet," he sang out. "To-morrow! No later than to-morrow! Brothers, I know that the Hip Leungs will be gathering outside the shop of Lee Wong Chung at eight o'clock, to attack us. We will be there, eh? *Hai-ya!* We will be waiting for them—"

It seemed to Jimmy Wentworth as if the speaker were telling him of the rendezvous, of the place, the time. Why? So that the police might stop the slaughter? No! Wentworth recognized this member of the Yee Yick tong as a bloodthirsty, opium-smoking Chinese. Undoubtedly, like Ko Fan'chi, he was contemptuous of the police, and especially of Jimmy Wentworth, the beat patrolman. To discuss their plan before the white man meant that the policeman was considered as having entirely "lost face"—that he was believed as brainless as the floor on which he stood.

Wentworth said, "That's the guy, huh?" and then added, "Well, Mr. Ko Fanshee, you tell him to come to headquarters an' tell my chief who done it, an' how, an' we'll arrest the murderers an' hang 'em."

"I will be delighted to convey your message to my friend," said Ko Fan'chi amiably. "Perhaps he will avail himself of your offer of assistance. Now, if you will pardon me, officer, I have duties to perform."

"Sure, mister. Say, you better give me the name of this guy who knows all about the murder."

"He only knows it *was* murder," said Ko Fan'chi gently. "And that it was done by a Hip Leung. He does not know who did it."

"I never seen him before, have I?"

"No; our tong member only recently arrived from China. It was there that he learned about the murder of our brother."

Jimmy Wentworth nodded as if completely satisfied. He wasn't—not in the least. He didn't like the looks of this new Yee Yick one particle, and he was willing to gamble that the fellow had been smuggled across the Canadian border, instead of being legally passed through the Angel Island immigration station. Aloud, he said only, "Well, you see that there ain't no monkey business in Chinatown. We don't want no more killings."

"Of course not, officer! Why, we would not—"

There were two shots, and then a dozen, coming from the street below. Jimmy Wentworth rushed to the window, and jerked aside the thick silken hangings. Instantly the glass was shattered, not by a bullet angling up from the street, but by a shot from an opposite building.

A Chinese in the Yee Yick rooms screamed in death agony.

3

KONG GAI

BLOOD ON HIS face, where glass had cut him, Jimmy
Wentworth dropped to his knees. Oblivious of the terrific
din behind him, where the inflamed Yee Yicks were shouting, *"Sha! Sha!* Kill! Vengeance!" the detective peered
cautiously out. His gun was ready in his hand.

There was a black-clad body lying on the cobblestones.
Six living Chinese were fleeing. One of them held his hand
against his thigh, where the black silk must have been turning moist with blood.

Whether any of the Yee Yick hatchetmen guarding the
lower door, or all of them, had been killed, Wentworth
could not know. He was now genuinely alarmed. This
wasn't the customary sniping tong war. A frontal attack,
instead of the usual mysterious murdering! Were the Hip
Leungs taking a lesson from gangster warfare?

Behind him, the Yee Yicks were milling about. Some
had rushed to the racks of swords and knives, tearing blades
down and brandishing them in the incense-blue air. Lean
hatchetmen waited, horribly grim, for orders. But no one
advanced to the windows. Wentworth said sharply, "Keep
out of the way! Ko Fan'chi, tell every one to get away from
this window!"

The head of the tong snapped, "Go away, oh, white man! Begone! Or—"

The detective's gun swung about, covering the room. In a cold voice Wentworth said, restraining himself from speaking in Chinese with an effort, "Ko Fan'chi, a murder has been done, and the police have seen it. Another murderer is in the building across the street. If he is staying there, concealed, I may be able to catch him. Now, tell your men to keep away from the window, and to keep away from me. Otherwise, somebody else is going to be killed!"

The man who had made the harangue before, the stranger Chinese, shrilled, "Oh, Ko Fan'chi, to-morrow morning is the time appointed for vengeance! Do not stand in the way of the gods, Ko Fan'chi!"

As if against his will, the head of the tong gave the order.

Even while Jimmy Wentworth was carefully pushing aside the hangings, to see if it would draw another shot, he was thinking that again this was an unusual procedure. A recently arrived tong member giving orders! What did it mean?

Nothing followed Wentworth's moving of the heavy curtain. No shot. Absolutely certain that the sniper had fled after the attempted attack, the white detective stood up, and looked squarely out of the window. Again nothing happened. There was no reason for him to leave the Yee Yicks rooms by a rear stairway and search the other building; the sniper was gone from his lair.

While Wentworth was wiping blood from his face, the Chinese, at Ko Fan'chi's demand, picked up the body of their brother who had fallen victim to the random bullet.

Carefully they placed him in the red coffin, putting the doll on his breast.

"To-morrow at eight we will avenge you," the shrill-voiced Yee Yick screeched. "To-morrow at the shop of Lee Wong Chung—"

"Silence," Ko Fan'chi hissed. "Tell not everything, oh, brother! This white man may not be the utter fool we believe!"

"He *will* be a greater fool than any one could believe," retorted the stranger Yee Yick.

Ko Fan'chi shifted suddenly to the intricate Mandarin dialect. "Careful," he said very softly, glancing not at Wentworth, but toward the red coffin. "Before, the policeman spoke in the language of the streets. When he was excited, he spoke as educated white men speak. Perhaps he knows Cantonese also. If so—"

Wentworth could have sworn that the stranger Yee Yick's eyes were smiling. "If so," he said, "we will find out." He, also, spoke in polished Mandarin.

The detective said to Ko Fan'chi, "I'm going down to see the guy who was killed." He must never again slip into good English. "Then I'll come back an' get the name of the feller up here, too."

As he started to walk away, the stranger Yee Yick said, " '*M sai kam fai hu cho che!* Wait, man of police; I have something to tell you."

Jimmy Wentworth's face did not move a muscle as he continued to walk toward the door.

"You see?" the new tong member said. "He knows no word of our language." And then the stranger Yee Yick laughed.

Wentworth thought, I don't believe you're laughing just because you've made a monkey out of me. Something's behind all this! You're too anxious for me to be at Lee Wong Chung's shop.

TWO OF THE door guards were carrying up the dead hatchetman. Wentworth stopped, and waited while the Yee Yicks crowded about the body, cursing it and the Hip Leungs. Ko Fan'chi said firmly, "Brothers, this is a dangerous business. I do not recognize this Hip Leung highbinder. The Hip Leungs must have imported hatchetmen in addition to their own. Our new brother from China, Yee Yong Mi, has spoken wisely. We must act in the morning, after prayer, and wipe out these fiendish Hip Leungs before we ourselves are all exterminated."

"I will examine his token bag," said Yee Yong Mi, the stranger. Bending, he fumbled under the dead man's coat, and drew out a silken sack which had been suspended from the hatchetman's neck.

Sure enough, as every one suspected, the token of the Hip Leungs was in the bag. There were, in addition, several charms against death. A small purse, containing only a few pieces of silver and one silver dollar, proved that the Hip Leung had not been paid for any recent killing.

What interested the alert Wentworth most of all was that the stranger, Yee Yong Mi, took one object from the bag and kept it concealed in his hand without showing it to any of the Yee Yicks, who were too excited about the whole affair to notice what happened. Wentworth alone saw what it was… a tiny king cobra in gold, his hood outstretched as if ready to strike.

The sign of Kong Gai, the King Cobra of Chinatown,

the deadly, mysterious Chinese whose path Jimmy Wentworth had crossed again and again!

What did it mean? Was Kong Gai backing the Hip
Leungs? If so, why? Or was Kong Gai lending, for pay, his
deadly killers? Kong Gai! Anything was possible!

Could the venomous King Cobra have incited this
tong war himself, to reduce both the Yee Yicks and the
Hip Leungs in power, so he could set himself up as the
controlling figure in Chinatown, unafraid even of tong
influence?

The Yee Yicks were becoming more and more unfriendly
in their glances at the white officer. Wentworth had a thousand questions he would have liked to ask; he knew he
could ask none, nor, even if he dared, would the truth be
told him. Only one thing was clear: the Hip Leung hatchetman was Kong Gai's killer, since he carried the sign of
the King Cobra! Jimmy Wentworth thought grimly that
a tong war was bad enough, without having the terrible
Kong Gai mixed up in it.

There was nothing for him to do now, but report the
matter completely to his chief, Captain Dunand. Over the
telephone the captain of detectives said, "It seems to me
you've done a thorough and capable job, Jimmy. You have
been able to tell us the time and the place of the Yee Yick
attack. We'll be there, plenty of us, and round up the whole
outfit of hatchetmen. After that we'll talk some sense into
the heads of the two tongs."

"It looks mighty funny," Jimmy Wentworth insisted.
"I can't make anything out of it, chief. If I had a scrap of
anything to go on, I'd say that this is a lot more than even
a bloody tong war."

"The Chinks won't think it's funny when we pop out on 'em with the riot squad! Shotguns'll make 'em quit laughing, boy. To-night we'll go over the details—"

"I don't like it," the detective sergeant insisted. "Here they let me in on their plans—"

"By accident!"

"And tell me how everything is going to break—"

"They didn't know you understood Chinese."

"And Kong Gai has something to do with it all. He knows I understand the language—"

"And a lucky thing for us that you do, boy. Stop worrying! By to-morrow we'll have all of the Yee Yick and Hip Leung highbinders down here in the Hall of Justice and the battle will be over before it starts. Kong Gai may not be in this at all, Jim. The dead hatchetman may have worked for him before, and gone over to the Hip Leungs for more pay."

Just the same, knowing the devilish cunning of Kong Gai, the King Cobra, Jimmy Wentworth was as uneasy as ever. What was Kong Gai planning? Why the war between the two tongs? *What was up?*

By night Jimmy Wentworth knew no more than before, but as he left his beat to confer with Captain Dunand, he was still just as positive that something was in the wind, something evil and deadly. And behind it, involved in some terrible way the detective was unable to fathom, was the ominous figure of Kong Gai.

4

THE HORROR AT PIER 134

AT FIVE MINUTES to eight, when the members of the Hip Leung tong were walking up the street, well guarded by hatchetmen, toward the shop of Lee Wong Chung, Jimmy Wentworth, several blocks away, saw a covered truck drive slowly past him. The burly driver did not so much as glance at the blue-clad Chinatown detective, although Wentworth knew that the man behind the wheel was Officer Mulcahey.

Inside the lumbering truck, Jimmy knew also, were twenty picked men, including the well-trained riot squad. The gray-haired captain of detectives, unable to resist taking part in this round-up of murderous hatchetmen, was in direct charge.

Captain Dunand's plan was simple. Wentworth had assured him, from his knowledge of Chinese customs, that the attack would take place exactly at the appointed time, unless the strange Yee Yick tongman, Yee Yong Mi, had lied in everything he said. If eight o'clock were determined upon as the time for vengeance, it was because the gods had been consulted. The hour would not be changed.

Therefore, at a minute to eight, the rumbling truck was to stop a hundred feet from the door of Wong Chung's shop. Officer Mulcahey was to get down instantly, and raise the hood over the engine. When he saw the Yee Yicks swarm out from their places of concealment, he was to swear. This was the signal to the blue-coats concealed inside the truck.

The plan was so simple that Wentworth believed it would work. He himself, following Captain Dunand's orders and common sense, was to stay away from the scene until he heard shots, in order to preserve his disguise as being only the Chinatown patrolman.

At three minutes to eight, the Hip Leung tongmen were filing into the shop of Wong Chung, member of the same company.

At two minutes to eight, doors on the far side of the street opened a cautious inch or so, and the beady, drug-inflamed eyes of murderous Yee Yick Sun hatchetmen peered into the daylight.

At exactly one minute to eight, Officer Mulcahey, bending over his engine but missing nothing, cleared his throat warningly.

Eight o'clock! The great bell of the old cathedral struck the hour melodiously. Before the sound died away, and while Mulcahey gave the signal, a Yee Yick darted from a dark doorway, and a watchful Hip Leung hatchetman instantly pulled trigger. The Yee Yick, shot through the heart, whirled around horribly and fell with a thud to the cobbles.

Twenty blue-coats rushed pell-mell out of the truck. Dunand's gun, fired over the heads of the Chinese, stopped the meeting of the rival, vengeful tongmen in the middle of the street. Hip Leungs, armed and prepared, had immediately raced out of Wong Chung's shop.

The riot squad went into action, not to kill, but to capture every one of the hatchetmen.

And down in the gray Hall of Justice, which the riot squad had left only a quarter of an hour before, the emergency gong was beating its summons, telephones were ringing furiously, and the signal of Box 78C, down at Pier 134, was flashing again and again before the startled eyes of the desk sergeant!

Jimmy Wentworth was right; something had happened!

Desk Sergeant Reid, telephone to his ear, shouted even while he was listening: "Box 78C! Pier 134! Motorcycle squad!" and pressed the button which set a piercing whistle blowing all over the building. The whistle which was the signal for the riot squad—and the riot squad was up in Chinatown, out of touch!

Something had happened, something which set every traffic officer's call box to buzzing as Desk Sergeant Reid sent out the warning to stop all traffic. Something which sent motorcycles, throttles wide open, roaring down toward the wharves to Pier 134. Something which forced Sergeant Reid to organize a makeshift riot squad composed of detectives, patrolmen off duty, and rookies, and rush them in automobiles toward the bay. Something so unexpected and seemingly impossible that the guards in the Federal Reserve Bank unlimbered their Lewis gun—the chopper—and wondered what was coming next. Something so fearful that the San Francisco Mint demanded a detail of soldiers from the Presidio.

Fourteen men were dead, and a million dollars in gold—

gold bars and newly minted gold coins—had been stolen down at Pier 134—at eight o'clock!

THIS IS WHAT happened, while Captain Dunand and the riot squad were breaking up the tong war.

The liner Asamako Maru, from Japan, was warped into Pier 134, with her passengers eager to land, with her flags flying, after an uneventful voyage. Almost before the gangplanks for them were pulled to the ship, stevedores swarmed aboard, forward, where the Asamako Maru's tank had been opened, from which the shipment of gold consigned to several international banks was being taken and checked by the purser.

Down on the pier, the armored car of Whitefield's Express was waiting. The car's body was made of steel, with slits out of which high-powered rifles protruded. The windshield was of bullet-proof glass. The driver's compartment was also furnished with slits, out of which the driver and the seatguard (four other guards rode in the rear, with the gold) could shoot.

Standing near the armored car, alert and watchful, were four motorcycle policemen with their sidecars. Each officer who would ride in the sidecars as convoy for the gold on its way to the Mint was armed with a chopper. Officials of the consignee bank and the express company waited to check the shipment as it was loaded into the armored car.

While gay and talkative friends and relatives greeted the descending passengers, the lumpers—stevedores—were carrying the small, one hundred-pound wooden boxes containing gold, to the pier. Rope handles fastened through end cleats marked those boxes which held Japanese twenty-yen gold coins; the shipment of Chinese bar gold was without handles, heavier by fifty pounds or more, and more difficult to carry.

Quietly and efficiently, the million dollars in gold were checked as it had been done a thousand times before, and placed, box after box, in the rear of the Whitefield Express car. In a few minutes, with motorcycles ahead and behind, the gold would be on its way to the United States Mint. A million dollars in pure gold!

The Asamako Maru lay at Pier 134; at Pier 132, a hundred feet away, was an old Chinese tramp, the Taipi'ng Shan, rusty and discolored. She had steam up, and was sailing at eight, although obviously she had been slightly delayed. While the gold was being carried to the dock, the Taipi'ng Shan moved slowly away from her berth, her whistle blaring hoarsely once. She swung slowly as the tide hit her, so that the stern moved toward the Asamako Maru's stern, and then the Chinese ship began to churn forward.

As her screw revolved, sending froth to the surface, a cloud of what seemed white-hot steam shot up, almost under the stern of the Asamako Maru. Instantly there was a series of sharp explosions, so like the sound of guns that the police reached for their own weapons, and the White-field Express men leaped into the car and slammed the doors, protecting their gold.

Then, for the fraction of an instant, every eye went toward the stern of the Asamako Maru. A sheet of flame was rising high into the sky—red, lurid flame!

For only the fraction of an instant the police, the express guards, the bank officials, glanced down toward the end of Pier 134... and that instant was their undoing.

From under the pier black-clad men crept—white men, Chinese, half-castes—men with the staring, inflamed eyes of opium-smokers, men with the white, dead expressionless faces of professional killers, men moving their hands and arms with the strange boneless motions of ex-convicts. They must have been concealed under Pier 134 all of the night, waiting, waiting for eight o'clock in the morning, when a million dollars in gold would be taken from the steel tanks of the steamer, and transferred to the armored car of the express company.

Two machine guns in the hands of the black-clad men began to chatter instantly. The sound was covered completely by the noise of the explosions, which continued steadily, and by the shouting of the hundreds of people on the wharf. The sheet of flame reached into the sky like a furnace blast; the whistle of the Asamako Maru began to roar the signal of fire.

A slim, yellow-faced man rose to his feet the moment the machine gun clattered into deadly action. He ran to the armored car, and thrust an oblong object through the slit in the protected driver's compartment, pulling back a spring as he dropped the deadly gas bomb inside. Another of the gang did the same thing in the rear of the car, where four guards were crouched, all looking out of the end slit, toward the explosions and the fire.

A horrible odor of cyanide, sweet and deadly, began to seep at once through the slits. Inside the car, the driver tried to press his foot against the starter, and then fell forward in death agony. The guard beside him writhed on the leather seat, clutching at his throat. In the rear, four men were dying also.

One of the motorcycle officers tried to raise his gun, but the chopper of the deadly assassins cut him down.

Dead men on the planks of the wharf, dead men in the armored car! Seventeen men had been about the armored car or in it, and fourteen of them were already dead. The other three were unconscious, but still alive—O'Hearne, of the police; Jefferson, from the bank, and Richards of the express company.

And as yet no one on Pier 134 realized that anything was amiss!

One of the black-clad killers, with something shining in his hand which was smaller than a gun, was already at work on the bullet-proof glass. In almost no time at all he had made a hole in the glass, and had the door open. As he stepped aside—everything had obviously been perfectly planned to the last detail—two other men ripped the coats from the dead Whitefield guards, took their caps, and shoved the bodies to the pier's floor. One of the men slipped into the driver's seat behind the wheel, and pressed the starter gently, capably.

Already the killers were disappearing from the wharf.

On the far side of the pier, a power boat slid against the piles. One by one the black-clad men, after crossing under the floor of the pier, dropped into her, and she slid silently out toward open water. At the end of the dock the power boat crept closer to the shadows, and let the summoned fire tug race past her. Then, looking like any inoffensive pleasure craft, with no one in sight except the man at the wheel, the power boat continued quietly out into the stream, headed northward as if toward the boat club.

The Whitefield car, without any fuss, was driven off the

dock. Here and there men were running toward the pier, attracted by the explosions, the sight of flames, and the sudden blaring of the Asamako Maru's whistle, but no one paid any attention to the armored car, since all were intent on reaching the scene of the real excitement.

The armored car was driven along the water front (it went past Officer 1187, who supposed that since no guards followed the Whitefield car that it was going somewhere, empty, to pick up a shipment) until it came to the deserted streets lined with black, silent warehouses filled with coffee and spices and goods from the Orient.

Here a moving van was waiting. The armored car was driven up a runway, inside. Carpets were thrown over it, and furniture lashed to the roof of the van were piled about the rear of the armored car. The door of the van was not closed, but, so cleverly did the black-clad men do their work again that the presence of the express machine could have only been discovered if the carpets and chairs and tables were removed in the search!

By the time the people who had rushed out on the pier saw the shambles, by the time the report was made to headquarters, the van was lumbering toward Pier 188. Here, after being weighed, the van was driven on one of the ferries which, after crossing the bay, proceeds up the river toward the inland cities. The driver and his assistants, burly men (with the tinge of red in their eyes, however), left the truck when the river boat's paddle-wheel began to churn, and went on deck.

By the time the word was rushed to the head of the detective bureau, up in Chinatown, the river craft was puffing along across the bay, and a million dollars in gold had disappeared.

A million dollars vanished, fourteen men dead, and three more expected to die, and not a clew!

5

THE FIEND OF CHINATOWN

IT WAS A grim assembly which was meeting in Captain Dunand's office. The gray-haired captain of detectives said, "Excuse me, gentlemen," and answered the demand of the telephone.

He said into the instrument, "Hello. Dunand... Eh? What?... Well, *Daily Sentinel*, I can't tell you any more than your reporter knows... What? I can't help it if you are the city editor. You've got the names of the men who were killed, and how much was stolen; if we knew who did it, we wouldn't be sitting here!... What? It would be better if we went out and made some arrests, instead of sitting around talking? Oh, you were just speakin' to yourself, eh? Well, then you don't need me!"

Dunand banged up the receiver.

"We're in for a ride," he snapped.

The head of Whitefield's Express said thoughtfully, "And you can't blame the papers, captain. A million dollars stolen. Fourteen men—perhaps seventeen—dead. Right under your nose, and while you were giving a party up in Chinatown."

"Party, hell," Dunand shouted. "A tong war!"

In the office was Jerome Whitefield himself, J.J. Knowles,

from the Mint, several representatives from the bank, and Hewitt Sexton from the company which had insured the shipment, and which was out the million dollars.

It was the latter who said, "I know how you feel, Whitefield, at having six of your men murdered. All ex-army officers, weren't they? I knew a couple of them—fine fellows. But no good can come of blaming the police, can there? Let's go over this thing soberly, gentlemen, and have Captain Dunand tell us what he has learned, and what deductions he has drawn."

Dunand said, "I've put my best men on the case. In spite of the tong war—and there'll be more killings by night, unless all signs fail—I've taken Sergeant Wentworth off his beat up there and put him to work. As—as a matter of fact, he asked for the assignment," the gray-haired captain admitted somberly. "He is of the opinion…" Pausing, Captain Dunand said wearily, "That's putting the cart before the horse. As Mr. Sexton suggests, gentlemen, I'll give you what facts are at our disposal.

"The gold shipment of the Asamako whatever-her-name-is was stolen at approximately eight this morning, when she docked. Some one on a Chinese freighter threw a chemical into the water when the Chinese ship was leaving. We have determined that this was a compound which bursts into flame, and continues to explode, when it touches water. At the same time, during the diversion, the attack was made on the armored car. Guard Richards, who was conscious for a few moments while the surgeon was preparing to operate and remove the bullets, says that he thinks more than twenty men were involved in the attack.

"Richards, as Mr. Sexton knows, accompanies the armored Whitefield car in an automobile, and is in charge of the protection of the shipment. He was unable to identify any of the murderers; he says that he was looking toward the stern of the Jap liner, at the flames, and the first thing he knew was when he was hit. By a machine gun bullet. We are aware of that, of course.

"The car was driven away under her own power. Detective Williams found the piece of glass which was cut out of the door of the driver's compartment. And, gentlemen, that is absolutely all we know, except—"

"Except what, captain?"

Dunand rubbed his hand over his chin. "You tell 'em, Jimmy," he said wearily, and the men in conference with the captain of detectives turned toward the young detective sergeant.

Jimmy Wentworth said softly, "There isn't anything really to tell. It is all conjecture. However, my theory is this. The gold was stolen either by Chinese, or by men directed by Chinese."

"WHY?" JEROME WHITEFIELD said sharply. "It sounds to me like a gangster outrage, committed by daring men, totally without fear."

"That is my opinion also," Sexton agreed.

Knowles, from the Mint, said nothing, but continued listening.

"Firstly," Jimmy went on, "there was a riot in Chinatown—which the police knew about!—and it was scheduled to occur at eight o'clock. Secondly, we are practically positive that the sodium—the chemical—was thrown from the Taipi'ng Shan, which is a Chinese ship. Thirdly, three-quarters of the gold—all of the gold bars, in fact, according to Mr. Knowles here—was sent to this country from China. Fourthly, the wholesale murders sound like the work of a fiend, and I know a Chinese fiend. Those are my reasons for saying that the crime was committed by Chinese."

Whitefield said, "Then, Sergeant Wentworth, all you need to do is to get this Chinaman. Why hasn't it been done?"

"If I knew where he was," said Jimmy Wentworth quietly, "I'd have arrested him six months ago."

"It shouldn't be difficult to get one Chinaman!"

"One devil," Captain Dunand grunted.

"What's his name?" Whitefield asked. He added unpleasantly, "Or don't you know that, either, sergeant?"

"Kong Gai," said Jimmy Wentworth. "He poisons with cobra venom. He has kidnaped white women and children. He drugged the girl I am to marry, and kept her in his power for months, to satisfy a grudge. He controls the opium smoking in the State. He almost wrecked the canning industry, when he tried out a form of racket white gangsters taught him. The Federals are positive he is behind every smuggling of drugs, every smuggling of coolies and hatchetmen into this country. That's the sort of man Kong Gai is. A fiend. A horror. Nor do we know when he is about to commit a crime, except, as I think happened in this case, he tells us for some reason of his own."

"Wentworth believes that the tong war—several Chinese have been killed already, gentlemen—was incited by Kong Gai to occur at the exact time the attack was to be made on the shipment of gold."

"It doesn't make sense," Whitefield protested. "Why would he do that?"

"He knew," Jimmy Wentworth answered slowly, "that the one chance of failure lay in the police—in the riot squad."

"Which means," the insurance man, Sexton, said, "that he—this Kong Gai—was afraid the police might arrive on the scene before the armored car and the gold had been driven away?"

"Possibly," said Jimmy Wentworth. "That's the way it sounds, when you first think about it. The men Sergeant Reid assigned to go to the pier got away rapidly, but the riot squad would have beaten this time by three or four minutes. It was necessary to collect men, and use a patrol wagon. The riot car, on the other hand, would have been on the way before the warning bell stopped clanging.

"There's another angle. The armored car must have been driven through the streets. It might have been possible for the riot car, rushing toward the bay, to have seen it. The Whitefield machine, in my opinion, was driven along the water front, where it would not attract any attention, and the murderers wanted the riot car out of the way."

"That's a grand deduction," Whitefield growled. He threw away his unlighted cigar. "As a vague theory, it's a beauty!"

The telephone jangled again, and Captain Dunand answered it. He said, "Yes, Reid?" to the desk sergeant, and then listened a moment. After that he said, "I'll want him right now; call him off his beat."

To the men in the room, Dunand said shortly, "Officer 1187, patrolling the water front, reports that he saw a

Whitefield car drive north along the Embarcadero, gentlemen. He says that he observed nothing unusual about it, and that the men in the driver's compartment wore the usual Whitefield uniforms—"

"An armored car can't vanish into thin air!" Whitefield cried. "Where is it?"

"The State traffic officers have already been warned," Captain Dunand told the express company owner. "They will stop every car bearing the slightest resemblance to your machine, no matter what the color is. Every avenue of escape is closed, although—"

"The car," said Sexton, "was probably taken to an old shed, or an abandoned garage, owned by the gang. There the steel sides were cut through, and the gold removed—"

"What will they do with the bodies of the four guards?" Whitefield broke in. "My four men, dead without having a chance to fight! Killed by poison gas, just as the two men in the front seat were gassed! Captain Dunand, those men have wives, families. The poor women don't want to believe their men are dead..."

Dunand said wearily, "All we can do is wait, Mr. Whitefield. Sooner or later the bodies will be recovered... somewhere."

"If Kong Gai is behind this crime, the bodies will be thrown in the bay, when the tide is going out, and never found," Jimmy Wentworth said. "Or—"

"Or what, sergeant?"

The Chinatown detective had been about to say, "Or he will play some devilish trick with the bodies, something he considers a joke on the police and on all white men." Instead, he said quietly, "Or he may become careless, and show us the trail by simply leaving the bodies wherever the armored car is opened, sir."

"And what good will that do?"

"In solving a crime, anything we learn helps. As it is, we are almost completely in the dark."

WHITEFIELD STOOD UP. "I'm going to employ private detective agencies," he announced. "A million dollars stolen, white men murdered, and all you do is sit here, talking!"

Gently, Jimmy Wentworth said, "Captain Dunand has put the case in my charge, Mr. Whitefield. We are doing everything possible. All I ask is one thing. Since we have told you in confidence what our one theory is, please say nothing about it to whichever agency you hire. I mean by this that I do not want any private detectives in Chinatown, sir."

"I see no reason not to tell them to rip the roof off Chinatown!"

The young detective explained, "If they do that. I'll never learn a thing. Kong Gai will be on the alert. I have sources of information in Chinatown. I have one scant clew to run down. If you want this crime cleared up, if you want the murderers brought to justice, say nothing about Chinese being involved."

"Rubbish!"

"Sergeant Wentworth is right," said Dunand.

"You are only trying to cover your failure to get on the trail of these arch-criminals by talking about Chinese," Whitefield blurted. "You can't stop me from telling what I know—"

Shrugging Wentworth said, "If you do send private

detectives into Chinatown, I'll know within an hour whether Kong Gai is the man behind the crime. It will make my own job easier, but—"

"But what?"

"I hate to see more murders. Because if Kong Gai is involved in the theft of the gold, your detectives will be knifed before they are out of sight of Grace Cathedral!"

Wentworth stood up.

"I'm not bluffing," he said. "Now you can suit yourself." Young, competent, he dominated the meeting. "You think the police are being lax. That is not so, sir. Although I am working on a Chinese angle, the remainder of the department are all starting from scratch, working with open minds. I feel strongly that this tong war is part of the plot, and I am going to find out about it."

The representative from the United States Mint, Knowles, had never taken his eyes from the young detective. He held up his hand now, silencing a new outburst from Whitefield. It was obvious that of the three men, Whitefield, Sexton, and himself, that Knowles was the most important. Also, that he was actually in charge, and that the other two respected his opinions. So far, he had voiced none at all. He looked at Wentworth, his keen eyes fastened on the detective's face.

"Sergeant," he said, "I have listened to everything you have said. Let me ask you one question? Do you believe that Kong Gai—if he is responsible—will attempt to market the gold bars? Do you hope to catch him when he does?"

Jimmy Wentworth almost smiled. He said, "No, Mr. Knowles. A man who is smart enough to start a tong war to get the police out of the way, a man who is capable of planning every detail of the theft, a man who was able to escape, untouched, with the entire shipment of gold, is certainly going to be intelligent enough to realize that gold cannot be sold!"

"I wanted to see if you knew that," said Knowles. "Gold, pure gold, cannot be sold. That is true. I will be in my office to-morrow. Will you come and see me, please?" The man from the Mint turned to his companions. "I am satisfied to leave this case in the hands of Detective Wentworth. He is one of the very few men I know who understands that there is no way of selling a large quantity of pure gold. I believe that the case is in excellent hands, and I advise strongly that nothing be done to interfere with Wentworth's investigations."

Whitefield bit off the end of a fresh cigar.

"You think there's something to all this talk about Chinks, Mr. Knowles?"

"I do," said Knowles crisply. "And I also think Wentworth is the man to ferret it out!"

6

THE TWO COBRAS

JIMMY WENTWORTH MADE his next arrangements carefully. He impressed upon Captain Dunand the necessity of immediate peace in Chinatown. Without a cessation of hostilities, he would have no chance at all really to work on the gold theft and the murders; if peace was not declared at once, valuable time would be lost. Through the police department an ultimatum was delivered to the Yee Yick Suns and the Hip Leungs, and after much verbal argument, delivered through a Chinese interpreter, the two tongs agreed to meet in the neutral chambers of the Suey Chok company—the tong to which the Wangs, father and son, belonged.

Since there was no time to be wasted, the police brought every ounce of pressure to bear, and the meeting was scheduled for the same evening. The Yee Yicks and the Hip Leungs, for the first time in their history, found that even the Chinese Bank, where many had borrowed money to conduct their business, were insistent that they meet and hear what the police had to say. The Chinese Bank had listened to the voice of the great American banks in San Francisco.

In the Suey Chok chambers were the Three Wise Men

of that tong, one of them old, impassive Wang Yu. The Yee Yicks and Hip Leungs were each represented by three men also; one Wise Man, one influential merchant, and one of the younger, vengeful members. When Captain Dunand, the interpreter, and Wentworth, again in blue uniform, entered, they found the Chinese split into different parts of the room. The Yee Yicks stood under a scarlet and blue banner; the Hip Leungs stood near the door; the three Suey Chok Wise Men sat placidly on high teakwood chairs.

"There will be no ceremonial tea," said Wang Yu, the oldest of the Wise Men. "A superior man, in a time of mourning, does not enjoy pleasantries," with this brief introduction, he said sonorously, to open the discussion, "How abundantly do spiritual beings display the powers that belong to them. We look, but do not see the gods; we listen, but do not hear them. Yet they enter into all things, and there is nothing without them. The gods are here. Let the talk commence."

The interpreter said to Captain Dunand, "We talk first, please. Wang Yu say, 'Begin.'"

Jimmy Wentworth stood stolidly, looking his part as the beat patrolman, as Dunand said:

"Gentlemen, there is war between your tongs. I wish to know why."

It was a matter of vengeance, both rival tongs insisted, and had nothing to do with white men nor the police. When this was repeated in English to Dunand (Jimmy Wentworth's face did not indicate that he understood a word) the captain of detectives suggested that the tongmen explain further. This they were not anxious to do, since it would tell the police that the killings had been determined upon in the tong meetings, and make them all guilty.

Then Dunand, who had been coached by Wentworth, asked, "Who was killed first?"

Bit by bit, the tale of murder was related.

Finally Dunand said, "And this stranger, named Yee Yong Mi, a Yee Yick, told you how the first man was killed by being thrown down his cellar stairs. Do you believe Yee Yong Mi?"

Yee Yong Mi had come to them all the way from China to tell the tale. He was a brother. His letters to them were signed by officials high in the tong.

"Where is Yee Yong Mi now?"

He was in another room; he was one of the guards for the delegation.

"Send for him," ordered Captain Dunand.

When the stranger Yee Yick entered the room, Jimmy Wentworth saw that another hatchetman was with him, and that this second man slipped out of the door and down the hall toward the steps. The Chinatown detective caught old Wang Yu's wink, but saw no way to inform Dunand what had happened.

Through the interpreter, Dunand went to work.

YES, SAID THE Yee Yick, his name was Yee Yong Mi. He had been born in Canton, in the year of the Black Rat, which made him twenty-seven years old now. His father had been a Yee Yick member also, although his father was now dead. The Yee Yick company, with headquarters in Canton, had selected him to bring a sacred message to the Yee Yick tong in San Francisco. He did not know what was in the writing. Yes, now that things had happened, he could guess, although he himself had not killed any one.

Wentworth whispered in Dunand's ear, while Yee Yong Mi was talking, "Make him prove he belongs to the tong, chief. He's got to have the Yee Yick charm in his token bag." Jimmy Wentworth wanted to see more than the tong symbol! How he could accomplish this, he did not know.

"We must have proof of all this," said Dunand gravely. "Also, since you came to this country, the police wish to see your papers of entrance."

Yee Yong Mi showed his immigration certificate grandly; it seemed to be in order. Then he launched into a suave oration about the Yee Yicks, and the Wise Man of that tong agreed that their brother was a member in good standing.

When Dunand demanded again that definite proof be shown, Yee Yong Mi's face showed both distrust and anger, possibly because his word was doubted.

After a word with his tongmen, old Wang Yu said tonelessly, "Yee Yong Mi will have the sacred sign of his tong in his charm bag. If we may see it, we can inform the police that Yee Yong Mi is a true Yee Yick, although, for my part, I fail to see how it is of any importance to the white men."

"Show the symbol of the sacred Yee Yick god," commanded the Wise Man of the Yee Yicks. "There is no way of understanding white men, Yee Yong Mi. If it will satisfy them, by all means expose it to their gaze."

Yee Yong Mi bowed and drew a silken sack from beneath his jacket. He undid the cord, and it seemed to Wentworth that the Chinese was in no hurry to take out the symbol of the tong, and that Yee Yong Mi gave the appearance of a man waiting for something. The next moment Wentworth was disappointed, for Yee Yong Mi took out a bit of priceless jade carved like a Chinese god.

"I had it from my honorable father," said Yee Yong Mi, and handed the symbol to old Wang Yu.

"It is real," Wang said judicially. "It is—"

A shot crashed through the window of the Suey Chok chamber. Dunand whirled toward the window; Wentworth watched Yee Yong Mi. The eyes of the Yee Yick became bright, and then he turned and rushed to the window. Drawing aside the hanging, he cried, "I see… *hai-ya!*… I see a Hip Leung! I see him run! I see—"

And then he struck out with his left fist.

Jimmy Wentworth, approaching silently, had jerked the charm bag out of Yee Yong Mi's hand, and his gun was thrust into the belly of the slender hatchetman.

Captain Dunand's own gun was out. "Tell everybody to stand still," he ordered. "Nobody's to move!"

The interpreter squeaked the command.

Old Wang Yu said placidly, "Let us wait until we see what this means," and folded his hands.

Wentworth handed the charm bag to his chief. "Spill it on the floor," he said in English. He knew that the two younger Chinese in the room, Yee Yick and Hip Leung alike, could understand English; he must be careful. "Maybe there's more proof in the bag."

According to custom, the rival tongmen had come to the Suey Chok chambers unarmed, but the young Yee Yick glared at the Hip Leung for what appeared to be a violation of the truce, and the Hip Leung glared back venomously as if he were glad that it had happened. Only the guns of the white officers kept the two men from each other's throat.

Old Wang said sharply, "Peace!" and then Dunand held the bag upside down.

Yee Yong Mi's right hand was creeping slowly toward his middle, the fingers working up under the jacket. Wentworth did not dare look to see what came out of the charm bag… and did not need to look, for a great shout went up in the room.

"The Cobra! The King Cobra! Kong Gai!"

On the rug were two little gold cobras, like as peas; cobras coiled to strike, with their hoods outstretched. The symbol of Kong Gai the Evil One.

OLD WANG SPOKE first. Fear must have been in his heart, but could not be detected in his manner. "No man," he said, "can serve two masters. Is Yee Yong Mi a servant of Kong Gai the Deadly, or is he a member of the Yee Yick Sun?"

"It is a plot," the Wise Man of the Yee Yicks shrilled. "Oh, Hip Leungs, will you say with us that there shall be peace? We will worship at your shrines, and you at ours. For we have fought only to give pleasure to the Evil One."

"Peace," said the Hip Leung's Wise Man. "We, also, wish peace. We have all been fools, oh Yee Yick! For a man like this Yee Yong Mi came to us also, and poisoned our ears—"

Never once did Wentworth take his eyes from the slender hatchetman. At the exact instant that Yee Yong Mi's hand flashed out from under his jacket, with a heavy assassin's knife glinting viciously, Jimmy Wentworth drove his left fist squarely at the Chinese's jaw, a terrific uppercut. Down went the hatchetman, the knife falling noiselessly to the rug.

It was all that Wentworth and Dunand could do to keep the Yee Yicks and Hip Leungs off the unconscious body.

Wentworth whispered hastily to his chief, and Dunand said at once, "Gentlemen, in view of what has happened, we will make no arrests of men in either tong. We, in return, ask that nothing be said of the true reason for declaring peace. Say anything you wish, but do not mention this Yee Yong Mi, or Kong Gai, or what has taken place! The police have something else to learn. If you say nothing you will help us."

"It is agreed," said the two tongs, and called upon their gods to witness the promise.

When they were leaving the tong room, Wentworth said to Captain Dunand, "When the hatchetman sneaked out, I was pretty certain, chief. Yee Yong Mi was taking no chances that we might force a declaration of peace, so Kong Gai's hatchetman—employed by the Yee Yicks, I suppose—went across the street and fired into the room. He fired high, careful not to hit any one, although he'd probably have liked to get you or me. The bullet just touched the upper pane. I saw the hole in the hanging. If we hadn't seen the little cobras, the Yee Yicks would have walked out of the conference. Now are you convinced Kong Gai robbed the shipment of gold, chief?"

"I—I don't know what to think, Jimmy! Say, boy, I think this, anyhow; we ought to take Yee Yong Mi along with us for questioning."

"Waste of time. He wouldn't talk. Even if he knows what happened, although it isn't likely Kong Gai told him more than his part in the performance. It would only show Kong

Gai we're wise to him. Leave Yee Yong Mi to the Yee Yicks. His brothers will take good care of him."

"We can't permit another murder, Jimmy."

"Yee Yong Mi's? They won't kill him, chief. They'll give him a—a little lesson, maybe, and keep him out of sight, and then send him back to China. By that time, if we have any luck, maybe we'll have this gold robbery solved."

"Find Kong Gai, and you find the gold!"

"That's it, chief."

7

A NEW YEAR CUSTOM

IN THE MORNING, after a night in which he pondered in vain for a clew, Jimmy Wentworth went to the Mint. He was admitted to Knowles's office at once. On the government man's desk were many boxes, tins, sacks, and other objects.

"Good morning, sergeant," Knowles said pleasantly. "I'm glad to inform you that I have been able to keep Whitefield from raising a fuss. You can't blame him. His finest men murdered. And it sets a bad example. It shows that the armored cars are vulnerable. However, Whitefield is already at work on a different type of slit, which will be kept closed except when a gun is thrust through it, and that ought to thwart a similar outrage. Now, have you learned anything, sergeant?"

Jimmy Wentworth told him briefly what had transpired in the Suey Chok chambers, and added that no reports had come in concerning the missing Whitefield car, nor the dead guards. Nor, of course, the gold.

"It was the gold I wanted to speak to you about, sergeant. I had no idea that you realized that gold, in any quantity at all, cannot be sold. Certainly not gold bearing the assay marks stamped on it in China. It would necessarily need to be assayed again in the United States, and the instant it was taken to an assay office the robbers would be caught. Now, detective, I asked you to come here to explain a few things about this shipment. I believe it will be helpful."

"I need plenty of help," Jimmy Wentworth admitted with a grin. "We're fighting not only an unknown enemy, sir, but a terrible one."

"That's what I thought. Naturally, any discovery of the gold containers will be valuable to you, eh? I thought so. Let me explain, sergeant.

"The Japanese ship us practically nothing except newly minted twenty-yen gold coins, which are sacked two hundred and fifty pieces, or five thousand, to the sack. One like this—linen. There are ten sacks to the box, making a gross weight of about one hundred and eight pounds. The Japanese boxes, of wood, are tin-lined and soldered; we open them with an ax, by the way. The size never varies, sergeant. Nine and a half inches by eight and a half inches by fifteen inches. However, nothing can be done with these coins in this country by the robbers, unless it is melted down.

"If they attempt to make disposal of anything, it will be the Chinese gold, especially if the thieves were Chinese. Chinese gold, shipped to this country, is in bars, sergeant. Like a chocolate bar—see? Here's one. Sometimes the bars are stamped, sometimes they are unstamped. The bars are packed in threes or fours in red-and-gold enameled tin boxes, and these boxes are cut to fit the gold bars! That is a fact, sergeant. By weight, the tin boxes, which are quite small, range from one hundred and two to one hundred and four taels by Chinese weight. The gold is nine hundred and ninety-five fine. 'Touch,' the Chinese say. Each individual Chinese gold merchant assays his own gold.

"On these red and gold tins, sergeant, is pasted a sheet of paper with the number of the particular tin in Arabic numerals, and on the tin, in Chinese, is written the number of bars contained within, and the name of the gold merchant.

"Let me emphasize this fact: as you know, gold, except as old gold, or jewelry, cannot be sold. There is no fence in this country who would dare handle a million dollars' worth. Even if the bars are melted down, the thieves would not—if they are as clever as you and I believe—attempt to sell the gold in small quantities, losing almost all their profits to the fences. They have some other plan."

Knowles leaned back in his chair.

"I have one thing to request, sergeant. I am not skeptical. Let me know every development in the case. Ultimately, the gold must be disposed of; I may see something in a fact which to others might appear unimportant. Remember, the government is interested in this case. It might be repeated in the case of one of our own shipments of twenty-dollar gold coins."

"It's a rule that a thief hates to let his loot out of sight," said Wentworth, "but suppose the gold is reshipped, somehow, to China—concealed in a cargo?"

"It might be, sergeant. However, the Chinese authorities will examine every shipment except those consigned to reputable firms. I do not believe the gold could be smuggled into any Oriental port—and we are going to make that plain, in the newspapers, to prevent an attempt. That will keep the gold in this country, and it puts it up to you, Wentworth."

"And the one fact I have to go on," said Jimmy, "is that the crime was committed by Chinese, led by a fiend whose name is Kong Gai."

"I asked you here, sergeant, to give you what information I could about the gold itself, and for one other purpose. It is this: the gold is going to be worked back into circulation. Somehow, somewhere, the criminals are going to attempt to market the gold, and, Wentworth, they can't do it! That's where we'll catch them, sooner or later."

"Suppose Kong Gai has thought of a way to sell it, Mr. Knowles?"

"He can't."

"The Evil One has done the impossible before." Jimmy Wentworth smiled grimly, and then said, "Well, I've got to go to work—be on my beat."

"You are going to stay right in Chinatown?"

"It's the only place I can learn anything."

UP AND DOWN the steep streets the young detective paced, as if nothing had happened. The truce had been confirmed by the two tongs, and Chinatown was as busy as ever. To celebrate the signing of peace, the Yee Yicks and Hip Leungs intended giving a great feast, in which birds' nest soup and duck dumplings and braised squid served in a gravy of pigs' ears would figure.

There would be many speeches and protestations of friendship and love undying by the same men who yesterday were willing to murder one another.

Chinatown was again itself. The alleys throbbed with business. Children in yellow and red and blue played in the sunny doorways. Flat-breasted matrons padded into the shops. Tourists wandering under the lanterns spoke feelingly about the peaceful attitude of the Chinese.

The newspapers' excitement continued, the flames fed by plenty of fuel.

Late in the morning, the body of one of the armored car guards was found floating in the bay near the east shore. The Coast Guard experts stated that, according to the drift and tide, the body had probably been thrown from a boat, perhaps near Pier 134 itself.

The police boat Eben Prentice dashed about, searching for other bodies, but found none.

At five in the afternoon the second body was discovered, two hundred miles down the coast!

Since the government itself was vitally interested, the destroyer Hemingway was wirelessed, and the swift craft altered its course and, at eight in the night, stopped the Chinese freighter Taipi'ng Shan at sea—and learned exactly nothing.

At midnight the police at Sacramento, a hundred miles eastward from San Francisco and a hundred miles from the coast, found the third gassed guard, dead from the same deadly poison, and the following morning, seventy miles north of the city, the fourth body was found on the highway!

North, south, east, and west—which way had the murderers gone?

It seemed impossible for the armored car to have escaped the cordon of State officers, and it was impossible. On the third day an abandoned car was reported to the Stockton police; it was seen on a deserted road near the river. And the abandoned car was the Whitefield armored automobile, with the steel neatly cut through, and the gold vanished.

The men of Kong Gai had taken the gold, and disappeared without a trace. They might have gone anywhere except to sea. They might have gone north toward Canada, south to Mexico, or east over the Sierras… but they were gone.

Grimly the State police followed every highway, questioning at gas stations; all week long the newspapers demanded arrests. Dunand's best men were unable to pick up a shred of information. Again and again Jimmy Wentworth sought to discover Kong Gai's secret lair, to no avail. The Wangs, father and son, were able to furnish no information of any nature.

A second week, and a third passed, with Chinatown placid, and Jimmy Wentworth baffled.

Only O'Hearne, of the three men who had not died instantly on Pier 134, struggled back to life, and he was unable to give any description of the attackers. There was absolutely nothing to go on!

THE LILIES OF the new year began to bloom. Chinese children filched firecrackers from the long strings which would be exploded to frighten away devils. The Chinese of the district paid all their past debts, that they might not lose face by owing money after the fresh year. Wentworth was given presents by the merchants: a glazed duck wrapped in bright paper; a rock from the Sacred Mountains; a square of pink-and-yellow cake made with addled eggs. From the Yee Yick Sun and the Hip Leung tong came an enormous watch, engraved "To the Peacemaker" on the cover. On the morning of the new year, with open house being held in every shop, Wentworth's progress along the street was slow...

"Honorable officer of the law," called young Wang Chen-p'o as Wentworth was passing the bowl shop, "we have a small present for you. Will you enter?"

Smiling, Jimmy Wentworth went inside. Old Wang, dressed in his best, was behind the counter; he bowed ceremoniously to the white detective, and accepted the silver-handled writing brush which Wentworth gave him in honor of the new year.

"We, also, have a miserable offering for you, my son," the old man said in Chinese, as he gave Wentworth a magnificent jade ring. "Wear it because we love you, my friend. And it comes to me that we have another present for you." The ancient Oriental smiled as placidly as before. "Yes, it may be a present of value. My son, months ago we lent Gee Ming a sum of money. He is not a good man, Gee Ming, but his wife is a relative of my cousin in China. A hundred dollars in gold. And to-day, to save face, Gee Ming returned this money."

Wentworth did not see the point to all this. Did Wang Yu mean to give him the hundred? He couldn't take it, of course.

"Gee Ming," said old Wang, "has saved face. He said to me, 'Say nothing of this money' and therefore, being curious, I have learned that Gee Ming also paid three other men. Now where did Gee Ming get such a sum?"

"Hatchetman?" Jimmy Wentworth asked.

"No. Coward. He departed from here four months ago,

to work as a laborer. Do laborers have several hundred dollars in gold?"

Wentworth was listening very attentively.

"Making a long story short, Jim," said young Wang Chen-p'o, "Gee Ming was engaged, together with a few more men, four months ago, as a common laborer. He is leaving to-night, for wherever he's going. I don't know where it is. But, James, Gee Ming is so virtuous now that he hasn't had a drink of *ng ki po,* and hasn't hit the pipe. If I were you, Jimmy—which is what my honorable father is indicating in his roundabout way, with his usual politeness—if I were you, I think I'd see where Gee Ming is going."

"Why?" Jimmy Wentworth demanded, his eyes beginning to shine.

Chen-p'o shrugged. "Firstly, because he is secretive, and secondly because my father is intelligent. Gee Ming, according to my father, has callouses on his hands, such as come from handling a pick, and Gee Ming said, 'In the mountains, one has trouble sleeping.' Then—"

"You believe Gee Ming is working in a mine."

"I'll make a dick out of you yet, Jimmy! Of course, he's been doing it for several months, long before the gold was stolen, but it is said that the eyes of an evil man see far ahead. Such a complicated plan is the kind Kong Gai would select. You know his ways."

"Can I get a look at Gee Ming without his seeing me?" Jimmy asked.

Hours later, detectives supplied with a description of Gee Ming were at every ferry entrance. Jimmy Wentworth himself dressed in rough clothing, watched the gates through which eastbound passengers must go if they take the most-traveled route toward the Sierras.

Captain Dunand insisted that it was a wild goose chase, based only on the fact that gold came out of mines, and a Chinaman was a miner. Knowles, at the Mint, said that crooks had never operated a fake mine in order to market stolen gold—never before. He admitted that the thieves could do it without detection.

"Some mines are equipped with apparatus for making bars or bricks," he said to the Chinatown detective. "Your Kong Gai could smelt the gold, and feed it, little by little, through the assay offices and down to us, where we would buy it without question, since it would bear the assay stamp. You haven't much to go on, sergeant, although it is the first clew any one has picked up. Do you want a few Federal operatives to go along?"

"I'd rather have a look-see myself," Jimmy said. "I don't want to frighten them off—if there's anything to it. It is a shot in the dark, sir, but I have been listening and watching in Chinatown all month, and it is the first shred which might work out to be anything. I'm not counting on it. It is simply a case of not neglecting anything."

And so, later, Jimmy Wentworth was sitting in the smoker of an eastbound train. Several seats ahead of him, sucking coconut candy, was Gee Ming, the supposedly penniless Asiatic who had nevertheless saved face by paying his debts on Chinese New Year.

8

HANGTOWN ATTACKS

SLIDING THROUGH THE brush like a snake, Jimmy Wentworth approached the cabin in the Sierra cañon. It was
broad daylight, and the dazzling sun half-blinded him as
he advanced.

To have followed Gee Ming, who had been met by a
buckboard driven by another Chinese or half-caste, when
Gee Ming had left the train after midnight, had been
entirely impossible, but in the morning the manager of the
town assay office had given Wentworth the information
he desired; that the old Grizzly Mine had been reopened
by some syndicate, and that it had a tough looking gang
of miners.

That was all the detective needed to know. The assay
office man had driven Wentworth within a mile of the
mine, where Wentworth left the battered automobile and
continued on foot. He kept off the road, but did not see a
soul on it.

The assayer was curious, but Jimmy Wentworth did not
enlighten him, although he felt that the man was probably making an accurate guess of what Wentworth was
after. Jenkins, the assay office man, had already told Jimmy
Wentworth that the Grizzly Mine owners had not brought

any gold to him, and that people in the town believed the Grizzly was worked out.

Cautiously, Wentworth came to his knees, and then to his feet, peering inside the cabin.

At first glance, there seemed nothing out of the way. In one corner was a bunk, in another the cook stove, over which a Chinese—not Gee Ming—was stirring a pot. There was a large table in the room. Obviously it was where the men ate. The cook hummed to himself as he stirred. Then Wentworth saw, beside the cook's bunk, a shining opium tin—smuggled, bearing no government stamp. The tin was almost full. Camp cooks could not afford such a supply of opium.

While Wentworth spied, his ears alert to catch any sound of footsteps, the cook turned away from the stove. Still humming, he reached inside his greasy black jacket, and drew out his charm sack.

Instead of hanging in soft silken folds, it appeared stiff, oblong. And while the Chinatown detective watched, the cook undid the cord, and drew out a red-and-gold lacquered box, bearing black characters in Chinese... a tin such as had been stolen at Pier 134, a tin which had contained Chinese gold bars!

Opening the red-and-gold box, the cook removed nothing more dangerous than a felt-wrapped pipe, into which he put a pinch of silky Oriental tobacco flavored with opium, and, sitting on the edge of the bunk, smoked in perfect comfort.

Here was proof! Somewhere about the Grizzly Mine was the stolen shipment of gold. What, also, was more reasonable to suppose but that the mine workers were the servants of Kong Gai who had done the stealing and murdering?

Silently Wentworth stole away. He had learned what he wanted to learn. The idea of capturing twenty or more desperate, opium-inflamed men was utterly ridiculous; it would only result in complete failure. On the other hand, Jimmy Wentworth did not know if there was a Kong Gai spy in the village at the railroad, who would report the arrival of strange men, either by train or automobile. In which case the mine workers—the servants of the King Cobra—would vanish, either taking the gold or leaving it securely concealed.

Back in the village, the detective made up his mind. He again sought out the assayer, Jenkins.

"Look here," he said. "I think you've guessed what I'm doing up here, since I come from San Francisco and I'm looking into gold mines. Well, you are right. It's the missing gold shipment—and the murderers! If I send to the city for help, the fiends will be tipped off. If I try to make an arrest myself, that'll be my finish. You know what happened, Mr. Jenkins. The worst crime in years. Men shot down in cold blood. Now, I haven't the slightest authority to ask it, but I need assistance, and the sooner the better. I'm absolutely positive the gold is at the Grizzly Mine. Will the people here be willing to surround the mine? They don't need to do anything more, unless the Chinese start something—"

"Stranger," drawled Jenkins, "My grandfather came here in '50. We've all been living here a long time, and we're all native sons. They call this place Hangtown, because we hanged a sluice-box robber back in '51. We're white men, sergeant, and we read the daily papers. When do you want to go?"

"I don't want to expose any of you to danger—"

"When do we go!" Jenkins snapped.

Jimmy Wentworth grinned. "Get your men," he said.

When Jenkins picked up the old-fashioned telephone, and began to crank it to call central—who was the proprietor of the general store—the Chinatown detective slipped out of the assay office. In a few minutes he was standing where he could see the one Chinese laundry in Hangtown, but where the Orientals could not see him.

FOR FIVE MINUTES nothing happened and then two white men marched down the plank walk past the laundry; two bearded men carrying Winchesters, in high spirits. In another minute an old Ford raced along the dirt street, carrying three armed men, one of whom, in sheer excitement and despite Jenkins's warning, discharged a thirty-eight into the air.

Out of the stores came other Californians, as Jenkins's message came to them. The Hangtown barber rushed into the street with a bear gun. Behind him, his face half-shaven, hurried his patron on the way home to get his own weapon. A rider came tearing on horseback down the street, head low, gun-scabbard under his knee.

White men were out to avenge murder, white men breathing the desperate spirit of the days of gold.

Wentworth thrilled to the response to his plea. It would be necessary for the town constable to swear these men in as deputies. It was possible that some of the men would be dead from Chinese bullets. But Wentworth's heart leaped at the way the Hangtown men were responding.

In against the walls of the building a Chinese was scurrying. He slipped inside the laundry, and Wentworth heard his shrill, excited voice: "They go to the place-where-gold-is-tested," the Asiatic screamed." Come, brothers! We go by the hill road and tell what we have seen!"

The same Chinese rushed out, followed by two others. In the alley beside the laundry was an ancient machine—which popped and banged and rattled as the Asiatics started it.

Wentworth waited until the old machine was opposite him. Then, gun out, he leaped to the running board, and while his gun covered the three jammed in the front seat, he snapped off the ignition.

"Don't move," he ordered in Cantonese.

The driver's hand was working into his coat sleeve. Where he kept his assassin's knife. Wentworth did not want to fire; he brought the heavy butt of his gun down on the Chinese's head, but while he was doing this two other knives were in the air.

The nearest knife was flashing in the air when a gun cracked, and the knife dropped from the bloody hand holding it.

Up tore a mounted man, waving his gun.

"Right through the palm," he shouted. "Shall we hang 'em here, like my granddad used to do, or save 'em for Sunday?"

"We'll lock them up," Jimmy Wentworth said. "Lay off the hanging talk, old man. That will be done in San Quentin. And thanks for the help!"

"Any time, any time," the rider shouted jovially. "You're

th' stranger Jenkins told me about, huh? Ready to go, mister? The clans is already gathered!"

At half past five when the sun was sliding down into the Sierra peaks in a red haze, forty grim-faced men circled the cabins of the Grizzly Mine. They advanced step by step, rifles ready. Wentworth had warned them that the men of Kong Gai would be opium-users, jail-birds, Chinese, and desperate men, and that they would have the machine guns which were used on the guards at Pier 134. The Californians did not seem alarmed. They promised to show Wentworth some real shooting if a defense were attempted.

How good this shooting would be the Chinatown detective realized when a watchful Chinese saw at last the approaching white men, and, shouting, turned to run and give the alarm. One of the Californians beside Wentworth leveled his rifle, and fired. The Chinese dropped.

"He ain't hurt, much," said the mountaineer. "I only knocked off one of his toes, even if he thinks he's dead."

Out of the eating cabin streamed men. Some were armed with only knives, which they jerked out as they ran. Others were drawing guns.

Wentworth cried, "You are under arrest! Surrender! If you fire, we will attack!" He repeated this instantly in Cantonese, to the amazement of the posse.

Some one cried, "What's this mean? Who are you?"

Then another voice shrieked, "Wentworth! *Sha!* Kill! Out of the way!"

Up went the muzzle of a Lewis gun, but before the chopper's trigger could be pressed, the machine gunner fell with a dozen bullets in him. Another of the gang reached for the gun. Before his fingers touched it he was writhing on the hard, sun-baked earth.

The motley horde wavered.

"I warned you," Wentworth shouted. "Drop your knives and guns! Throw the machine gun out in front of you!"

THE CALIFORNIANS WERE acting with great restraint. Wentworth had feared that the first sign of resistance would mean the wiping out of the entire gang, even if some of the native sons were killed in the battle.

The Chinese who had demanded Wentworth's death screamed now, "Here is only death, brothers! We are honest men! Nothing can be proved against us!"

Wentworth laughed grimly.

"Then—surrender," he demanded.

The Californians took no chances. One by one they searched the Chinese and ex-convicts for weapons, and then tied each one separately, using a coil of rope in the supply cabin.

Jimmy Wentworth went up to the leader of the Grizzly Mine gang. He said gravely, "Why have you a machine gun?"

"White men tried to rob Chinese," whined the Asiatic, although his eyes burned with rage.

"White men were killed with a machine gun, in San Francisco, at Pier 134," said the Chinatown detective. "I arrest you, and these men, for robbery and murder."

The Chinese spat.

"Prove it," he said shortly. "We will have lawyers—many lawyers. White lawyers. We laugh at you, oh fool!"

"You and Kong Gai?" Wentworth asked slyly.

The Asiatic spat again, this time trying to reach the

white man's face with his spittle. He cursed horribly in Chinese.

Wentworth walked over to the cook, and, while the man glared hatred, took the charm sack from under the cook's jacket. "This," he said, showing the Californians the red-and-gold box, "contained one hundred and two taels of fine Chinese gold—and it is enough to hang them all."

The gang began to curse the cook. Many of the renegade white men had long prison records. Even if they did not swing, they knew that it meant life, as three-time losers, in Folsom. On the rock pile. The cook began to whimper.

Wentworth said quietly, "Now, where have you hidden the gold?"

Even the frightened half-castes, having less courage than the others, began to smile; perhaps it was not as bad as they supposed, and they might be able to bargain. It was well known how much white men loved gold.

Gee Ming sneered, "Try and find it, fool!"

"It is safely hidden?" Wentworth asked.

"Where no white monkey will ever look!"

"String a couple up by their toes and we'll find out where it is," said one of the Californians. "That's the way our grandfathers worked it."

"The Chinese," said Jimmy, "won't talk."

"Try it on th' white scum," suggested Jenkins. "They'll talk! They're a crumby lookin' lot, anyhow."

Wentworth said, "They don't know where the gold is," and, from the expressions on the ex-convicts' faces, he knew that he was right. In the same sober voice, addressing Gee Ming, he went on, "So the gold is well hidden, Gee Ming?"

The Chinese shivered when Wentworth called him by

name, but snarled, "Well hidden! And you had better hide well also. Kong Gai will take care of you."

"All in good time," Jimmy Wentworth smiled. "So only you, and Kong Gai, and the gods, know where the gold is concealed?"

The Californians wondered what the quiet detective was driving at, always repeating the same question.

In Cantonese, Gee Ming shrilled, "Ask the gods where it is, white slug! Ask and see what they tell you!"

"Now," said Jimmy Wentworth to Jenkins, "I'll find the place where the gold is hidden."

For a moment Wentworth looked around him, toward the cañon and the river. He searched the landscape carefully, and then said, "Mr. Jenkins, do you see that curve in the hill, with a little stream running before it? It looks something like the letter 'U.'"

"Down over yonder?" Jenkins's eyes were wide with astonishment.

"That's the place. It is so situated that favorable *feng shui*—spirits—can blow with the west wind toward it. It's curved in a 'U.' The Chinese call such a place a horn of the dragon. It's the luckiest and safest hiding place, especially if a stream flows in front of it, to carry away the thoughts of any one who might suspect the place of concealment. From time immemorial Chinese bandits have hidden loot in the 'horns of the dragon.' You'll find the gold buried there."

In a man-made cave covered with giant bowlders from the river bottom, the Californians found the vanished shipment—the gold bars and gold coins, heap on heap of shining gold. There also was the diamond glass-cutter, the acetylene tank, the copper can of poison gas.

And for future use, they found a small smelter which would have put Chinese bars and Japanese gold into a shape which could be safely taken to the local assay office as the product of the Grizzly Mine, when it would be announced that the mine had discovered a gold ledge! Kong Gai would have waited until no one save the police remembered the murders on Pier 134, and then would have converted the gold into checks from the United States Mint—and done it safely, and without danger!

It was Jenkins who said, "Sergeant, this's the strangest thing I ever hearn tell about, the way you knew where t' look for the gold. We could've searched for weeks, and not hit on the spot. You know the Chinks' habits!"

"Right," grinned Jimmy. "Now let's herd this gang back to town and lock 'em up. I'll feel better when they're finally in Murderers' Row, Jenkins!"

"Back in '50," mourned the assay man, "we'd of had a grand necktie party! Oh, well, we're civilized now. I'll talk the boys out of it!"

Back in Hangtown, before he sat down to his dinner in the little hotel—as Hangtown's guest—he sent off a telegram to Captain Dunand:

TWENTY-ONE MEN UNDER ARREST HERE
ARRANGE TRANSPORTATION SAN FRANCISCO
ENTIRE GOLD SHIPMENT RECOVERED

He wished that he had also been able to wire that Kong Gai had been found at the mine, although, even without the arch-fiend's capture, it was the real thing the young detective sergeant had accomplished.

Knowing how Dunand would fume at the laconic tele-gram, Jimmy decided it would serve him right to be forced to wait for more complete information; the captain of detectives had called this a wild goose chase. The thought of this made Jimmy Wentworth grin as he entered the hotel dining room, where an old-timer was telling, what would have been done to the gang in the days of '49.

"Now," said the old miner, "all they'll do is hang 'em, boys!"

"Right, old-timer," said Jimmy Wentworth cheerfully.

Hangtown was yelling for a speech, but the young Chinatown detective, blushing, shook his head.

"Three cheers for Jimmy Wentworth," yelled Jenkins, and the Californians gave them with a will.

www.ingramcontent.com/pod-product-compliance
Lightning Source LLC
Chambersburg PA
CBHW031203020726
47499CB00002B/467